Countdown

Also by Carey Baldwin

Stolen
Notorious
Fallen
Judgment
Confession

1-9-18
$16 89

Countdown

A Cassidy & Spenser Thriller

CAREY BALDWIN

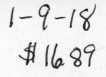
WITNESS
IMPULSE

An Imprint of HarperCollins Publishers

HarperCollins
PUBLISHERS
Since 1817

Digital Edition NOVEMBER 2017 ISBN: 978-0-06-249563-1
Print Edition ISBN: 978-0-06-249564-8

FIRST EDITION

17 18 19 20 21   LSC   10 9 8 7 6 5 4 3 2 1

For my father

Chapter 1

Six Months Earlier
Late Morning
Riverbend, Texas

FOR THE SECOND time since Rose Parker entered her target's backyard, the Ruger LCP nearly slipped from her sweat-slicked shaky grip.

Damn nerves.

Careful to maintain her hold on the pistol, she halted, wiped her palms on her jeans, one at a time, and then resumed forward progress. Papa hadn't raised her to be a weak-willed helpless woman. If only he were here to give her a steadying slap—because she was going to take care of Tommy Preston or die trying.

Scratch that.

Dying wasn't an option.

Then there would be no one left to get the job done.

Suddenly, the pulse in her ears seemed loud enough to burst her eardrums.

You don't have to do this.

She checked out her toes. Dust obscured the newness of the two-sizes-too-big men's Nikes that had arrived in the mail yesterday.

Yes, you do.

A bitter taste worked its way up the back of her throat. She spat onto the ground and instantly regretted it. Could they get DNA from dirt-spit? Better keep her saliva to herself from here on out, just to be on the safe side. She wasn't worried about shoe prints though. If documented as evidence, these would only mislead the cops—something that was easy to do, and a skill she'd mastered at a too-young age.

She pulled her shoulders high and tilted her face up. The rays of the white, west Texas sun had blanched the color from the heavens, changing them into a transparent film. Sweat trickling down her forehead stung when it reached her eyes. Longing to shuck out of every stitch of clothing on her body, she unbuttoned the top of her blouse. Weird how claustrophobia could hit you out in the open like this, but the soaring temperatures and the sheer, heat-wrinkled sky made her feel as though she were trapped in a giant earthen bowl covered by Saran Wrap.

Gulping hot air to prove there really was oxygen to be had, she shaded her eyes. Her Ray-Bans would be nice to have right about now, but she had no purse to dump them in, and when it came time to set that bastard in her sights she couldn't afford to have glasses slipping down her nose. Even on a good day at the shooting range with no pressure on her, she wasn't a great marksman. So under circumstances like these, any distraction would add an unnecessary layer of risk.

Up ahead, a column of dust lifted off the ground, stretched vertically, and then spun itself into a dust devil.

Willing her heartbeat to slow and her mind to still, she curled her finger a hair's breadth away from the Ruger's trigger.

Settle down.

To kill a man she needed her head level and her blood as frosty as that mug of beer she'd been wishing for even though it was not yet noon.

You can take care of your own self, girl. Don't let anybody tell you different.

She had to give Papa his due about one thing—he'd set no stock in the notion that a woman was less than. Sis claimed that had just been his excuse to be harder on them than he would've been on any son. But Rose disagreed—yet one more example of how she and Sis didn't always see eye-to-eye. The way she looked at it, Papa had done them a favor by teaching them to live by their wits. Sure, they'd paid a high price for the lesson, and yes, she'd promised herself she wouldn't carry on the Parker family's vocation once Papa was gone, but at least life with him had prepared her to outsmart any trouble that came her way. So, no, it didn't matter if she couldn't match Tommy's physical strength—she had a gun.

And she might not be a stone-cold killer, but she could get the job done all the same. Her whole life had been about doing things she either didn't want to do, or was ill equipped to do in order to please Papa and protect the family. And today, she was pushing her boundaries for a righteous cause. Not to mention she had to get rid of Tommy Preston if she was ever going to have that normal life she and Sis had always dreamed of.

A normal life.

Surely killing a man wasn't the way to go about getting one.

What if they lock you up and throw away the key?

She couldn't think about that.

She had to act.

Her unreliable breath hesitated yet again.

There was still time to turn back. Why not just go to the police and tell them everything she knew about Tommy?

Steer clear of the cops.

The memory of her father's words rebuked her hard. There was no exception to this rule.

Parkers got a problem? Parkers take care of it.

Of course, Parker wasn't her real name—Papa had stolen it from history. He'd robbed it off the guy who used to sell the Brooklyn Bridge to "marks" several times a week—but paired with her true Christian name, it had come to feel as natural as her two green eyes and her straight small nose, and the dimple in her right cheek that was a mirror image of the one in Sis's left.

She squeezed her eyes shut.

Pictured Tommy prone on the floor of his luxurious home, a bullet in his back, blood pooling around his lifeless form, ruining his expensive Persian rug. But instead of steadying her, the image made her want to puke. She opened her mouth for more air, and her chest locked up. For a good ten seconds or so, she truly couldn't breathe—maybe the world really was covered in plastic.

One thing was sure—she was going to be sick.

She eased her finger away from the trigger and covered her mouth, trying to quiet the sound of her revulsion, which had now become a physical, unstoppable force. Milk and soggy, undigested Cheerios, and a fluid resembling her morning coffee spewed around her hand and through her fingers.

Oh, lord.

She had to get it together.

She mustn't lose her nerve.

In light of the very personal, present circumstances, Tommy was her responsibility. It didn't figure into it that every cell in her body recoiled at the thought of taking a human life.

She couldn't let it figure in.

Pretend you're Anna.

Her chest loosened at the idea. She should've thought of it before. When she and Sis were small, and Papa needed one of them to do something a good little girl would never do, he'd have her pretend to be a fearlessly naughty little girl called Anna.

Make believe you're someone else—someone who doesn't mind doing the things you cannot bear to do.

Like playing dress-up in your mother's shoes—only she and Sis didn't have a mother.

The Anna game was a simple concept that even an eight-year-old could understand. One that had steeled her nerve and saved her ass on many occasions.

Pretend you're Anna.

The tingling in her fingers disappeared.

She looked down at the pistol, now steady in her hand.

In the stillness, she heard branches crackling behind her.

She whirled around to find Tommy's black Doberman, Vader, lumbering toward her. A current of fear electrified Rose's blood, but *Anna* refused to heed the warning.

Instead, she wiped her hands on her shirt, met the guard dog's big chocolate brown eyes, and willed him to be civil. He tilted his head in a not unfriendly fashion. Extending an open palm, Anna whispered, "Hey, buddy, it's me."

The animal made a welcoming noise. She patted the top of his head, and when he didn't sound the alarm, she set her pistol on the dirt and took his face between her hands. "Good boy. Sit."

Vader did not break eye contact with her as he lowered himself to the ground—a strange mix of sharp teeth, sinewy danger, and unconditional doggie love.

"Stay." She retrieved her Ruger and started to back away slowly.

When Vader made a move to follow, she put up her hand in a stop sign. "Stay!" Hard to make a whisper sound commanding.

Vader obeyed, but ventured a yelp of protest.

She gripped the pistol, and holding her breath, dared a glance over her shoulder at the house. No curtains lifted. No face appeared in the window to check on the canine's concerns.

She backed up some more, keeping her eyes glued to the dog. Luckily Vader had seemingly lost interest in following her. He stuck his nose to the ground, sniffed her vomit, cautiously at first, and then, happily, he began lapping up the remnants of her breakfast . . . and along with it her DNA.

Good boy!

She sucked in more air, filling her lungs with oxygen and her heart with courage.

You got this.

She turned her back to Vader and with a determined step, crept closer to the house. She noticed a new coat of white paint refreshing the shutters and trim on the exterior of Tommy's redbrick home. Had this estate been parked in a Dallas suburb, it would've been nothing remarkable. But in Riverbend—a low-end-of-the-middle-class county—the property drew envy and admiration. Here, six thousand square feet plus guest quarters, presiding over a two-acre lot, was more than a mansion.

It was a dream.

Proof of good character.

A promise of what life could be if you worked hard and could coax a bit of luck your way in the process.

Casting her gaze down, she noted new sod had replaced the gravel that had previously led up to the perimeter of the lap pool. Atop the back porch, colorful urn planters overflowing with cheery geraniums had appeared. Tommy must've added these touches in anticipation of bringing home his new bride.

A new spasm of sick washed over her.

Play the game. Pretend you're Anna.

A hot breeze blew around her ankles, bringing with it the smell of mown grass and summer flowers. Scents as wholesome and optimistic as the man Tommy presented himself to be. Tommy Preston wasn't just a pretty face that turned the ladies' heads. He was an industrious man. A solid citizen. He loved dog and country and minded the rules of the homeowners' association. Ask anyone who lived in this town and they'd all tell you the same thing. He was a good neighbor—and a good guy. He was the first friend you'd call if your car broke down in the middle of nowhere. The Samaritan who'd dig out his cables and jump-start a stranger in the Kroger parking lot. He paid his bills on time and went to church regularly. He'd earned a master's degree in marketing from the University of Texas at Austin, and now he owned his own small business—lots of them, in fact. Preston Enterprises employed nearly a third of the workers in this community.

He was the kind of man men wanted to be and women just plain wanted. A favorite son in Riverbend, Texas. And that was precisely the reason she couldn't back down or go to the police.

Who would believe her—the daughter of a two-bit con man— over Tommy Preston?

Her own *sister* hadn't believed her.

And she had no real evidence against him, only the whispered words of a stranger: *Find Sadie.*

She tapped the pistol's magazine against the palm of her hand.

Tommy Preston was an evil, dangerous man.

And she sure as hell wasn't going to let him marry her sister.

Chapter 2

Present Day
Monday
Papeete
Tahiti Nui

THE CAREFULLY ORCHESTRATED plan Anna Parker had initiated back in Riverbend, Texas, hadn't exactly gone off without a hiccup.

But no matter.

Any successful venture required a willingness to reevaluate along the way and make adjustments as needed. And that was just what Anna intended to do. She slipped on her Ray-Bans to cover her startling green eyes, smoothed the plain, conservative skirt she was wearing and smiled down at her dowdy low-heeled pumps. She'd chosen the perfect outfit for the occasion.

She was going to meet Papa's banker.

Her step quickened.

Right now, she was supposed to be at the spa with Sis getting a pre-wedding massage. She'd begged off, claiming a migraine, but she couldn't stay away too long. After the spa, her sister would feel the need to check on her, and she needed to be present and accounted for.

The small satchel she'd slung across her shoulder banged her hip as she hurried along. When she'd decided to walk the two miles to the bank, she'd been in high spirits. The morning air was still cool, and she'd had just enough time. She'd planned to cab it on the way back—by then she'd have plenty of cash—but at the moment, all she had on her was five hundred CFP francs, worth slightly less than five bucks. Now, her previously unworn pumps were working up quite a blister on her right heel.

She wanted to hail a cab, and to Anna, lack of funds had never been an impediment.

She halted in front of a bakery and stepped into the shade of its covered stoop. From the fold-over clutch she was carrying, she removed Anna Parker's passport, driver's license and birth certificate, along with Papa's death certificate, and then transferred them into her small shoulder satchel.

Clasping her five hundred francs, she snapped shut the now empty clutch and waved at a smiling, long-legged teenager across the street. He waved back before returning to his engrossing task of chasing something on the sidewalk. A lizard? Maybe a frog?

She waved again, this time with a more obvious *come-here* motion.

He pointed to his chest.

She nodded.

He looked both ways and crossed to her side of the street. Then he slowed his approach, as if torn between curiosity and timidity.

She removed her sunglasses and waited for him to work up the nerve to meet her eyes. "Thanks for coming to my assistance. You speak English?"

His smile revealed a set of crowded teeth and, she thought, a friendly disposition. "Yes. My English is good."

"Hooray. I'm Anna. What's your name?"

"Antoine. Are you lost?"

She shook her head. She not only knew where she was going, she knew what she had to do to get there.

"But you need help?"

"Are you a fast runner?"

His shoulders lifted. "I won a medal in school for the relay."

"Excellent," she said, but nothing more.

She didn't want to come on too strong. Better to let him draw it out of her.

"You need me to run somewhere fast for you?"

"In a way."

He scratched his head. "Maybe my English isn't so good."

"Oh, no. Your English is perfect. It's my fault for not explaining properly. It's just that I hate to ask such a big favor."

"Go ahead. I don't mind."

She shifted back and forth on her feet, as if nervous. "I need to play a trick on someone, but I can't do it alone. I'll pay you five hundred francs."

His grin widened. "You don't have to pay me. I like jokes."

"It's only fair I pay you since the joke is a little . . . well, it's different than what you might expect. I want you to steal my purse." She held up her clutch.

He scratched his head and stared at the purse. Stuck his hands on his hips.

"It's okay, really. It's only a trick."

He twanged his bottom lip with his fingers.

"I won't let you get in trouble. But you have to do exactly as I say." She reached out, and when he didn't back away she put one hand on his shoulder and leaned in to whisper instructions.

"What if I make a mistake?" he asked.

"Then I'll fix it. I'll explain it was only a game, and you'll still get your five hundred francs." Stepping back, she swept her hand to indicate his long legs. "But you'll have no problem. You won the relay medal."

Laughing, he reached out and snatched her purse.

"Not yet." She pressed the money into his hand and exchanged it for her clutch. "Be patient. We have to wait for our mark."

As she chatted with Antoine about nothing, her heart sped up, and a rush of endorphins bathed her brain. Much like running, the anticipation of a good con often triggered a physical high in Anna.

She was ready.

And just in time.

A man, midthirties, with *short* legs and expensive shoes, waddled toward them.

"Leave me alone!" She took a sharp step back from Antoine and cowered.

A big grin lit his face, and then he grabbed her clutch. To a count of ten, she struggled with him and then released the purse.

He ran, clutch in hand like a relay baton.

"Help!" she screamed. "Help!"

The waddler rushed his steps into a semblance of a trot. "Stop! Stop thief!"

Bringing her hands to her mouth, she bit her nails and bounced on her toes, watching the little man go. His arms pumped furiously, and he picked up so much speed for a second, she thought he might actually catch Antoine.

But Antoine's timing, like hers, was perfect.

Antoine tossed the clutch behind him and disappeared into the alleyway.

Her mark pulled up short, grabbed his knees and wheezed like a set of bagpipes that had seen better days.

Nice work, Antoine.

Red-faced and sweaty, Anna's hero scooped her clutch from the sidewalk and limped back to her. "I believe this is yours, mademoiselle."

"Oh, thank you, sir. Are you okay?" Her hand flew to her heart. "I—I was so frightened. I—I mean what if that young man had had a weapon?"

His bright red face blanched. "I hadn't thought of that."

"Well, you're very brave just the same. Let me give you a reward." She huffed out a breath and held out her hand for her purse.

"I couldn't possibly take a penny."

"No. No. No. I insist." As she opened her clutch she bit the inside of her cheek, making her eyes fill with tears.

He peered inside her purse along with her, and sweat dripped from his forehead into her beautiful bag. That was going to leave a stain in the silk lining.

"Your purse is empty," he said, brilliantly.

"I—I can't believe it! I had five hundred dollars in there. That's fifty thousand francs, my money for the whole month."

"Let me give you something to get you home. How about two thousand francs?" Now it was his turn to pat her shoulder.

She stifled a sob. "Th-thank you but I can't accept. I mean what good will it do me anyway? I—I don't get paid again for two weeks."

"Two weeks?" He put his hands in his pockets.

"Y-yes."

"I could maybe spare a little more."

"Oh, no. Unless . . ." She touched her index finger to her lips. "What about a loan? I insist on paying you back. Let me give you my number. Do you have a pen?"

"No. But I'll add you to my contacts." He sounded pleased.

And why not? He'd rescued a woman in jeopardy and then gotten her number. It was a story he could tell his friends at the bars.

While he typed into his phone, she dictated her favorite phony number.

"I've got ten thousand five hundred francs."

"I'll take ten thousand." She'd leave him what she'd had to begin with. "Call me!" she cried as she hailed an approaching cab.

"Where to, mademoiselle?" the cabbie asked.

"Première Banque Nationale de Papeete."

"Tout de suite."

She kicked back in the cab and transferred her papers into her purse once more. The traffic was light and within minutes she pushed through the door of the First National Bank of Papeete—an establishment large enough to handle major transactions yet small enough to know your name. Papa's name anyway.

She stopped in front of a chest-high counter, cleared her throat and signed the book.

Rightly interpreting the throat clearing as impatience, a slender woman dressed in much the same manner as Anna headed toward her. "Sorry to keep you waiting." The woman glanced at the sign-in sheet. "If you'll follow me?" She indicated a desk situated near several other desks, distinguishable only by the family photos and knickknacks on display.

Anna adjusted the satchel over her shoulder. "I'd like to speak to the manager please."

"I'm the assistant manager. How may I help you?"

"I—I'm afraid I'll need to s-speak to the manager."

The assistant manager quirked an eyebrow. "I'll see what I can do, mademoiselle."

She straightened her back and infused her voice with authority. "Tell him it's Anna Parker. George Parker's daughter."

Another lift of the brow and the woman left.

Anna stood, eschewing the leather chairs until a beefy-faced man hustled into the waiting area. He extended his hand while still a good yard away. "Anna Parker?"

He arrived, and she shook his hand. "Yes."

"I'm Bertrand Fontaine, the bank manager. I was sorry to learn of your father's passing. A wonderful man."

"Thank you." She cast her gaze around. "Is there somewhere private we can conduct our business?"

"Mais oui!" He reached his hand toward her shoulder but it didn't land. He directed her, by only the insulation of a touch, into his office. Like the lobby, the walls were painted in vibrant colors. The desk looked to be genuine wood rather than veneer and thank goodness there was a door for privacy. After pulling out a chair for her, he took his place behind his upgraded desk and tapped his fingers together. "Such a pleasure to meet you, Mademoiselle Parker . . . but before we speak further I'm afraid I'm going to need to see proper identification."

She slid her papers across the desk and studied his bald spot while he examined them.

"It all seems to be in order. How may I be of assistance?"

Smiling, she leaned in close and asked, "May I count on your discretion?"

Chapter 3

A BLADE OF light cleaved the sky into halves, giving Dr. Caitlin Cassidy the feeling she inhabited two worlds at once. In the distance, blood red dripped from cottony clouds over the South Pacific. But closer in, the sunset drama had not yet percolated through the pastel skies, and crystalline waves gently lapped the beach, imparting a sense of peace. When the tide retreated, it left behind a treasure trove of broken shells and polished stones.

Even a starfish.

Though the girl in her itched to claim the beautiful sea star as her own, she was a grown-up, and too conscious of its nature—it was a living, breathing creature—to grab it for herself. She settled for pointing it out and kept walking. The memory of its stunning blue arms sparkling in the sun would be souvenir enough. As she stored the image in her mind, a breeze lifted her long dark hair off her bare shoulders and played with the straps of her cotton sundress. The misted air felt wonderful against her basted skin and teased her senses with a delicious fragrance. "Is it my imagination, or does Tahiti smell like sugar?" She smiled at the man next to her, who kept shortening his stride to allow her to keep up—her fiancé, Special Agent Atticus Spenser.

"It does." Spense tightened his hand around hers, and her heart squeezed, as though he held it, too. "Science might assert the salty ocean breeze, by contrast, brings out extra sweetness in the scent of tropical flowers, but you know what the natives say it is."

Of course. Leave it to Spense to solve the puzzle. "Mana."

The life force. The sweet spirit surrounding the soul.

"They say you can touch it, taste it . . ."

"Smell it." She took a deep breath.

"Everywhere on the island. Happy?" The look he gave her was enough to make her burst.

"Sort of." There had never been a more perfect day in the history of the universe. She was certain of it. But a single adjective couldn't fully describe her feelings at the moment. She was a bit like the sky—one part calm and at peace, the other, teeming with tumultuous color and excitement—and with trepidation, too.

According to her mother, Arlene, all brides-to-be had the same nervous worries. But Caitlin didn't think so. She didn't have cold feet. Not at all. And considering how warm the sand beneath her toes was, and how high her spirits soared every time she caught so much as a glimpse of Spense's profile, she couldn't imagine such a thing to be possible.

He was her world.

Their wedding day couldn't come soon enough.

He stopped and turned to her.

"I was hoping for a *hell yes*," Spense said.

"Then *hell yes*, I'm happy."

"But?" He arched an eyebrow, and she couldn't help noticing how devastating he looked with his thick brown hair, normally clipped Bureau short, grown out longer than usual and blowing in the breeze. Greg Peck anyone?

"But nothing. I am happy . . . and nervous." She recognized how ridiculous she was being. There was absolutely nothing to worry about . . . only . . .

"You nervous about the ceremony? And here I thought I had the only bride who didn't go bananas over the little things. It'll go off without a hitch. I promise."

"I hope so, but even if it doesn't, as long we're together when it's over, that's all that matters to me."

"So what's wrong? Are you thinking about your father?"

"Keep moving." She tugged Spense's hand, leading him farther down the beach. They were here to pick a site for their nuptials and hadn't yet found the perfect stretch of sand. She missed her father terribly, but that wasn't the problem—not directly. "Of course I wish my father were alive to share my wedding day. But I truly feel his presence—like he's here with us."

"Good . . . and . . . I'm still listening." Spense sounded the soul of patience.

Which was very un-Spense-like. Maybe the slow pace of the island was having a soothing effect on those hypersensitive neurons of his. She should just come out with it before her hemming and hawing became too distracting. In fact this was usually the point where he'd pull out his Rubik's cube and solve it in order to sort his unruly thoughts.

"Caity?"

She met his gorgeous brown eyes and, like always, melted inside.

Life was so good, so perfect, and *that* was the problem.

The last time she'd felt this secure, this happy, she was a teenager planning a month-long tour of the national parks with her dad. The cross-country trip was to have been both a high school graduation present and a reward for her becoming class valedictorian. At the time, she'd believed she'd had the world by the tail, and in typical adolescent fashion, she'd been sure she always would. But then, without warning, the universe had spiraled out of control. She and her father had never taken the trip—because he'd been arrested, and later, executed for a murder he didn't commit.

She watched a plumeria blossom drift down from a nearby tree, and her hand fluttered to her stomach. She'd tried, but she couldn't ignore the uneasy feeling that had been gnawing at her since yesterday when they'd arrived in this island paradise. "It's as if this is all too good to be true." Though complaining that life was *too good* certainly made her seem a grade-A dolt, if she didn't explain herself, Spense might get the wrong idea and think she was having second thoughts about marrying him.

His lips tensed, as if he had something to say, but he didn't interrupt.

"I haven't exactly been walking through life with a lucky charm in my pocket."

He nodded.

"So it's hard for me to believe this is really happening. I want a life with you in it—I want that so badly I'm worried something will go terribly wrong."

"You mean like a natural disaster? Are you cooking up a tsunami in your head?"

She forced a laugh. "More like man-made trouble. I dread the phone ringing because I'm afraid it will be the Bureau. 'We've got a serial killer loose in French Polynesia and the locals are in over their heads. We need you to postpone your big day and come up with a profile ASAP,'" she boomed out in her best imitation of their boss, the special agent in charge of the FBI's Behavioral Analysis Unit, thus owning up to one of her fears, but not the other. Not the one that made her shiver, even on balmy days like today.

If anything ever happened to Spense . . .

Why hadn't she thought to bring a sweater?

"That's one of the reasons we chose Tahiti for the wedding. Remember? Murder rate: zilch. I give you my word there are no psychopathic killers here, and the BAU will not come calling. And even if there were and it did—which there aren't, and it won't—we would simply say *no*."

She realized he was being utterly sincere, but . . . . "We never say no."

"Then this would be a first. We're getting married. Nothing will stop that, because I won't let it." His gaze fixed on her with an intensity that made her tremble. "You have my word of honor. Five days from now, I'm going to make you my wife. I'm going to prove to you that life is good . . . *great*, in fact, and it's going to *stay* that way. So start the countdown, Caity." He checked his watch. "Sunday at sunset we're going to be standing up in front of a preacher, somewhere on this very beach, gazing dumbstruck into each other's eyes."

"Not a preacher. A Tahitian priest."

He waved his hand in the air. "The point is that *nothing* is going to get in the way of me making you mine forever."

Her heart steadied. "I'm already yours forever."

Spense closed his arms around her waist and pulled her against him. She looked up, blinking a moment, before the best face in the world descended to hers and literally blotted out the sun. She had more to say to him, but as his delicious, sun-warmed lips pressed against hers, she knew a longer conversation would have to wait. Sparks were flying over every inch of her skin, short-circuiting her brain. She couldn't remember how to breathe. Her mouth opened beneath his and, as his tongue swept hers, she became completely lost, tasting a strange and compelling sweetness.

Mana.

SPENSE COULD KISS Caity all day long, but if he didn't end this right this minute, he wasn't going to be able to walk down the beach without embarrassing her. Reluctantly, he broke their embrace. Keeping hold of her hand, he moved to her side and waited for her to open her eyes.

She took her sweet time before allowing her lids to open, and when she finally did, he saw that her irises, usually a stunning, bright blue, had darkened to a color that reminded him of the ocean at midnight.

His fevered blood climbed another degree.

He'd done that to her—and it had been so easy.

While he stood there, admiring his handiwork, trying to decide whether he should comment on his kissing prowess or wait for her to bring it up, Caity suddenly pointed down the beach.

"There!" she cried. "That's it! The perfect spot."

She meant for the wedding. To him the entire beach seemed

like the perfect spot, but he followed her gaze anyway. "I see what you mean." And he did. Thirty yards or so down, the sand formed a smooth crescent with an outcropping of rocks on one side. On the other, a line of thatched huts rose on stilts out of the ocean. To add to the idyllic scene, moored to a nearby dock, a group of brightly painted boats bounced atop the waves, their reds and yellows reflected off the ocean's surface, transforming it into a churning kaleidoscope of color.

The setting sun hit the shore in such a way that the wedding party would not be squinting. The angle of light was ideal for photography, and, it seemed, another couple had arrived at the same conclusion. Spense's gaze homed in on what appeared to be a bride and groom posing for post-nuptial photos.

Spense didn't see any guests, but they had probably already headed off to the reception. Judging by the abundance of equipment the photographer was wrangling into submission—tripods, cases, lights, and a giant reflective umbrella—this wasn't a Tahitian quickie but rather a planned affair, and, like his own upcoming wedding, would entail at least a few family and friends flying in to help celebrate.

The bride, whose long blond hair kept whipping into her face, wore white: a slim-fitting gown that revealed an impressive amount of cleavage, elaborately shored up with expensive-looking beadwork. The gown had a long train, but in keeping with the destination-wedding style—something Spense had heard quite a lot about lately—an absence of poof and net. It was a look he found pleasing. Caity hadn't let him see her gown, but he suspected it would be simpler and would probably show a bit less—still he wouldn't complain if it hugged her slender curves. Truthfully, he wouldn't complain if she wore a T-shirt and jeans, or layered herself in big fancy petticoats, or wound a stuffed swan around her neck, as long as when the preacher said *do you take this man?* She did.

Like Spense, this groom was tall—well over six feet—and in shape. He was suited up in a gray tux. Spense had yet to be fitted for his, and he made a mental note to confirm his appointment at the rental store. Both the bride and groom were barefoot. Two pairs of shoes had been left to sun atop a large boulder, safe from the whims of the swelling and receding tide. The couple frolicked, not a word Spense used often, but it was an apt description, along the shoreline. The photographer shouted instructions Spense couldn't quite make out over the roar of waves and wind. With an obviously practiced eye, the man choreographed the shoot, directing the couple from a hand-holding stroll, to a cheek-to-cheek dance, to a bent-over-backward kiss.

Beside him, Caity seemed mesmerized by the happy couple's antics.

"Want to get closer?" Spense asked.

She shook her head. "I don't want to intrude. I feel a little guilty, staring."

"This is a public beach. You can't go putting on a show like that and expect no one to notice. In fact, I think it would be an insult if we didn't stop and stare." He let go of her hand to shade his eyes, watching the man lift the woman in his arms and carry her along the water's edge. Sea spray bounced off the rocks, getting her good. The man turned, facing the ocean, showing them his back. He continued his forward march until the waves were up to his ankles.

Spense paced ahead with Caity on his heels. "Spense," she called after him. "Not too close."

"I'm sure they don't mind." He strained his neck as the groom carted his bride farther into the ocean—the water was past his knees now. "What the hell's he doing?"

"Not too far!" the photographer yelled. They were close enough now to make out his words.

Spense frowned. He'd never been one, but he couldn't imagine a bride wanting the train of her wedding gown dragged through the water like that. The thought unsettled him enough to make him pick up his pace, but Caity, who'd caught up to him, didn't seem the least bit bothered.

She beamed her beautiful smile. "I give up. Let's go watch. This is going to be fun."

The bunched muscles in his shoulders loosened. Caity was grinning like she was in on a private joke. She obviously knew something he didn't, and since it had to do with wedding photo-shoots, she was more the expert than him. "What's going to be fun?"

"Trash the dress. Sign of a free spirit. Wish I were brave enough to throw convention to the wind like that." She passed him up. "Hurry up. I've changed my mind. I'm all in."

She trotted ahead, not giving him a chance to remark that she was the bravest woman he'd ever known, or to ask what the hell *trash the dress* meant. But he didn't have to wonder long. With the camera clicking away, the groom carried his bride waist deep into the water, and then the real action started. Making a big show of it, he dumped her into the waves. She screamed, a laughing, happy scream, and splashed water in his face. The wedding dress was definitely a goner, but the photos and the fun would preserve a priceless memory. Maybe more so than a fancy dress packed away in mothballs for a hypothetical daughter who probably wouldn't want to wear her mother's outdated gown at her own wedding anyway.

Trash the dress. Got it.

"You're asking for it." The groom's deep voice boomed over a lull in the wind. He grabbed his bride by the hand and ran farther into the ocean. She resisted, trying to hang back, or maybe it only seemed that way because she was struggling against the train of her dress, which seemed to be tugging her down, as if it had caught on something underwater.

A wave crashed over the couple, and the dress broke free from its unseen anchor, its long white train now topping the water like frosting on a cake.

"Too far, Tommy!" The photographer stood at the edge of the sand, motioning the couple back in. "I need closer shots."

Tommy seemed not to hear.

But the woman looked back . . . and when her gaze landed on Spense, adrenaline blasted through his body, shooting his pulse into the red zone.

The groom dragged the bride against him, locked both arms around her and began swimming, towing her out to deep water, with the train floating behind.

Spense kicked off his shoes so he could move fast.

A person who hadn't experienced the perils of this world firsthand might have hesitated. Might have reasoned away the rush of blood to his gut. Told himself the distress signal he picked up from the woman's body language was a product of his imagination or just his eyes playing a trick on him.

Spense did not.

It didn't matter that there might be a logical explanation for the groom hauling his bride farther and farther from shore.

He didn't hear the photographer over the wind.

He didn't realize how quickly the bottom would disappear.

Nor did it matter that Spense couldn't clearly see the woman's expression. The moment she'd jerked her head around, he'd known, with a certainty that came from too many years of chasing down trouble:

This woman was in it.

Chapter 4

Tuesday
Plage Des Dauphins
Tahiti Nui

THE PHOTOGRAPHER EITHER sensed something was wrong or didn't have a long enough lens for a decent shot. He lowered his camera and began pacing the shoreline.

"FBI! Stop!" Spense shouted the words, so loud and hard his vocal cords continued to resonate afterward.

The photographer dove for the sand.

Guy must've thought he was talking to him.

Elbows tucked to his sides, Spense sprinted into the ocean.

Cold.

And then warm.

Far in front of him, the couple disappeared beneath the waves.

Spense ran, knees high, all but hitting his chest, until he was in deep enough to get his six-foot-four body horizontal.

His feet left the sand.

Keeping his head up, he swam toward the long white train bobbing in and out of the water, his cupped hands motoring salt and water and wind into his open eyes. Despite the painful burning, he didn't close them. He had to keep the target in sight. The telltale train might sink at any moment.

The woman's arms appeared, flailed, disappeared.

The world went quiet.

As if someone had dialed down the volume on a pair of headphones, the seagulls cawing, the ocean crashing around him, the voices shouting from somewhere behind him faded to black.

His heart thumped powerfully in his chest.

This, his body's reaction to danger, felt safe, and familiar. Adrenaline fired up his muscles while his pulse beat strong and steady. His body didn't panic.

And neither did he.

He was trained for this.

His arms surged and pumped, like pistons, propelling him forward, through water that seemed to absorb his body heat. It felt hot and hard around him, like a cocoon of molten glass he had to break through over and over again.

Until the silence broke.

A distant voice—the only one he could never unhear—was calling his name.

"Spense!"

Caity.

She'd be right behind him, he knew, but he didn't turn, didn't stop.

He trusted her, not because he had to, though in a moment

like this he really had no choice, but because she'd earned it. Whatever she meant to tell him, he couldn't stop. Probably she was just letting him know she was here. By his side. Which was good.

Always.

But now especially, since both the bride and groom had disappeared beneath the water. There might be two people drowning.

As he stroked furiously across the ocean, it occurred to him he had no idea what the hell kind of a mess he was swimming into.

CAITLIN'S FEET KICK boxed the surface of the water as she swam straight toward the waves, diving under before they broke to avoid being towed back toward the shoreline. Unlike Spense she wasn't a strong enough swimmer to power over the cresting waves, but she was strategic. Each time she pulled her body beneath a wave, she lost her sight line for a moment, but it was worth it to maintain forward progress. And Spense was making enough of a splash up ahead to guide her, creating a road map of turbulence for her to follow. She'd have to trust that he had the couple in his sights even if she didn't.

Another wave broke and she dove a split second too late.

A gush of salt water seared her nostrils, driving pain up her sinuses. The pull of the current was strong, and the muscles in her arms complained. She dove deeper, swimming under the surface, not coming up for air until her head threatened to explode from lack of oxygen.

But her strategy was working. Swimming deep and under the waves, she was making progress. She'd caught up to Spense's wake, and then she saw them.

The bride and groom, underwater.

The bride kicked hard, blasting to the surface, and the man, hanging on to her by one arm, went with her.

Caity rocketed to the surface just in time to see the couple butt heads and go back under. She was dizzy from holding her breath, and her vision dimmed by the salt water. She'd only caught the briefest glimpse.

Who had head butted whom?

SPENSE REACHED THE spot where he'd last had eyes on the couple.

He dove beneath the surface and kicked in a circle, spotting them, underwater at 2:00.

Gun!

The bride had a gun in her hand.

The groom's foot flew up, catching her beneath the chin.

Blood poured from her mouth, swirling in the water like red finger paint.

The groom grabbed her by the elbow, applied torque, and they rolled, weightless in the water, moving with the rhythm of the ocean, gun pressed between their chests.

Spense kicked toward them, his eyes locked on the compact pistol in the woman's hand. There was a chance it wouldn't fire under water, but it wasn't one he was willing to take.

Spense pulled water with all his might, kicking at the same time.

The couple summersaulted.

The woman jammed her knee into the man's groin, used her feet to push off, and broke free, floating backward in a sea of blood.

A muffled boom.

A ball of gas in the water.

The groom's body flew back, knocking Spense in the chest, and they spun together like shirts in the wash. With a series of tiny shockwaves reverberating in his ears, he locked an arm across the man's chest and dragged his dead weight toward the light shining through a curtain of blood. When he popped through the ocean's surface, his eyes scanned everywhere.

No bride.

No Caity.

He mashed his fingers on the man's neck checking for a pulse. Found one.

His thoughts turned back to Caity. She was a good swimmer. She knew how to handle herself in just about any kind of mess, but he didn't like how long . . .

Caity popped out of the water and signaled an *okay* with her thumb and fingers.

Spense could breathe again.

In a few strokes she was by his side. He treaded water, half floating, with an unconscious man's head on his chest. Guy was still in his tux. Breathing. He'd been knocked out only an instant before Spense got him to the surface. There was a lot of blood, but it didn't seem to be coming from the groom.

"Where is she?" Caity panted.

He jerked his head in the direction of a white gown, its long train floating atop the water in a pool of red.

"You've got your hands full." Caity dove under.

An eternity seemed to pass.

Finally, she resurfaced, shaking her head. "Just the dress."

Still hanging onto the groom, Spense started swimming in a clockwise circle while Caity swam counterclockwise, trying to spot the woman. No luck. If she was under, she didn't have long. He considered passing his guy off to Caity in order to search for the bride himself, but he didn't want to risk the man coming to and in a panic taking Caity down with him.

He was a really big guy.

Spense noticed, for the first time, the muscles in his arms slackening, as if he'd just finished his last set of bench presses.

"Caity . . ."

But she was already under again, searching.

Then dead ahead, Spense spotted something.

He blinked hard, trying to clear his vision, but the view remained the same.

He slapped the water, signaling Caity to come back up. He knew she'd have no luck, because the bride wasn't underwater.

She wasn't drowning.

And from what he could tell, she might be more in need of a lawyer than a lifeguard.

When Caity resurfaced, he shook his head and pointed.

"What the hell?" she asked breathlessly, then swam to his side to take some of the groom's weight from him.

Together, they watched in silence as off in the distance, the bride, dressed in her underwear, hefted her weight over the side of a yellow motorboat and fired up the engine.

Chapter 5

Tuesday
Plage Des Dauphins
Tahiti Nui

TOMMY PRESTON TURNED his head to the side and vomited. Like a fist slowly opening, fingers of fluid spread across the sand next to him. He wasn't sure whether it was the ocean or his stomach contents that stank of fish, but whatever its source, the smell had him battling another wave of nausea. His vision floated in and out of focus. It hurt to breathe—like that time in college when he'd mouthed off to a bouncer at a strip club and paid for it with two cracked ribs.

Someone was moaning.

It took a minute, but then, recognition dawned—that whimpering loser was him. He was lying flat on his back on a beach with itchy sand crawling all over his body.

"Sir, are you okay? Do you know your name? Can you tell me what day it is?"

Who the hell cares?

He rolled his head back and squinted up at a woman with great bone structure, killer blue eyes, and long dark hair—it was wet. She knelt beside him in a see-through dress. He swiped one hand over his eyes and checked again. Yeah. He could still see two peaked nipples and full, round breasts through her clinging, transparent dress. He decided she deserved an answer. "Tommy."

"Your name is Tommy. Good."

Her smile made him want to taste her lips. Most dancers couldn't pull that off without lipstick, but this one was one of those natural beauties. Her breasts even looked real.

"Do you know where you are?"

She didn't sound like a stripper. She sounded . . . official . . . or something . . . and he hadn't been to a club in years. Didn't behoove a man who was president of the Riverbend Better Business Bureau. He studied her, fog rolling on and off his brain. "What?"

"Do you know where you are?"

He raised up on one shoulder, then got himself into a full sitting position. The woman reached out and took his hand.

Soft palms.

Long fingers stretched over his wrist.

"Tahiti." He got that right. He was sure of it. Hopefully, she wouldn't ask him what day it was again.

"Good." She seemed to be counting his pulse. "Seventy-five. Strong and steady. Respirations normal. Mental status improving."

She was some kind of doctor. If more doctors wore see-through clothes it would make the world a better place.

"Tommy . . ." A deep voice set his ears ringing.

He thumped them with his palms and water came out.

"You've had an accident." The man with the deep voice, also

wet, squatted to meet his gaze. These eyes, he didn't enjoy looking into. They were a nice enough brown, but too inquisitive. This
fellow could be trouble. Tommy sensed it instantly.

He shook his pounding head. "This was no damn accident.
Rose shot me—on our wedding day. I can't believe it." He really
couldn't. Rose was capable of deception for sure. She was a con
woman—but supposedly a reluctant one. Turned out she'd conned
him. He'd believed her when she'd told him all she wanted to do
was to go straight.

Straight to hell.

That's where he'd send her as soon as he got his hands on the
ungrateful woman. A man of his social standing needed a wife,
and he'd picked Rose. To be chosen by him was a great honor,
every woman's dream. And he actually enjoyed her company. She
was lively and smart—he had a weakness for smart women. He
would've given her anything she desired. And this was how she'd
repaid him.

He squinted against the sun, trying and failing to recall exactly
what had happened out there in the water. But beyond the gun in
her hand, he wasn't too sure.

"Witnesses. There have to be witnesses and . . ." He looked
down. His shirt was in pieces. A coating of sand covered the fine
hairs on his chest, and there was a bright red dent near his left
nipple.

Shot through the heart.

Her aim was decent.

Bitch.

And now his shirt was ruined. "This was a rental."

"Sorry. I had to tear it to check for any wounds you might
have." The big guy didn't sound sorry.

And he'd torn Tommy's pants off, too. Damn brain fog rolling in again. "Who did you say you are?"

"Name's Spenser. I was in the water. And I saw some of what happened, but honestly, I couldn't say for sure—"

"My wife had a gun. I've been shot." He pointed to the dent under his nipple.

"You have been. And looks like she hit her target, but when the bullet met the resistance of the water, it lost velocity too fast to kill you. I'd say you got something more like a punch in the chest than anything. You're lucky. At slightly closer range, you might've been killed."

Too bad for Rose he wasn't dead, because she would be soon.

She'd shot him, and he wasn't even bleeding—but he remembered blood in the water. He hoped it had been Rose's. He hoped he'd punched her in the nose or kicked her teeth in. The next breath he drew took too long and hurt like hell. "You seem to know a lot about underwater shootings."

"I'm FBI." The man looked at the doctor with the nipples. "But not today. Dr. Cassidy and I just happened to be in the neighborhood."

Tommy could see from the look that passed between them, the doctor meant something to the FBI fellow. He filed the observation away for future reference, just in case he needed to poke a potential weakness in him someday. Noticing what made others tick was a finely honed skill that, to Tommy, was automatic. He'd gotten where he was today because he knew how to work people, and working people meant paying attention, even when you had no agenda, even when you were confused and vulnerable.

Especially when you were confused and vulnerable—and probably had a concussion.

A flash of memory, his head butting Rose's, came back to him along with a shooting pain behind his eyeballs.

Then a man he recognized, mainly because he was carrying a tripod beneath one arm, appeared in his line of sight.

How many people were in this nightmare of his?

The wedding photographer did not get down to eye-level but stood over Tommy with a red puffy face, all screwed up like he was the one whose wife had just tried to murder him. "Agent Spenser pulled you out of the water. He saved your life."

Tommy made eye contact with Agent Spenser. As far as Tommy was concerned it was the man's job to stop crime and rescue people from unnatural deaths, so he didn't really deserve gratitude. On the other hand, there was no upside to not saying and doing what was expected in this situation. "Thanks. I owe you one."

"Just doing my job."

"Not today you weren't. You said you were just in the neighborhood." Tommy put his hands together in a thank-you gesture, and for the first time, really looked around, getting a broad view of his surroundings. To this point, he'd been focusing only on what arrived in front of him, and he was getting tired of surprises. Little by little his brain function was returning, and he wanted to get a better grasp of his current predicament.

Which was: He was sitting on the beach in what was left of his wet clothing after having his pants and shirt shredded by Agent Spenser. A few feet up the sand, a gendarme, dressed in uniform, held off a group of onlookers. To Tommy's left, a lanky man with curly hair, a mustache, and spectacles that looked more like they belonged on a librarian than a grown man hovered, arms crossed, listening intently. So when this new player stepped into the inner circle, Tommy wasn't caught off guard.

"You said your wife shot you. Do you have any idea why your bride would want to hurt you?" Spectacles asked.

"And you are?" Tommy made his tone polite before asking the obvious and completely sincere question, "Shouldn't you people be getting me to a hospital or something?"

"I'm Inspector Brousseau. I was having dinner at the Hôtel De Plage Dauphin." He pointed down the beach. "I heard the commotion and saw the crowd from the terrace dining room. As for your second question, I've summoned an ambulance. It should be here shortly."

Tommy scratched his head. "*Inspector Clouseau.* Why does that name sound familiar?"

"I'm *Brousseau*. Jacques Brousseau. Not Clouseau from *The Pink Panther*." A pained look came over the man's face. "And yes, my first name is also Jacques, like in the films. You're not the first to make the joke."

"I'm not trying to be funny, here. I think I have a concussion or something." That was half true. He still couldn't fully remember what had happened to him, but he'd heard the inspector correctly the first time. Tommy simply wanted to see how hard it might be to knock Brousseau off balance, and it had proved to be no challenge at all. It was going to be simple to put one over on the fellow. From what Tommy had heard there were virtually no murders in Tahiti. The inspector had likely never even investigated one before, so how would he *solve* a murder when one occurred?

Which it would . . . just as soon as Tommy found a way to get his hands on his lovely bride, Rose.

Chapter 6

SPENSE PUFFED OUT one cheek and debated the most polite way to say "get the hell out of our bungalow." It was after ten p.m. and the inspector as well as the two gendarmes who'd been on beach patrol earlier that evening still hadn't left. Caity smothered an exaggerated yawn, for what seemed like the hundredth time, but the gentlemen didn't seem to be taking the hint.

Brousseau pushed his spectacles up and flipped a page in his notebook, his pen poised and ready. "So then, let's review what it was that made you think the *bride* was in danger. You said that was the reason you raced into the ocean in the first place."

Spense reached out his hand to the inspector for a good-bye shake. This would make the third time he'd answered the same inquiry. "It was mostly gut instinct. I'm sure you've had a few of your own. Thanks for agreeing to take our statements here in our hotel room instead of down at the station. Caity and I appreciate the courtesy, but we've said all there is to say. It's been great meeting you. Good luck with the case, and let us know if—"

Ignoring Spense's extended hand, the inspector said, "No. No, I haven't had any."

Caity went to the door and opened it. It had been a memorable day, and Spense intended to make it an even more memorable night. Judging by the look on Caity's face and the way her foot tapped impatiently as she held the door, they were in accord on that point.

Brousseau stood his ground.

It wasn't that the inspector was dim-witted, Spense thought, he simply didn't intend to leave before he was good and ready. The problem was Spense was ready enough for them both.

"I say I haven't had any gut instincts regarding attempted murders. Do you know why that is?" Brousseau asked.

"I'm guessing because you haven't handled an attempted murder case before," Caity answered.

"Exactly right. And there are American citizens involved in this situation and you are the FBI."

"We're on leave," Spense said. "We came to Tahiti to get married, not pad our résumés. We have no jurisdiction in this case. Is there an old phonograph in here? Because I think I hear a broken record playing . . . no, wait . . . that's me."

"But if I invite you to assist, informally, I'm sure your superiors wouldn't object. And you're already involved. You're both eyewitnesses. I'm not asking you to oversee the investigation. I assure you my men are quite capable."

"No one doubts that. And the answer is still no." Apparently there was only one way to end this. Spense turned his palms up and attempted a joking tone to soften the blow of his next words. "So will you please get the hell out of our bungalow?"

"If you don't mind, I'm going to take my leave." Caity sent a smile to each man in the room, and then, without giving anyone time to protest, disappeared into the other room—Spense hoped it was to slip into something more comfortable.

Brousseau slapped shut his notebook. "Isn't the FBI supposed to be eager to overrule the local police? I must say I'm disappointed you're not living up to what I've seen in movies. But we'll carry on without you if you insist." He turned to his men. "You two will remain on hotel property long enough to interview the personnel at the desk and restaurant and housekeeping of course. Find out if they've overheard any arguments between Tommy and Rose Preston and make sure they know to alert us right away if they spot Rose."

He turned back to Spense. "It's very cozy that you and Dr. Cassidy are staying at the same hotel as our newlyweds."

The news flash hardly surprised Spense. After all, the couple had gotten married on the beach attached to the hotel, just as he and Caity planned to do. "We'll keep an eye out if that's your point. You think Rose might come back for Tommy to finish the job?"

"Not if she has a brain in her head. But you never know. Which is why we offered him a protective detail."

"Sounds like a good idea."

"Not to him. He adamantly refused the offer." The inspector shrugged. "Are you sure you won't reconsider giving us a hand?"

"Can't do it." Spense offered to shake again, and this time Brousseau took him up on it. "We'll keep our eyes open, and we'll be available for any *new* questions you think of, but I'm afraid we can't get involved beyond that, either formally or informally. It was a pleasure, sir. Wish you the best."

CAITLIN HUMMED "HARD Day's Night" under her breath. Her shoulders felt lighter than they had when she'd woken up this morning. Today hadn't gone quite as she'd hoped, but then again, she'd been expecting *something* to go wrong. To her way of thinking it was better to have gotten the trouble over with. Surely a near drowning billed as an attempted murder was enough to satisfy any bad mojo that might be following her around.

From here on out, it should be smooth sailing.

Still humming, she drew back the curtains to reveal a breathtaking view of the South Pacific Ocean, moonlight burnishing its surface into smooth silver. Next she opened the sliding doors, welcoming the sweet smell of paradise into their overwater bungalow, and stepped outside. Behind her, she heard footsteps padding across the wooden floor. She turned and looked up at Spense, just as he ducked to avoid the fringe from the thatched roof at the terrace entrance. "Did I ever tell you that you're my hero?"

"You're in a lyrical mood," he said.

"Got a song in my heart. Nothing wrong with that is there?"

"Not a thing." He joined her on the terrace, and together, they walked to the edge of the deck.

"I thought they'd never leave. They did leave didn't they?"

"Yes. Want to go for a late-night swim?" Spense asked, rattling the ladder that led down into the ocean.

This was the most amazing setup she'd ever seen for a hotel. Luxury bungalows climbing out of the water on stilts—nothing behind them except ocean, and to the side—half a football field between them and the next bungalow—truly a private paradise. "I think I've had enough water for one day." Not to mention she'd just changed into a satin negligée, and she had something other than swimming in mind. She leaned back against Spense's chest, and he kissed the top of her head.

Happiness spread over her like a warm blanket.

"So go on. Tell me more about how I'm your hero." He whipped his T-shirt off over his head, then flexed. "Is it because of the way I swam into danger and saved a man's life today? Because, honest, I couldn't have done it without your help on the way back in."

"Liar." She tilted her face up and touched his lips with her index finger, imagining tasting them in the very near future. She faced him, her eyes traveling over the tanned skin of his powerful torso. She laid her palm on his arm. "Nice guns, by the way. But, no, I wasn't talking about your daring rescue. I was referring to what you told Inspector Brousseau when he asked for our help with the investigation."

"You mean *no*?"

"You've never been braver. And I've never heard a sexier word."

His gaze probed hers like he was trying to mind meld with her. At last, he said, "I gave you my word, and I meant what I said. This is our time, Caity. Nothing, not an attempted murder, not a fugitive bride, not even a dogged French police inspector is going to stop me from making you my wife in front of our family and friends and the preacher—"

"Tahitian priest."

"At the appointed time and place—on the most beautiful beach in the world, with the most beautiful woman in the world."

"Sounds like a plan to me." She thought she detected a flicker of guilt in his expression but maybe that was just the moon bringing out the catchlights in his eyes. "It's the right thing to do. We have an obligation not just to ourselves, but to our moms and your brother. Then there's Gretchen. They flew all this way. And you've already saved Tommy Preston's life. That ought to be enough. We've done our duty." Any reasonable person would agree.

They both turned to look at the king-size bed inside the bungalow, with big pillows and soft lighting, a gauze canopy billowing in the breeze. The ambience in this place could convert anyone into a hopeless romantic. If only all those depressing French philosophers had convened their annual meetings in Tahiti there'd be a lot less angst in the world.

"You don't need to convince me." He swept his hand in an *after-you.*

"It's arrogant to think we're the only people capable of solving a crime." She eyed the bed, but her feet remained inexplicably planted on the terrace. Maybe she was the one who felt guilty for turning down the inspector's request.

"Well, I wouldn't say arrogant. Brousseau's trying his damnedest to reel us in. It isn't like we're trying to butt in on his territory."

"If the locals don't have experience, then all the more reason for them to handle this case on their own. Brousseau seems sharp to me—and persistent. We could barely get him out of our living room. And since no murder took place, only an attempt . . ." But here her voice trailed off as she thought about the fact there was a fugitive still out there. *Preventing* a murder was more important than solving one after the fact. That was one of the main things that had attracted both her and Spense to profiling.

And the case was intriguing—one of those she'd dub a *fascinoma*. In spite of Tommy Preston's statement, and in spite of being an eyewitness to the crime, she hadn't yet decided whether it was the bride or the groom—or neither—who was the innocent victim. One minute they'd appeared so happy, and the next . . .

When the couple had disappeared beneath the water, to Caitlin, it had all seemed an accident. Then, when she'd seen them struggling in the water, she'd assumed the bride was the victim. And that wasn't Caitlin jumping to a stereotyped conclusion. She was a profiler, and profilers believed in science, facts, numbers. Statistically, a man is far more likely to commit a violent crime. And if the plan was to make it look like an *accidental* drowning, and the gun was a backup, which was about the only thing that made sense to Caitlin, why would a petite woman think she could defeat such a large man in an underwater struggle?

Caitlin made a scoffing noise in her throat.

If she needed a surefire way to get rid of Spense, luring him into the ocean for a wrestling match would not be her method of choice.

On the other hand, there was no disputing these facts: It was the groom who'd nearly drowned—if not for Spense he'd be lying in the mortuary instead of the hospital under twenty-four-hour observation. And it was the bride who'd fired a gun, and then swum, like an Olympian, to a nearby motorboat and fled the scene. "I have to admit I'm more than a little curious about how this will all end up."

Spense lifted her in his arms, carried her inside, and deposited her on the bed. He sat down beside her and slipped a finger under each strap of her negligée. "And I have to admit I'm more than a little curious about where your tan line ends." He flicked his fingers and the straps fell from her shoulders, revealing just enough of her décolletage to satisfy his curiosity. Only he didn't seem satisfied, not yet.

His eyes roamed hungrily over the tops of her breasts, making her shiver.

"You cold?" His voice held a low tingle. "I think this calls for skin to skin contact."

With a single tug, the satin dropped to her waist. Spense gathered her against him, his bare chest hard where hers was soft. "I love you, Caity." As he whispered the words, he guided her down to the bed and crawled on top of her, his weight pinning her to the mattress, but leaving her room to breathe.

"Love you more." Already, she ached to take him inside her. "Now, *s'il vous plaît.*"

"No," he growled.

"There's that sexy word again."

He trailed his hand between her breasts, and then lower, pushing the gown off of her hips. Somewhere along the way, his pants disappeared. She closed her eyes, reveling in the sensation of his slick, hot skin sliding against hers, the sweet smell of the island mingling with the musky scent of their desire.

His mouth on her.

Hers on him.

Hands crossing paths as they pleasured one another.

She became completely lost, aware only of this man in her arms until a sound that didn't belong—a floorboard creaking in the night—intruded on her bliss.

Spense's arms tensed, then his body flattened, spread-eagle, over hers. "Don't move."

She couldn't, even if she wanted to. Not with nearly two hundred pounds of FBI muscle on top of her.

The floorboard creaked again.

Her heart shot to her throat.

Spense's arm lengthened, and she knew he was trying to reach his Glock. She also knew he'd left it on the coffee table.

"Freeze or die," ordered a female voice.

Sounded like the intruder was at the foot of the bed.

Despite Caitlin's heart thudding loudly enough to wake the couple in the next bungalow, the irony of this was not lost on her.

So much for *no more bad mojo*.

Caitlin could guess who their intruder might be, but from her position she couldn't see anything except Spense's shoulders and the ceiling. She understood he was using his body as a shield, to protect her, but there was a problem. "P-please, let him roll over." With great effort, she managed to croak out the words. "I can't get enough air."

"No," Spense and the woman said in unison.

When Caitlin tried to get her next breath, a weak, whistling sound filled the deathly silence in the bungalow.

"Roll off of her, but take it easy," the woman said.

"I'm fine where I am," Spense answered.

"I said get off of her."

A thunk, like the sound of someone tapping a pistol sounded, magnified a thousand times to Caitlin's ear.

Spense lifted his chest. Thank goodness. She drew a much-needed breath.

"I'm gonna lift one hand and then flip onto my back." Spense spoke slowly but moved fast. Before he'd finished his sentence he was beside her. In a sudden change of heart, he'd decided better to be facing the enemy.

Caitlin quickly glanced around the room, taking in the scene.

A slender young woman, looking to be in her early twenties,

with her hair pulled back into a wet braid, and clad in a corset, crouched at the foot of their bed in a Weaver stance.

Their fugitive bride.

The compact pistol she held out front was trained on Caitlin, and trembling.

The room was dimly lit, but the woman was close enough that Caitlin could see streaks on her face, maybe dirt.

Maybe tears.

Against all reason, and in spite of the fact that the intruder held them naked at gunpoint, a wave of empathy rushed over Caitlin.

What terrible trouble would drive a woman—she was barely more than a girl really—to do what this one had?

What might motivate a bride to carry a gun on her wedding day—to shoot her groom on what should've been the happiest day of her life?

And why come back to *their* bungalow, in the dead of night, and risk being caught? This couldn't be coincidence. Caitlin wasn't sure how the woman found them but it had to have been by design.

More streaks appeared on the young woman's cheeks. No doubt about it now. She was crying, and her body shook from cold or fear or both. Since she was dripping wet, Caitlin assumed the woman had climbed the ladder that led from the ocean onto the terrace in the back of the bungalow.

"Hands up. Both of you!"

They raised their arms in the air.

Spense kept eye contact with the woman. "Your husband's alive. Not hurt badly so you don't have to—"

"Shut up." The bride's eyes darted from Spense to Caitlin and back.

Spense was right, with a good lawyer the woman might have a way out of this mess, as long as she didn't make it worse by killing someone.

By killing *them*.

Caitlin's empathy evaporated. "May I cover myself?" She didn't give a damn that she was nude. But she needed this woman to see them as people, not objects. She needed to appeal to her humanity.

"I said shut up. And do *not* move." The woman swung the pistol, aiming it back and forth between Spense and Caitlin.

Chapter 7

Tuesday
Hôtel De Plage Dauphin
Tahiti Nui

WHEN A GUN-WIELDING intruder appeared at the foot of their bed, Spense's first thought, his first instinct, had been to protect Caity.

And that he would do at any cost.

But his second thought?

Here we go again.

Despite his promise to Caity that the wedding would take place as planned—and he'd damn well make sure it would—the other matter was out of his hands. There was no staying out of the case now. This wet puppy of a woman, all the more dangerous because she clearly didn't know how to handle her pistol, had put them squarely in the thick of whatever the hell this was.

With a quick glance, Spense checked in with Caity. Her expression told him she was rattled—but ready for whatever might come. He dared a brief nod to her, and then, after waiting for his pulse to settle down, he leveled his gaze at the bride. "You're Rose?"

They'd heard her name, along with a number of choice expletives, from Tommy Preston, earlier this evening.

"I'll ask the questions," Rose said.

Spense gave it some time, but none were forthcoming. And it wasn't long before his arms stung like hell. His muscles were bathed in lactic acid from the ocean rescue, so after only a couple minutes of holding his hands high in the air, the pain became excruciating. "Rose, I'd like to lower my arms. I've had quite a workout today. How about if Caity and I both keep our hands folded in our laps?" He'd chosen his words deliberately. It would be harder for Rose to shoot Caity now that she knew her by name. They might not be friends, but they were no longer strangers.

Rose nodded.

He heard a big sigh of relief beside him as Caity slowly lowered her arms and clasped her hands.

"Thank you, Rose," Caity said, her tone both grateful and sympathetic.

If Spense knew Caity, and he did, it would be all too easy for her, no matter the circumstance, to develop a soft spot for a kid with big green eyes and a tear-streaked face. He firmed his jaw and sent Caity another glance, meant to remind her their first priority was staying alive.

Caity's eyes jerked and her teeth clamped down tight.

Message received.

For another few beats they all remained silent. Spense's heart thumped in his ears. Outside, waves crashed against the bungalow's stilts. Rose must be tired, too, since she softened her elbows and straightened out of that deformed Weaver stance some well-meaning Joe at the range must have taught her.

"Put down the gun," Spense said.

She shook her head. "I know who you are, Agent Spenser. If I put it down, you'll arrest me."

She must've seen tonight's news. The ocean rescue had taken the lead. "I won't. I have no authority here. Just put down the gun, and we can have a conversation." She might look innocent, but she'd already shot one man today. "You got no beef with us. We got no beef with you. So just take it easy and lower your gun."

The gun sank, maybe a few inches.

"Good. Now put it on the floor," Spense said.

She shifted her aim off to the side.

Okay, progress. At least if she discharged the pistol by accident, her victim would be that sumptuous arrangement of tropical fruit the management had sent up.

"I can explain everything." Rose's green eyes glistened with fresh tears.

The more she cried, the more Spense worried she might fire on them. Rose was desperate, and desperate equaled dangerous.

"Put the gun down, and we'll be able to listen a lot better," Caity said. A soundtrack of soft thuds accompanied her words.

At the front of the bungalow, a door crashed open. Rose whirled, pistol out front as two men in uniform—Brousseau's men—burst into the room.

Dammit.

"Police! Drop the gun! *Dépose ton pistolet!*"

Spense froze, his mind calculating the best move. With Rose's back turned, he could go for a surprise attack, but that would almost certainly startle someone—either Rose or the officers—

into pulling a trigger. If only he'd had another minute, he was sure she would've surrendered her pistol voluntarily, but now, they were in a guns on gun standoff, and unless Rose cooperated fast, it was not going to end well.

"Drop it!" shouted the officer, again.

"Don't shoot!" Rose cried, but kept her weapon out front.

"Put down your gun, Rose. If you don't, we can't help you," Caity said evenly.

The police pressed in closer.

"Please, put it down, Rose," Caity repeated. "You don't want to die."

Rose's gun clattered to the floor.

"Hands behind your head. On your knees!"

Rose sank to the floor.

A click sounded as handcuffs snapped over her wrists. "Please, just give me a chance to explain."

"Don't, Rose. Don't say anything else without a lawyer." Caity was on her feet.

Spense tossed her a sheet.

Before addressing the two uniformed men, Caity covered herself. "We'd like to speak to Inspector Brousseau—ASAP."

Chapter 8

Tuesday
Police Station
Papeete
Tahiti Nui

ROSE PARKER UNDID her braid, and her damp hair cascaded in crimped waves around her shoulders. The cheap cotton uniform the female intake officer had provided scratched her sunburned skin, but she welcomed this small discomfort compared to that of the miserable, wet bridal corset she'd been strapped into all day and night.

Good riddance.

After being searched and given a change of clothes, she'd been handed over to a male guard and brought here, to a holding cell.

At least she had it to herself.

As she took in her surroundings, full body exhaustion swept over her. The cell walls were gray and glossy, like a kitchen, and smelled of fresh paint. The place was surprisingly clean, and she wouldn't mind drifting off to sleep on the built-in concrete bench—far better than on a feather bed with Tommy Preston.

But there would be no rest for the wicked . . . or for the foolish tonight. She'd made one mistake after another—unworthy of her upbringing.

It was time to play it smart.

Parker smart.

So instead of crashing for the night, as she longed to do, Rose wandered to the front of the cell. The thought of what she was about to do next made her cringe. But in order to trade in this crazy, chaotic life for a fresh start, she had to keep going. Pulling a con might not be the only possible way to get out of a desperate situation. But it was the only one she was any good at. She took a deep breath and recalled what Papa used to say to her and to Lilly.

If you don't care to do what you must, pretend you're someone else.

Be Anna.

Play the game.

She took a determined breath and stepped forward as Anna Parker. She pressed her chest against the bars, knowing that in her loose-fitting top, they would outline her assets.

There was no need to offer a come-hither look.

The guard didn't seem to be able to take his eyes off her. Before she could so much as bat her eyelashes, he approached. When he'd locked her up, he'd been staring at her, too. At the time, she'd assumed, that like most men, he liked what he saw. She wasn't vain. It's a tough world, and you should recognize and use all the resources you've been given.

Anna's good looks were a tool, and she'd use them to her advantage if needed.

The more the guard stared, the better her chances. Only there was something funny about the way he was sizing her up. Almost as if . . . "Have we met?" she asked. She couldn't quite place him—ruddy face, gray-shot, receding hair.

"*Non.*" He met her gaze.

His eyes were the color of slate, the type that change depending on the light, and veined with red. No malice in them that she could perceive. And she was the perceptive type. He seemed older than she, but not by more than a decade. For years, she and Lilly had been coming to Papeete with Papa, so it was entirely possible they'd bumped into one another. This was, thankfully, her first incarceration at the Papeete police station, but Papa had been an overnight guest a time or two. Perhaps she'd seen this guard when she'd come to collect her father. "I'm not trying to BS you. You look familiar."

"BS?"

"*No BS* means *for real.* I think I know you."

"*Nous ne nous sommes pas rencontrés.*"

She smiled. "English please. I heard you speak it earlier."

"We've never met."

"If you say so." She gave him a coquettish smile. "I just thought maybe I'd seen you around. Are you certain we're not old friends?"

He turned his back on her, rather abruptly.

"Hey." She tried to rattle the bars, but unlike in the movies, they didn't budge. "What's your name?"

He sighed, lifted one shoulder, and turned around, this

stepping close enough for her to catch a whiff of something sweet on his breath. Whiskey?

"*Je m'appelle Pierre.*"

"Nice name. I don't suppose you have something to drink around here, Pierre."

He shrugged. "I could bring you some water."

"If that's all you've got I'd be grateful, but it's been a heck of a day. You don't have anything stronger?"

"It's against the rules."

"You don't look like the kind of man who bothers much with rules." She hugged the bars in the most fetching pose she could finagle. "Besides, I promise not to tell. Nothing in it for me to get you in trouble."

"Mademoiselle, I'm here to—how you say? Enforce the law," he said stiffly, glancing up at the corner of the ceiling.

Ah. A camera.

"I bet things go on the blink now and then around here," she offered. Surely he knew how to turn the video off.

"*Non*, miss. I'll get you some water."

He left the holding area and returned a few minutes later with a tin cup—empty. He glanced up, seeming satisfied. The green light that had been blinking on the camera was no more.

"About that drink?" She tilted her head.

He smiled, a bit warily. Went to his desk and retrieved a bottle. Showed her the label as if they were in a fine restaurant—scotch.

ut a quarter full, then with a wink, handed

nd returned to his desk. Resumed shuffling

ed in the middle of the cell, staring down into

What now?

Pierre's overly careful stride suggested he'd been drinking awhile already. And the wink he'd given her had been conspiratorial. When she'd promised not to tell on him, he'd believed her.

And why not?

Why should she wish him any harm?

In truth, she didn't.

She put the cup to her lips. The scotch burned on the way down. She welcomed its warmth into her cold empty stomach. "You're very kind, Pierre. And a gentleman." As far as she knew this was true. Many a man in his position might try to take advantage of a woman in hers. Pierre had not . . . yet.

She needed to do something about that.

He looked back over his shoulder at her. "Would you like a blanket? No pillow I'm afraid. You look *fatiguée*."

"I'm not sleepy. Just bored," she said. "You won't get into any trouble, I hope, because of turning off the camera."

She wanted him to know she knew what he'd done. She wanted him to begin to think of her as being on his team, and by extension to think of himself as being on hers.

Us against them.

Pierre and his prisoner against the stodgy old rule makers—those spoilsports who forbid drinking and pillows in jail.

It would move things along quicker if she was up front with him—as up front as she could be, anyway. Truth telling was part of the game. Earn your mark's confidence first; slam down the hammer after.

"Don't worry. I turn the camera off, but no trouble comes for me. No one will know. No one watches." He laughed, a big hearty laugh. "Unless you try to escape. Then they watch."

The scotch went down the wrong way. She coughed. "Escape? Are you worried I might?"

"*Non.* Of course not. I am big. You are small. I make joke."

"Ha! You are fun. Too bad there's nothing else to do but talk. Don't you get bored doing nothing night after night?"

"I like talking to prisoners. I like talking to you."

."You don't happen to have . . ."

"More drink? So soon?"

"I've still got plenty. I was thinking maybe we could play cards. If you have some hiding back there."

"I do!" He rummaged around and pulled out a worn deck.

"You play with your other prisoners?" Papa had played poker with his Papeete jailor once. At least he'd told a story that he had. Claimed he won a pair of dry socks and a flask of red wine.

"*Oui.* A few times." His gaze swept over her. "We could play out here. But, I need to cuff you for that. Maybe you'd rather play from there."

"Either way. Like I said, I don't want you to get in any trouble."

"You don't run, no trouble for me."

She looked down at her feet. "Wouldn't get far. Your legs are twice as long."

"What kind of cards you want to play, mademoiselle? Poker?"

"Sure. Or . . . do you know three-card Monte? It's quite a challenge, but that's the point. And I bet you'd be good at it—catch on fast." Anna pressed her index finger to her lips as if something had just occurred to her. "Only trouble is for three-card Monte, I'd need to use the surface of the desk—to lay out the cards."

"So we play at the desk." He fumbled with his belt and unhooked his keys and cuffs. She held her hands out front, while he reached through the bars to cuff her wrists. As he snapped them in place and opened her cell door, inviting her to claim some small semblance of freedom, she noted a fine tremor in his hands. Which could mean he was more nervous about bringing her out than he let on, or it could simply be the drink. In either case best not to make any sudden moves or up the ante too soon. She walked, slowly, so as not to spook him, to his desk and took the chair farthest from the exit.

Outrunning him wasn't feasible—nor was it the plan.

Pierre set the bottle of scotch on the desk in front of them next to the deck of cards. "Help yourself."

She picked up the cards and rapped them on the desktop until the edges were even.

"I'll shuffle," Pierre said. "Might be difficult for you." He frowned at her cuffed wrists.

"No need. For this game we only need three cards."

"Thus the name." His lips spread wide to reveal teeth aged by smoke and drink.

"Told you you'd catch on quick." She returned his smile. "I'll take the ace of hearts—red." She plucked it from the deck. "The king of spades and the king of clubs, since they're both black. Make it easy for you."

"I would like the hard way—how you say it?"

"Challenge."

"*Oui*. Challenge me. *S'il vous plaît*."

Don't worry, I will.

The cards made a slapping noise as she placed them face up on the desk. "The red ace is here." She tapped it with her fingernail. "Got it?"

He nodded.

She flipped the cards facedown. "Now. Keep your eye on the red ace. This is your only job."

"*D'accord.*" He was watching her face intently, with that look again, as if he knew her.

"No. Don't watch my face. Don't even watch my hands. Watch only the red ace."

"*Oui.*" He leaned his elbows on the desk and fixed his gaze on the proper card.

She looked up at him through her eyelashes. "Better. Here we go."

She dropped the cards quickly, switching up their positions, moving her hands not quite as fast as the cuffs allowed. "Show me the red ace."

Pierre thumped the middle card.

She flipped it over. "Too easy. That was just practice."

He waggled his brows with pride. "Faster. I can do it."

She glanced around the boxy room, missing her sister, Lilly. With Lilly as shill, she could convert the most cynical mark into a true believer. But if she couldn't figure a way out of this mess, she and Lilly would never be together again.

It was all because of Tommy, and she would not allow him to come between her and her sister.

She leaned forward intently.

Pierre's body canted forward, too.

Her scheme just might work. Pierre was indeed behaving as though they were on the same team—even his body language mimicked hers. And while Lilly might not be around to act as shill, the scotch would work in her stead. Maybe better, given Lilly's timing problems—she had a tendency to show her hand too soon.

Anna pulled in a determined breath and increased the speed of the game, keeping her movements regular. The more methodically she worked, the easier it was to spot the ace. The increased quickness only made it *seem* more difficult.

As she flung the cards, time after time, Pierre had no trouble keeping up. Soon he roared in triumph. "Too easy! Faster!"

She wiped a real bead of sweat from her forehead. "Going as fast as I can." It was true. The cuffs limited her speed—though not her guile.

Pierre took a swig of scotch. "Are you letting me win on purpose?"

"No. It's . . ." She glanced at her wrists.

He set his cup down too hard. "*Je comprends.* I'll take the cuffs off."

"I don't want you to get into trouble. This game isn't worth it. But I do wonder how well you'd do if we were playing for real."

He bent, searching for keys, then jerked upright, slamming his head against the corner of the desk in the process. A gash on his forehead seeped blood, and he wiped it off with his shirtsleeve.

"*Mais non!* Are you okay?"

"*Mais oui. Je vais bien.*"

The blood might've made the wound look worse than it was, or maybe the liquor was acting as a painkiller. Pierre seemed unfazed by his injury. He uncuffed her. "You care to make a wager?"

"A betting man. If we're going to wager the stakes should be worthwhile. That's what my papa always said."

Be careful.

She smiled to herself, imaging Lilly jumping in with *let's play a game of strip cards.*

But Anna realized that was far too obvious. It would certainly raise Pierre's level of suspicion. What woman would volunteer to strip for a jailor? *One with an ulterior motive.* Pierre was drunk, not stupid. He would likely see through that. She needed to tempt him without it seeming too far out of bounds. "What do you propose?" She leaned forward. "A kiss, perhaps. But only on the cheek."

His ruddy face turned apple red.

She'd made the right decision. No matter that he had her in his control, and was plying her with liquor, he considered himself an honorable man. He might fantasize about a game of strip with his prisoner, but he wouldn't engage in one. Such a suggestion might've landed her straight back in the cage.

"I don't want to take advantage."

She rubbed her forehead. "I'm very confident in my game."

"A kiss could cost me my job."

"Is that what you're worried about? Losing your job." Regret brought heat to her cheeks. If she succeeded tonight, he likely would. But she had no choice.

Be Anna.

"Playing cards is one thing. But I do not take advantage of a young lady in my custody. I cannot."

Quite liking Pierre, she sent him a genuine smile. "I'll say it again. You're a gentleman. How about this? We'll have the same stakes. If you find the ace again, I'll polish off my cup. If not, you drink yours. We Americans have a saying about a goose and a gander."

"I'm afraid I don't know that one."

"Just means things should be square—you know, equal between a man and a woman."

"*D'accord.* Shall we continue?"

He'd uncuffed her, so she'd better make a good showing. She made it hard on him, tossing her cards from the top in order to disguise the ace. After losing to her twice and downing two cups of liquor, he looked jiggered and flustered. Time to let him have his day. She tossed the ace from the bottom, methodically but quickly. When he spotted it correctly, she swigged what little scotch remained in her cup, as promised.

With a shaky hand, he refilled her.

"Oops," she said when liquid sloshed outside the cup.

He stole a shy glance at her, making her think he wanted to claim that kiss after all. She pointed to her cheek. "*Un petit bisou?* A little kiss?"

"I cannot."

The man was snookered, and still, he held onto his honor, and she felt lower than a rat snake's belly. She was slipping, slowly but surely out of character and had to remind herself often to stay focused on behaving as Anna would—*feeling* as Anna would.

When had the Anna game gotten so hard?

Pierre held out longer than she'd expected. By the clock on the wall it was after four a.m. when his head finally hit the table—again.

He was out cold.

She slipped his wallet from his pocket and slung his belt, loaded with goodies, pepper spray, baton, radio . . . over her shoulder. Finally, she removed his pistol from his holster and tucked it in the back of her pants beneath the tail of her shirt. Then she headed for the door.

Discarding the role of Anna, now that the game was won, she turned the knob.

Her feet froze.

Poor Pierre.

He'd been as much of a gentleman to her as any man in a long time. Though he'd clearly admired her, he'd kept his hands to himself.

Pierre's troubles are not your problem.

Costing him his job could not be helped. In fact it was good for him, right? It might be just the nudge he needed to stop drinking.

His liver would thank her later.

It might be a hard lesson, but it was his own doing.

She hadn't caused him to drink on the job. He'd been doing that long before she arrived. Still, as Rose, as herself, she couldn't help wondering what lay in store for Pierre. Suppose his superiors thought he'd done more than get drunk and succumb to trickery? The camera was off. It might appear as though he'd disconnected it to help her escape. As though he'd colluded with her. That would be a criminal matter, she was sure.

Her hand fell to her side. She turned around and went back to the desk, pulled a chair to the corner of the room, and climbed it—but the camera remained beyond her reach.

What now?

She hopped down and returned to Pierre. Gently, she turned his head to the side, so that he wouldn't be lying face flat on the table for hours, then she bent and untied his shoe.

She tossed it at the camera.

It took three tries, but she finally hit her target. The camera came bouncing down, hanging from the ceiling by its wires. She ripped the whole assembly out, and then knocked a chair to the ground and smashed the empty bottle of scotch over it.

A goose egg was already forming near the gash on Pierre's forehead.

While she couldn't *guarantee* he wouldn't be charged with criminal conspiracy, she'd set it up to make it hard to prove. She tucked the camera under her arm like a football. With it gone, no one would be able to say for sure he'd turned it off.

They'd find the broken bottle of scotch. He might be able to sell the story that she'd banged him over the head with it. He'd be suspended or fired for incompetency and drinking on the job— but not charged as a criminal. She hoped.

Best she could do.

Sorry, Pierre.

But she was using her get-out-of-jail card *now.*

She closed the front door behind her and headed down the deserted street, keeping to the shadows.

Busting out of a Papeete holding cell hadn't been difficult for a woman with Rose's skill set.

The hard part was up next: making Tommy Preston pay.

Chapter 9

Wednesday
Police Station
Papeete
Tahiti Nui

CAITLIN TWISTED THE diamond on the fourth finger of her left hand. The ring had once belonged to Spense's grandmother. The band was loose and spun easily—she should either get it resized or gain weight ASAP.

Eight a.m.

She and Spense had been waiting to speak with Inspector Brousseau, and hopefully, Rose Parker Preston, at the Papeete Police Station for more than an hour. She folded her hands and stared at the acoustic ceiling tiles lining the room's walls. They reminded her of every interrogation room she'd been in state-side: recycled pulp with punched holes to absorb mid-frequency speech. Apparently underfunding of law enforcement wasn't only an American problem. No one seemed to have a budget for actual soundproof panels.

The ring made another orbit around her finger.

Didn't these people know she and Spense had important matters to attend . . . like a cake tasting?

Spense smiled conspiratorially at her, and she knew he was thinking of Gretchen and Dutch left to do the honors: hosting the moms and fielding hard-nosed questions like *does anyone despise coconut?* while she and Spense got the fun of chasing down a case.

She sent him a stern frown.

They were in so deep now, it only made sense they would acquiesce to the inspector's request and bring their crime solving skills to the table. Any fun they might have in the process would be an unwelcome side effect.

Spense shrugged and checked his watch. "How long can it take to bring her around?"

"You think Brousseau will let us speak to her?"

"He asked us to help him close the case—so yeah."

"Is that what we're doing?"

"You tell me." Spense stretched his long legs out in front of him. "I know we promised we'd say *no*. I know we *said* no yesterday. Under the circumstances though, it might be best to help him fit the puzzle pieces into their proper slots—I don't want any other players surprising us in the middle of the night. Long as we wrap it up before the wedding, I think we should join the party." He rubbed a spot on his arm that had gotten more sun than the rest. "Stop for aloe vera on the way back?"

"Yes."

"To which? The aloe vera or the case."

"Both. And wrapping before the wedding goes without saying."

"No. We're saying it."

"Point taken." The ring twisting started up again. "There's something strange about this whole caper, don't you think?"

He reached for her hand, to stop her fidgeting. "What's wrong?"

"I have a gut feeling Rose needs our help. That she might be the injured party, here."

He squeezed her hand and released it. Tilted back in his chair. "Babe, you do remember last night. Hot-sex interruptus. Rose waving a gun. *Don't move! Hands in the air!*"

She did. She also remembered a tearstained face, a desperate woman, and a shakily uttered *I can explain everything.* They didn't have all the facts. "I don't think we should rush to judgment until we hear her side of the story."

He dragged one hand through his hair, and the chair thunked back down on all fours. "I'm not criticizing, but do you think maybe you're slipping back into an old pattern?"

"You mean not wanting to see an innocent person get railroaded into prison or worse? That kind of old pattern?"

"Rose Parker may or may not be guilty of the attempted murder of Tommy Preston. But she's far from innocent—she broke into our room."

"The terrace door was open."

"She climbed out of the ocean and onto our terrace in the middle of the night and held us at gunpoint. That counts as a break-in. Not to mention almost ruining our lovemaking."

Caitlin's cheeks warmed at the memory of what had taken place after Rose had been hauled away and she and Spense had been left to their own devices. "But she didn't ruin it," she whispered.

On the contrary, the incident had turned up the burner under their lovemaking from sizzle to sear.

"Being held naked at gunpoint did turn out to be an aphrodisiac . . . but that doesn't make what Rose did—"

The door swung open.

"To be continued," Spense said, as Inspector Brousseau stormed into the room, waving his hands like a chicken wondering what had become of its head.

Something was definitely up.

"What's up?" Spense asked, deadpan.

The inspector's face went purple. "She's disappeared."

"You mean Rose?" Caitlin couldn't hide her astonishment.

"Of course I mean Rose. Parker. Preston. The bride. She's fled—again. At least we think she's fled."

"Is she gone or isn't she?" Spense asked.

"There's no trace of her anywhere." With a heavy sigh, Brousseau scraped out a chair and plunked down in it.

"You make her sound like Houdini." The woman had, in fact, pulled off two confounding escapes. Whatever else Rose Parker was, she wasn't your run-of-the-mill criminal.

"Maybe she is some kind of magician. I don't know. All I can tell you is that her cell is empty. And the guard's disappeared along with her."

"Why is that all you can tell us? You must have surveillance equipment." Even Papeete with its low crime and low budget would have the basics. It was clear to Caitlin this *gosh-I-just-don't-know* routine was an act. To Caitlin, Jacques Brousseau seemed sharper than the third runner-up in a singing competition. He was holding something back. Covering something up. But was he protecting himself or someone else?

"Naturally we have surveillance, but the camera was ripped out."

Caitlin and Spense exchanged a glance. "Have you considered whether or not your deputy might have been susceptible to a bribe?" she asked.

"My deputy did not accept a bribe." The inspector straightened in his chair.

"How can you be so sure?"

"I know him."

"Seems like the most logical explanation." And it was better than the alternative. The missing guard could either mean he'd colluded with the prisoner or something worse. It could mean Rose Parker was every bit as deadly as Tommy Preston had suggested. "Any sign of foul play?"

"There's blood."

He'd been holding out on them all right. Her heart sank as her mind played out a thousand scenarios of what fate might've befallen the deputy.

"Why didn't you say so in the first place?" Spense asked, rapping his knuckles on the desk. "How about you give us the whole story? We can't help if you don't."

"Yesterday, as I recall, you declined to become involved, saying you must not be distracted from your vacation."

Brousseau knew it was more than a vacation. But his tone implied they'd been mean-spirited or selfish, refusing to help for some trivial reason.

Their upcoming marriage was not trivial.

She clutched her hands to keep from shaking a finger at him. "That was yesterday. Before Rose Parker broke into our room and out of your jail. Before there was a missing deputy and blood left behind. Maybe you don't want our help anymore. Maybe you'd rather no one learn the truth about what happened right under your nose. Good lord. What if your man's dead?"

Brousseau's Adam's apple dunked up and down. "It's not a lot of blood. A few drops and a long smear—confined to the desktop. And there's a broken bottle of scotch. Chairs knocked around. We don't think our officer's come to serious harm. We think it was what you Americans call a scuffle."

"Your man put up a fight," Spense said.

"*Oui.* Under normal circumstances a small woman couldn't have bested him. But it's possible he may not have been operating with all his faculties. It's possible he . . ."

"Your deputy was drunk," Caitlin surmised. Broken bottle of scotch. Not hard to figure.

"He's been known to take a nip here and there."

"On the job?"

The inspector shrugged. "We've warned him. He's supposed to be on—what's your phrase? The wagon."

"Risky to leave him in charge of suspects," Spense said.

Brousseau looked down at his hands. "I understand this makes a terrible appearance. But you must remember most of our prisoners are peaceful."

"I think you mean docile?" The inspector's English was excellent, but she wanted to be sure she didn't misunderstand.

"I'm trying to say not dangerous and not a flight risk. But as you are no doubt thinking, this woman has already attempted to murder one man."

"Allegedly." Caitlin crossed her arms over her chest.

The inspector's brows shot up. "Ah yes. Allegedly. But we have her husband's statement. And the evidence speaks to us. Her husband was hit by a bullet and Agent Spenser saw her fire the gun." He pressed both palms on the tabletop. "Which reminds me I meant to ask about something that happened last night."

"That's why we're here," Caitlin said.

"You, Dr. Cassidy, instructed the suspect not to speak to the police. *Allegedly.*" He drew the word out.

"I said don't talk without a lawyer. She's an American citizen and—"

"She is a guest in Tahiti. She must obey our laws. We are *French* citizens. We are a civilized people. We do not permit wives to shoot their husbands."

"Nor do we, in the United States," Spense said. "But in the U.S. we like to look at all the evidence before we reach a conclusion."

"Well, as you can see, we do not have the woman's statement, thanks to Dr. Cassidy."

Spense sent Brousseau a look that could fell an elephant at a thousand yards. "Dr. Cassidy isn't the reason you can't get your statement. You have no statement because you lost your prisoner."

"But we found the guard." A uniformed man butted his head in the room. "Pierre's back, sir. And he's ready to tell us everything—everything he can remember, that is."

Chapter 10

WHEN A BARREL-CHESTED man in uniform—split at the knees and muddied—sporting a square bandage on his forehead skulked into the interview room and seated himself next to the inspector, Spense kept his expression neutral.

"Where have you been?" the inspector asked, his tone stone cold.

"Looking for my prisoner," the deputy answered and lowered his gaze.

Brousseau's throat moved like he was choking on a piece of meat. It took a moment for the words to emerge. "You didn't call for help. We've had a search going since shift change."

"I—I . . ." He looked up. "I apologize."

Brousseau rubbed his eyes with his fists. "Don't apologize. Just explain it to me. Why didn't you call for help?"

"I tried to. I—I remember waking up . . ."

"Waking up?" The inspector scoffed. "That's what you call it?"

"I remember *coming to*, and seeing the door to the station open—and she was gone. I thought *I must go after her*. I remember running into the night and then reaching for my radio, but it wasn't on my belt and my belt wasn't on me . . . I don't know." He looked down at his torn uniform. "I can't remember what happened after that. I think I fell. I woke up at the bottom of *La Colline Du Français* an hour ago."

The inspector muttered something unintelligible and then turned to Spense and Caity. "Frenchman's Hill. It has a deep ravine at the bottom, not half a mile from here."

"I had a hard time climbing out, but I came straight to the station. I don't know what's become of my radio." Pierre paused. "Or my belt." He looked from Caity to Spense, clearly mortified. "She must have stolen my Glock."

"Agent Spenser, Dr. Cassidy, I present to you Deputy Sergeant Pierre Brousseau." The inspector's clasped hands were white around the knuckles.

A flush of red climbed the V of chest showing beneath Deputy Brousseau's uniform, past his neck, and upward, eventually leaving only a pale crescent of unaffected skin near his receding hairline.

"Pleased to meet you." The deputy's eyes darted around, probably marking the nearest exits.

"Likewise," Spense said.

"Pleasure. Sounds like you've had a rough night." Caity proffered a warm smile.

God he loved her smile.

Pierre Brousseau didn't reply, and a tense silence ensued. Spense thought about breaking it with the obvious question, but this was the inspector's show. If he wanted them to know his relationship to the deputy, he'd tell them.

"Oh, very well. If you must know," the inspector started.

Spense turned his palms up. "If we must know what?"

"Deputy Brousseau is my brother."

Spense felt a pang of empathy for the inspector. Spense understood a thing or two about troublesome brothers. And that might explain how Pierre kept his job despite his bad habits. And why the inspector would vouch for him about not taking a bribe.

"Pierre, Agent Spenser and Dr. Cassidy are interested in the Parker-Preston situation."

Pierre gulped. "But they're FBI. Why is the FBI on the case?"

"We're not, officially," Caity assured him. "We're merely interested parties who happen to . . ."

"We're aces at catching the bad guys," Spense said. "And we're willing to help, but you need to quit screwing around." He checked his watch. "Because I really don't have time. So how about you tell us what happened while Rose Parker was in your custody last night—before the coming to and finding her gone and falling down the hill episode, I mean."

Pierre's hands trembled a moment, but then he curled them into fists, and the trembling stopped. "My English is not so good as my brother's, but I can explain everything."

Something of a catch phrase around here.

"That's what she said." Spense winked at Caity. "But I've yet to hear anything resembling a satisfactory explanation for the strange happenings in and around Papeete. So if you can account for your own part in this mess, I'm all ears."

"You must think me incredibly, er, er, *stupide*. I'm sorry I don't know the word in English."

"Stupid," the inspector supplied.

"*Oui*." Pierre's shoulders lifted in self-defense. "And so I am. What I did was stupid." Pierre opened and closed his fists. "I have no excuse, but perhaps you will understand better when you hear the full circumstances."

"What exactly did you do?" Spense narrowed his eyes.

"I let Rose Parker out of the cell."

"For a drink?" Caity asked.

"*Oui*. And for a game of cards, but, you see, I did not believe her to be dangerous." He touched the square bandage on his forehead self-consciously. "Or a risk to flee."

"She's accused of the attempted murder of her husband," the inspector said, and raised his hands to heaven. "And she fled the scene of the crime in a motorboat."

"But the husband wasn't hurt."

"He has a bruised rib, and he would've surely drowned if Agent Spenser hadn't been there to pull him out of the ocean." Brousseau lifted his hands higher.

"But he *didn't* drown. And you must understand, Jacques." Pierre turned plaintive eyes on his brother. "I thought she was harmless."

"I understand you got drunk and let a dangerous prisoner escape. I understand you're lucky to be alive."

"*Mais non*. I do not believe Rose would hurt me."

"She hit you over the head with a bottle of scotch." The inspector's arms dropped to his side.

"*Mais non*. I did this to myself. I hit my head on the corner of the table . . . I think. It's a little hazy, I admit. I do not know how the bottle came to be broken."

Caity tilted her chin. "Why did you say Rose wouldn't hurt you? Sounds like you know her."

"I am—I *was* a friend of her father's. Well, perhaps not a friend so much as . . . yes . . . we were friends. Though he's passed now, less than one year ago, I believe."

Spense let out a whistle. "You know the father, too, Inspector? How much more have you held back?"

"I know *of* the father, but I was not his friend," Inspector Brousseau said. "I hold nothing back from you . . . from now on. As I said, you declined my initial request for help, so why would you expect me to give you all the details? Let's move on from this paranoia, shall we?"

"Not paranoia. You've been very cagey. But as long as you agree to be open with us from here on out, we want to help."

Caity glanced at Pierre. "You were going to tell us why you think Rose Parker is harmless."

"I know the father, George Parker, many years. I've never met the daughters. Last night, Rose did not recognize me, and I did not admit to knowing her. I'm acquainted with her and her sister only from a distance."

"There's a sister?" Spense pulled a pad and pencil out.

"A twin."

"Name?"

"Her name is Lilly. Lilly and Rose Parker, lovely like the flowers. George adored them. He spoke of them often. But he protected them, too. Never let me, or anyone else as far as I know, near them. I've seen them playing in the ocean, walking with their father, taking meals at local restaurants, and so on. In all those years, I've never observed any member of the family to be violent."

"Touching, Pierre. But it doesn't excuse what you've done. I am very tired of the excuses, and I'm embarrassed for you that you believe Agent Spenser and Dr. Cassidy will believe your actions were reasonable, justified even."

"I excuse nothing. I'm only trying to give you the context. I should never have let her out. I shouldn't have been drinking on the job. But sometimes I do." He lifted one eyebrow. "I'm off the wagon, *mon frère*. But I am ready for rehabilitation."

The look on the inspector's face made Spense's gut twist. It seemed he'd truly believed, or perhaps *hoped* might be the better word, in his brother's sobriety. And now that dashed hope might cost both of them their jobs.

"When I saw that my prisoner was one of the Parker sisters, my heart was touched. She lost her father."

"And the fact that Rose is a beautiful woman had nothing to do with you opening up that cell and sitting down to play cards with her?" the inspector asked.

Pierre, who did not seem to be able to meet his brother's gaze looked squarely at Spense. "Of course, it was a factor. I'd be lying if I said otherwise. But even so, a different beauty would have stayed locked up tight. I trusted Rose, because I trusted her father."

"How did you meet the father?" Spense asked.

"Here."

"In Papeete, I understand. But how?"

"No. I mean *here*. At the station. George Parker was detained on several occasions. Usually it was for public intoxication. But he was an affable drunk—like me, I suppose. He and I both had our struggles with the drink. It's how I came to be friendly with him."

"The man was congenial. I'll vouch for that," the inspector said sotto voce, as if reluctant to agree with anything his brother said.

"He was a drunk, but not a fool. He was quite clever and big-hearted. The first time he was brought in, I'd had a sad time of it. Our sister was in the hospital after a boating accident, and I was worried. George entertained me all night with stories of his adventures, and one tale in particular helped keep my mind off my troubles. He spun a fantastic story about one of Tahiti's most famous citizens. You've heard of Monsieur Paul Gauguin."

Caity whipped the pencil and pad from Spense's hand and scribbled *Gauguin*, then handed it back to him.

"That story circulated around town and eventually took on a life of its own," the inspector said. "Plenty of locals believe it, and oh how they love to repeat it."

"You were saying George made you feel better when you were worried for your sister," Caity addressed Pierre.

Spense made a mental note to get back to Gauguin, but Caity was right. They were getting far off the track.

"Yes. And the next morning, when George was released from jail, I saw his local address was near my home. I invited him to dine with me the following evening, and he agreed. We had wine and small plates. He inquired after my sister. When he saw my saxophone, he promised to come again and to bring his John Coltrane CD with him. And that is how George Parker and I became friends. And that is why I did not fear to let Rose out of her cell for a game of cards. It was stupid but I was influenced by my fondness for her father."

"And the scotch," his brother grumbled.

"Do the Parkers reside on the island?" Spense had assumed, until a few minutes ago, that the bride and groom had traveled here for their wedding.

"Not full-time, no. But George brought his daughters to Papeete many summers. They usually stayed a few weeks. Over the years, he wound up in my cell on occasion, but it was never for anything too awful."

"Besides the public intoxication, what other not-too-awful things are we talking about?"

"A picked pocket, once. And then there was the gold."

Caity borrowed the pad and pencil again. "What gold?"

"*Gauguin's gold*. Ah, perhaps I didn't finish that part of the story."

"The story George Parker invented." The inspector rolled his eyes.

"We assume he invented it," Pierre corrected his brother. "We have no proof it's not true."

"*Allegedly*, he invented a story," said the inspector.

"That the brilliant painter, Monsieur Paul Gauguin . . ." Pierre resumed . . . "hid a chest of gold coins somewhere in the Society Islands. At times, George claimed the gold was buried on Tahiti, other times he said it was on Hiva-Oa."

"I thought the painter died in poverty," Caity said.

"So it seemed, but Gauguin's family included a former president of Peru, and it was rumored that Gauguin hoarded gold from that country. That he kept it hidden to prevent his estranged wife from getting her share. That he preferred to live . . . and to die . . . in poverty rather than to share the fortune with *the witch* as he called her."

"I never heard any such rumor . . ." Caity flushed, and then smiled. "Of course I didn't."

"Because George invented it," said the inspector.

"But very believable, since Gauguin was, as I recall, connected to the president of Peru. Bravo for George Parker." Caity clapped softly. "I can see how the story could get going around town."

"Exactly. He told the story at the bars, and then the people of the town embellished it. It circulates without him now."

"So how did this story of Gauguin's gold land him in jail?" Spense asked. Though he could venture a guess. He was getting the distinct feeling this George Parker was a bona fide con man.

"George often peddled maps to the treasure—*Gauguin's gold.* Nothing too terrible about that, we thought." He glanced at his brother.

The Inspector shrugged. "As long as Mr. Parker stated up front that it was a *legend,* my thinking was that it was legal enough. Buyer beware, I think you say. We tended to look the other way."

"Harmless fun for the tourist to search for the gold." Pierre nodded.

"But occasionally, we did get a complaint from an unhappy customer. We'd bring George in for the night and remind him to be clear with the tourists that Gauguin's gold wasn't a sure thing. That it might be pure fantasy," the inspector said.

"No hard feelings on his part," Pierre continued. "He'd come by for dinner the next day, bring a bottle of wine. His family never stayed more than a few weeks, but they returned to the island often."

"Did they have business in Tahiti? Besides the treasure maps?"

"I cannot say." He hesitated. "George mentioned a banker maybe. I think he did have an account in town. But as for any other business, I don't think so."

"So George Parker was a charmer who sold fake treasure maps to tourists and made up fantastic stories about Paul Gauguin. Sounds like a con artist to me," Caity said.

"I believe he was a very capable one." The deputy nodded, and then looked at them earnestly. "Like father like daughter, *oui*?"

Chapter 11

"SPEAK OF THE daughter . . ." Inspector Brousseau said. "I have her right outside."

Pierre leaped to his feet. "You've found Rose?"

"*Non*. If we'd found her wouldn't I have said so right away? It's the other daughter, Lilly, who's waiting outside."

Caitlin, who'd been gathering up her things, dropped her bag with a thud. Spense turned his palms up. Per the clock on the wall, they could still make it to the pâtisserie to meet their family on time if they left ten minutes ago.

She sighed, faking disappointment that the cake tasting would have to wait a little while longer.

It wasn't that she didn't like cake.

It was only that she'd been trying to picture Lilly since the moment she'd learned of her existence. Caitlin had a thousand questions about the twins. Were they identical? Did they share some kind of uncanny, almost psychic connection? Did Lilly know her sister carried a gun? Would Lilly turn out to be a valuable lead, a thorn in their side, or just a regular family member worried about her loved one?

"And she's in a state," Brousseau added. "It's a good thing we have our American friends here to ease her mind."

"How do you mean?" Pierre asked.

"Rose called her sister for assistance when she was arrested last night. When Lilly arrived this morning to see her, and found we didn't have her, she became distressed. She seems to be under the impression that we've done something nefarious with Rose. Nothing I've said thus far has succeeded in disabusing her of this notion—though I explained that we are governed by French law not despotism. Suspects in our custody are as safe as they would be on American soil."

Caitlin understood French law enforcement to be quite sophisticated, but she didn't blame Lilly for her concerns. "Still, I can understand how she'd be mistrustful until she's provided with an explanation. I'm sure Pierre's account will reassure her."

Brousseau spoke into a radio, and a moment later an officer ushered Lilly Parker into the interview room.

She did not disappoint.

If you look out over the South Pacific Ocean in the morning, its color is deep, deep blue. Except near the shoreline where the white beach underlies it and the early sun shines down on it. There, it's a spectacular shade of green. One that Caitlin had never seen anywhere else, until now—in Lilly Parker's eyes, swimming with tears. Long wavy tresses, the color of sand, formed the perfect surround to a heart-shaped face. Lilly had a small straight nose and a dimple in her left cheek.

Beautiful.

And not identical to her sister.

Rose's features were, however, quite similar to Lilly's, though Caitlin hadn't seen Rose's eyes in the daytime. Last night they'd appeared jade-like. And wasn't Rose's dimple in the other cheek? She closed her eyes, and a flash of imagination conjured a brightly painted Gauguin, featuring Rose and Lilly surrounded by tropical flora. That would've made quite a portrait.

It didn't exactly astound her that Pierre had succumbed to Rose's charm.

The best word she could think of for the sisters was *mesmerizing*. She imagined that together they'd create quite a stir.

"I demand to see my sister, Rose, immediately."

Caitlin strained forward to better hear the surprisingly meek voice that emerged from this dynamic looking young woman. If this was how Lilly spoke when she was *in a state* her normal voice must be a whisper.

"We demand the same," said the inspector. "I'm afraid your sister fled, and she's destroyed government property in the process. There's a missing camera. She's accused of shooting her husband. These are very serious crimes, and I can assure you we are doing our utmost to apprehend—that is—to locate her. Once we have her in our custody, we'll notify you *tout de suite*."

Lilly's head turned left and right and back in a shake made more dramatic by its gentleness. "I demand to see my sister, *now*."

"Mademoiselle, you are understandably distressed by recent events." Brousseau went to her and guided her to a seat beside Caitlin.

Lilly placed her hand on the back of the chair but remained standing.

"Please, sit." Caitlin nodded in Spense's direction. "This is Atticus Spenser, a special agent with the FBI. I'm Caitlin Cassidy. I'm not an FBI agent. I'm a consultant. But I help on cases."

"*Dr.* Cassidy is my partner and a hell of a criminal profiler," Spense said, shooting Caitlin a look.

"Please sit," Caitlin invited the young woman again.

Lilly slid into the seat slowly, as if doing her best to resist a magnetic chair while her pockets were loaded with pennies. "I saw the news report. I know who you are. I was going to call the embassy, but actually I prefer the FBI look into my sister's disappearance."

"She did not disappear." Brousseau's fingers moved near his mouth. If he had a mustache, he certainly would be twirling it. "She broke out of jail."

"Not exactly." Pierre pulled his shoulders back. "I let her out of her cell, and she walked out the front door. I'm not sure that's the same thing."

"It is quite the same thing under the circumstances," his brother replied.

Lilly gripped the table. "This is nonsense. My sister wouldn't hurt a spider much less a person. What proof do you have that she didn't come to harm while in your custody?"

"Had she not ripped the camera from the ceiling, I'd be happy to provide proof," Brousseau said.

"Very convenient for you. I say you broke your own camera to destroy the evidence."

"Lilly." Caitlin decided to intervene. "I haven't seen any tapes of what happened in your sister's holding cell, but I can tell you she did come into our hotel room last night, brandishing a pistol. Two uniformed men took her peacefully into custody and brought her to the police station. You know she arrived safely, because she called you. Deputy Brousseau will explain what happened after that." She looked pointedly at Pierre. The man's story was too humiliating not to be believed.

As Pierre recounted his version of last night's events again, Caitlin studied Lilly's body language. Arms, initially tightly crossed, slowly loosened as the tale unfolded. Her lips quivered several times with what Caitlin interpreted as deep empathy. Lilly seemed to be putting herself in her sister's place. In fact at one point, she lifted her hand as if sipping scotch from a cup. If the sisters had that queer empathy that so many twins do, she might be able to accept the truth of Pierre's story based on intuition alone.

Assuming he was telling the truth.

But Caitlin would bet her mother's secret pound cake recipe he was.

"Three-card Monte?" Lilly's hands lifted as though flinging imaginary cards. "That's how she got away?"

Pierre nodded. "I had to drink every time I lost a round."

Lilly exhaled a long breath and then blinked away a fresh round of moisture from her eyes. "I believe you," she said.

"Very good." Inspector Brousseau folded his hands. "Now, as I said, we will notify you *tout de suite*—"

"No. My sister may have broken out of your jail, but I'm not letting you off the hook. She was in your custody. It was your responsibility to keep her safe. And now, she's out there, probably scared to death, afraid that if she turns herself in something terrible will happen. And what if she's in danger?"

"From whom? Her husband?" Caitlin asked.

"I—I don't know. I told you Rose wouldn't hurt anyone. I still don't believe she shot Tommy."

"But Agent Spenser saw her shoot him, and Rose fled the scene," Caitlin said.

"Maybe it was Tommy's gun. Maybe Rose and Tommy struggled and, and, she shot him in self-defense." Lilly gripped Caitlin's arm. "Please, will you help us? Rose and me? I don't know who to turn to. I don't have money for a lawyer."

"We can't act as your advocate. Or Rose's," Caitlin said. "I need to be clear on that."

Lilly ducked her head and drew a shuddering breath. "But you will help?"

"We'll look into things," Spense said.

"You'll make sure the police don't try to plant evidence or—"

Brousseau slammed his hand on the table. "Enough. I don't know where all this mistrust begins. But in Papeete we do not operate outside the law. Indeed, your own father was a friend to Pierre. He trusted him, as you have heard."

"My papa may have played cards and listened to jazz with your brother. He may have even liked him. But I promise you, he trusted no policeman. And neither will I."

It wasn't lost on Caitlin that by extension Lilly couldn't trust her or Spense either.

And if Lilly didn't trust them, how could they trust Lilly?

Chapter 12

KEEPING HER HEAD tucked, Rose lingered in front of the aluminum paneled concession truck parked midway down Dolphin Beach. She'd been to this particular truck twice before with Tommy, and she'd chosen it today for two reasons. First, the burgers were delicious, and second she'd seen the vendor trying to cheat the tourists out of extra francs and cuffing the ears of his assistant for no good reason. He was the antithesis of most of the island inhabitants who were among the friendliest folks she'd ever known.

Now, she pretended to study the menu posted below the vendor's serving window, but in reality, she was far more interested in the kicked-back guy she'd spotted on her six. Reflected in the shiny panels of the food truck, she could see, approximately fifteen yards behind her, a young man, late teens to early twenties. Obviously

American and surrounded by beach bags, bottles of sunscreen, and an assortment of feminine clothing. Shorts, cover-ups, and tank tops sprawled over three empty beach chairs like they owned the place.

Big brother turned designated stuff watcher.

Could've been the *Top Gun* shades pushing up his clipped brown hair, or his devil-made-me-do-it mouth, but whatever the reason, this kid looked the type. Rose could easily picture him buzzing the tower on a flyby—and getting away with it.

Unfortunately for him, he was perfect.

As for her, hiding in plain sight on a crowded beach had been a risky but necessary call. Dolphin Beach was familiar and close to the jail, and she was on foot—*bare* foot. Luckily plenty of folks were dressed with even less panache than Rose, who'd ditched the long pants that came with her jail uniform right out of the gate and tied the gray prisoner's top in a sailor's knot beneath her breasts. The top was plain enough to pass for an incredibly tacky bikini cover-up—à la your husband's old shirt—and her purple thong undies made barely acceptable faux swim bottoms.

She swept her gaze one last time over the kid guarding his sisters' gear.

If only there were another way.

But there wasn't.

She hadn't eaten since yesterday. She had no money. No *shoes*.

And she was on the run from the law.

She was going to need the beach attire to slip through the crowd unseen—eventually someone was bound to notice her odd getup, put two and two together, and call the cops.

It was time to put *Anna* back to work.

She'd hopped on one bare foot and then another across scorching sand to get to the food truck, and now she made a one-eighty and stared at Top Gun until he looked up and caught her. Instantly, she averted her gaze, turned around, and got in line. Counted to twenty. Peeked back over her shoulder and smiled shyly at the young man, who looked behind him, and then when recognition dawned, cocked his mouth into a bad-boy grin. Averting her gaze again, she stood on alternating legs until she reached the front of the line, then ordered a loaded cheeseburger. By the time it was cooked, so were her feet, and the other patrons had taken their taffy and sodas and moved on.

She accepted her burger, shoved a delicious bite into her mouth and began hopping away.

"Stop!" The vendor, a bulked-up gentleman with tattoo sleeves and thatches of greased black hair plastered over his bald spot shook his fist at her.

She froze.

Top Gun glanced up with just the *you-okay?* expression she'd been hoping for. Of course she'd never trade Lilly, but she'd sometimes fantasized about what it would be like to have someone looking out for her—like a big brother.

She smiled at him, feeling genuinely grateful for his concern, then turned back to the vendor. "Who me?"

"*Oui.* You no pay."

She scarfed two more bites, ingesting all the calories she could manage, and then wiped her mouth with the back of her hand.

"I gave you a five. I put it right there on the counter. Maybe now I want my tip back."

"Your tip back? You no pay. The cost is three hundred francs."

"I left you five dollars. That's more than five hundred francs. I know what a dollar is worth."

Big brother was on his feet, just as she'd known he would be. Her hands clenched at her sides.

You don't have to live like this forever. Just make believe. Play the game.

"Your burger tastes like goat meat. Did you serve me a goat?" Anna leaned in and whispered the words to the vendor, then made a gagging motion with her index finger.

His hand flashed by as he grabbed her collar.

"Help!" she yelled. "Somebody help!"

He released her so fast she stumbled back and the burger went sailing. She took the opportunity to pratfall, taking care to find a shady spot. She closed her eyes and counted to ten. Opened them.

Top Gun stood over her with his hand extended. "Are you hurt?"

She let him help her to her feet. "I don't know. And I don't know you."

"I'm Jonah. Don't worry. I'm American, too."

And there they were. Bonded. Strangers in a strange land.

"He grabbed me and he . . ." She started to cry. Just a little. Sputtering only here and there as though trying like mad not to.

Jonah took her by the elbows and steadied her. "Wait right here. I'll take care of this." He stalked over to the food truck and stuck his face in the window.

Before Jonah could make an accusation the vendor went on the defensive. "I did nothing! I didn't touch her!"

"I saw you." Jonah's feet came off the ground as he hefted himself halfway through the window.

"Rester dos!" The vendor's fists went up, and he ran out the side door of his truck. *"Je faire non vouloir a lutte!* I no want fight!"

Jonah darted around and now the vendor had the truck at his back and Jonah blocking his escape from the front. "You owe this lady an apology."

Anna backed away slowly until she reached Top Gun's beach chairs.

"She no pay!" The fists stayed up.

She slipped into a pair of shorts and stuck her feet in the flip-flops, then pulled one of the women's tops over her head.

Jonah widened his stance and crossed his arms. "Apologize to the lady before I call the cops. Or maybe I'll take care of this myself. You want the cops? Or me?"

She confiscated a wallet and a makeup bag from a beach tote, then mingled with the crowd gathering around the men. Quickly and quietly she backed to the edge of the group, turned and made her escape as fast as her flip-flops and enough decorum to blend in allowed.

When she cast one last glance over her shoulder to be sure Top Gun wasn't following her, a familiar face smiled back.

As a seagull dive-bombed into the waves after its prey, her heart plunged to her stomach.

Tommy.

She picked up her knees and ran, never looking back to see if Tommy was in pursuit. Though the soft sand and the distant hum of the crowd hid any sound but that of her panting breaths, she knew he was right behind her.

Because Tommy would never let her go.

She reached a grass-covered hilltop and veered left. Picked up speed. Without the deep vats of sand trapping every step, her legs felt suddenly lighter. But with each stroke of her foot against the grass, her heart grew heavier.

Because all she'd ever dreamed of was living the kind of life where she didn't have to run or hide or live in fear of being caught in a lie.

An ordinary life.

But her chance at *ordinary* vanished the instant she'd fired her gun at Tommy Preston.

She was wanted for attempted murder.

And all the evidence was on his side.

She froze, listening. Above her own heartbeat, she heard the *whoosh* of wind splitting through the trees. Grunting breaths not far behind her.

Run!

Her ears pricked at the sound of silence.

Had she lost Tommy?

He'd been so close on her heels.

A pain in her side struck like lightning but she didn't stop.

Ahead, a paved road came into view.

Her heart was beating too fast. Her legs threatened to give way.

She'd been running too long and too hard.

Air seeped from her lungs as though they were leaky balloons.

Hide.

If she didn't rest, she'd fall over.

But there was nowhere.

When she reached the road, her shoes made slapping noises on the pavement.

One slipped off, forcing her to stop and retrieve it.

As she slid the flip-flop on, she eyed the hilly landscape and noticed the smell of manure wafting toward her.

A farm.

There must be one nearby. Behind that slope?

She scrambled up it, and when she reached the crest, her heart lifted. At the bottom of the hill was a big red building—a barn. And a cornfield. And sheds.

She dropped and rolled.

Fastest way to get down the hill.

TOMMY PUT HIS hands on his knees, breathing heavily, and watched Rose tumble down the hill. He'd crested the slope moments after her, and he'd be damned if he'd risk life and limb to play Jack and Jill with her. He ducked and waited until she'd had plenty of time to reach the bottom and find a hiding place. Most likely she'd head for the barn. And while she was tucked in a hayloft, he'd catch his breath, get his strength back, and take his time getting safely down to the meadow.

His fingers stroked his Glock.

Rose was a beautiful, sexy woman with more spunk than most. It was a damn shame he was going to have to shoot her . . . in self-defense.

Chapter 13

AS SPENSE AND Caity shoved through the door of Juliette's bakery, Special Agent Gretchen Herrera whispered something into Special Agent Alex "Dutch" Langhorne's ear. Knowing Dutch, Spense figured they'd made a bet on exactly how late he and Caity would be. One hour and twenty minutes would've been the correct answer. Dutch passed a dollar to Gretchen—the apparent winner.

After interviewing Lilly Parker, Spense and Caity had stayed at the station another half hour in order to let Brousseau bring them up to speed on the results of his officers' findings to date and their meeting with Tommy, who'd been released from the hospital earlier this morning. And though Spense didn't mind keeping Gretch and Dutch waiting—they'd do the same thing if the situation was reversed—he felt a sharp guilt pang when he saw the moms.

The two women stuck their hands up and motioned excitedly, notifying him of their presence—as if somehow he and Caity wouldn't spot their own mothers hanging out at a table with Caity's best friend and Spense's half brother in an otherwise empty bakery.

All smiles though they were, Agatha Spenser and Arlene Cassidy looked done in. The wedding party, which consisted of the moms, Gretchen, and Dutch, had arrived in Tahiti last night, and no doubt jet lag was responsible for the older women's droopy eyes. Gretch and Dutch seemed none the worse for it. No surprise since those two thrived on lack of sleep. Back in the day, when Spense had served in the field with his half brother, he'd accused Dutch of grinding down his fangs to conceal his true identity as Lestat. It would've been a plausible theory if only the vampire had thick red hair cropped Bureau short.

"Sorry we're late." Spense approached the ensemble with up-turned palms.

His mom jumped to her feet to embrace Caity, while Arlene got up and roped him in for a big squeeze. Gretchen and Dutch waited their turns and then offered hugs to Caity and a clap on the back to Spense. On impulse, Spense pulled his brother back in for a last-minute bear hug. Afterward, Dutch looked away quickly, but not before Spense caught a hint of moisture in his eyes.

Real men do cry.

If you count a split-second sheen as tears.

Spense's throat welled, too. When he first learned his late father had sired an illegitimate brother, it had seemed like the universe had thrown him a curve ball. But now, with Caity in his life and a brother who could be counted on when the going got tough, it felt like he'd whacked the thing out of the park. Sometimes the balls with the most spin on them turn out to be the ones that fly the farthest. His relationship with Dutch had gone—with no small amount of effort on both of their parts—from outright dislike to grudging respect to true friendship.

"There are worse fates than being trapped in a sweets shop with Gretchen and Dutch," his mom said, as they all took a seat around a big round table. A dozen plates of cakes and multicolored marzipan confections encircled a table tent that read "Cassidy and Spenser Wedding party."

Arlene dabbed a clump of pink frosting from the corner of her mouth. "Hope it's okay we started without you."

"Sure, but, what is all this? I wasn't expecting . . . there are more cakes to taste than guests. We're only six people."

"And you only get married once. Agatha and I don't want you to miss out on anything, just because it's an intimate affair."

"I expected this from you, Spense. But I thought Caitlin would arrive on time for her own tasting." Dutch winked at Caity.

"Maybe they don't like cake." Gretchen stuffed a spoonful of something yellow into her mouth and sent him a look that told Spense she was on to them. The only question was how much did they know, and were the moms looped in?

Standing nearly six feet tall, and with more muscle than a lightweight boxer, Agent Gretchen Herrera wasn't the type to be intimidated by any man, but to Spense, the striking bronze-skinned blonde always seemed a bit off her game around Dutch. Like now for instance, she was patting one of those lacy things—a doily—between her palms. Soaking up the evidence of the effect his brother had on her?

Dutch was still mourning the recent death of his wife and

likely didn't even register Gretchen's infatuation. It was simply too soon for him to notice other women. Still, Gretchen was good people, and Spense wasn't unhappy the wedding had thrown her together with his brother.

"So here's the thing," Gretchen said. "In all seriousness, if you two are late, I'm sure you have a good reason."

The moms nodded their accord.

"But if you want the cake to be ready in time, you've got to make a decision today."

"Does anyone despise coconut? Because Caity loves it but it doesn't agree with her," Arlene said.

"Mom, please don't start." Caity wrinkled her brow. "One stomachache at the age of five does not a food allergy make."

"I love coconut." Spense grinned.

Dutch coughed into his hand. "We have three coconut icings and a dozen cake flavors to choose from so you're not done yet. And you were supposed to pick the beach location yesterday."

Spense shot a questioning look at Caity. Yesterday, she'd said that spot they'd picked on Dolphin Beach was perfect, but did she still feel that way after everything that had happened?

"We found an ideal place." Caity touched his shoulder and the warmth radiated all the way down to the bone.

"Yep." He should've known she'd be fine with it. Caity was a sport. One of the many, many things he adored about her. "And we took care of the license yesterday morning. We're right on track."

"Glad you managed to get your license, pick your spot, and save a guy's life. Sounds like you had a productive day yesterday," Dutch said.

Spense blew out a breath. Not that he thought the incident

wouldn't ever come to light. He'd just hoped to keep his mom and Arlene in the dark a few days longer. He didn't want them to worry.

"Look," Gretchen said. "We've *all* seen the news." She cast a side-glance at the moms.

"And what we'd like to know," Arlene said, "is are you two late because you were pre-honeymooning in your bungalow, or have the local police somehow managed to cajole you into helping them find the woman who escaped after allegedly shooting her husband?"

Like her daughter, Arlene was big on innocent until proven guilty. Of course what she didn't know was that the same woman had aimed a pistol at her daughter last night. And Spense would like to keep that information from her for as long as possible. But he wouldn't lie. If it came up, it came out.

"The French police aren't the cajoling types," he said. "But as a matter of fact, Caity and I did agree to help. When we went to the station to give our statements this morning things got complicated."

"Shocker." Agatha's fork clattered onto the table. "Atticus, I don't like to interfere . . ."

Since when?

"But I have to say, if you've given your statements and saved a man's life already then you've done your duty. This matter no longer concerns you."

"I'm afraid it does, Mom."

"Son, you may think planning a wedding isn't important compared to catching criminals, but . . ."

"I don't think that at all. And I promise we're going to wrap this up in plenty of time."

"But there are so many preparations and so little time," Arlene said.

Agatha touched Arlene's arm lightly. "We can help. And I'm not sure what's left to do except find a photographer and inform the minister of the location."

Arlene sighed. "What about the centerpiece? I suppose we could choose that for them. It's only that Caity has such a love of flowers."

"I'm sure you'll do a great job, Mom," Caity said.

"Fine. But I feel strongly you two should choose the cake." Arlene crossed her arms over her chest.

"Then let's get started. I'm ready to make a memory." Spense took a bite of something gooey and chocolate, then pointed. "Let's put this one on the short list."

Gretchen and Dutch came out of a huddle.

"How about we make a memory Cassidy and Spenser style?" Gretchen said. "You can update us on the case while we eat cake. Two birds. Dutch and I want to help out, and no one else is around to overhear."

Spense tilted his head toward the moms.

"If you think keeping us in the dark will stop us from worrying, it won't. We know your work can be dangerous. The truth is, knowing what's happening is better than imagining the worst. But maybe you think we can't be trusted not to leak something to the press," Agatha said.

"We trust you more than anyone," Spense said.

Caity shrugged. "I think it's a good idea. My head is brimming with questions."

As was his. He wouldn't mind using the others as a sounding board. "All right. I think I'll let Caity tell it." He wanted to let her choose how much to reveal to the moms. If she wanted them to know everything, that was good with him, but if she wanted to hold back what happened in their bungalow that was okay, too. Her call.

In the end, Caity told them the whole story, and he felt a weight lift from his shoulders. He preferred transparency whenever possible. He didn't like keeping secrets from his family. And in this case, he was under no obligation to do so.

He turned his palms up. "Any questions?"

"A few," Arlene said.

He suppressed a smile—it seemed she'd been taking notes on a napkin.

"First, I'd like to know, based on what you saw in the water, who was trying to kill who?"

And there you had it, the million-dollar question. "I don't know," Spense answered.

"But you saw it go down," Dutch said.

"We did. I saw the bride fire the gun. And because of what happened in our bungalow, and because she conned her way out of jail, the inspector is assuming the bride was the aggressor."

Caity straightened her back. "But it's not as clear-cut as you would think. Spense and I both saw a struggle. But neither of us saw where the gun came from. So I'd say that's on the list of unknowns—and a very important unknown in determining what really happened in the water."

Dutch pulled out a tablet and began taking notes, too. "Question number one, whose gun was it, and where did it come from?"

"Maybe the groom had that gun in his pocket. Maybe he was trying to drown the bride—that's what Spense thought was happening in the beginning—and she got the gun away from him and shot him in self-defense." Arlene was making napkin notes again as she spoke.

"You said it's a Ruger LCP II, that's under one pound," Gretchen said. "Rose could've hidden the pistol in her wedding gown. Maybe the groom saw it, and tried to dunk her in the water to kill the gun."

"I don't think she'd just stuff it down her dress. It would be too easy to spot. If she thought to carry a gun on her wedding day, that suggests premeditation. Maybe she had the dress made to conceal the weapon," Caity said.

Agatha tugged the tablecloth. "It's an odd theory though, that Rose might've brought a gun to her wedding. It doesn't make sense to me. I certainly would not marry a man I wanted to murder."

Good to know his mother was among the sane. Spense touched his heart and smiled at her.

Dutch began typing again. "I'll check with the local police and ask them to inspect the gown carefully. You say you think they're capable."

"We do," Spense said. "Otherwise, they wouldn't have caught Rose in our bungalow. I'm surprised no one wants to know how the cops found her."

"I do." Arlene shoved away a piece of carrot cake.

"It was strong work on the part of Brousseau's men. They were interviewing the front desk and learned that the only thing out of the ordinary that happened that night was that a woman ordered a fruit basket over the phone. It was sent to our room, but the credit card she used turned out to have been reported stolen. The men didn't think it was a coincidence, so they returned to our bungalow to check things out."

"So, you think Rose sent the fruit basket to find out where your room was? She followed the basket?" His mom would make a good detective.

"Apparently. It's the only thing that seems to make sense," he said.

"That doesn't explain how she knew you were staying at the hotel." Agatha was on a roll.

"She might have called around to ask, but the Dolphin Beach Hotel would be the logical place to look for us, since we were hanging out on Dolphin Beach that day."

"But why on earth would she risk coming back to the hotel to find you? And what did she mean when she said she could explain everything? And if she did plan to kill her husband, why not just shoot him dead someplace normal, like in a hotel room? Would she even know the gun would work underwater? And you said the groom refused police protection. That makes no sense to me. Something's off with this whole situation." Arlene finally took a breath.

"These are great questions, but we don't have the answers yet." Caity rested her chin in her hand.

Then Spense's phone buzzed, vibrating on the table. He checked the messages and looked up, licked his fingers and slid an outrageous piece of marble cake with orange coconut frosting Caity's way. "Check this out, hon."

Caity forked a big bite loaded with icing into her mouth. "Delicious. I'm calling it," she said with her mouth still full.

"We'll take this one." Spense got to his feet.

"But you haven't tasted the other flavors," the moms protested.

"We know what we like." Spense pulled Caity up by the hand then turned to Dutch and Gretchen. "And we gotta go."

"But we could definitely use your help with the case," Caity added.

"Name it," Dutch said.

"While you're checking on the wedding gown, I'd also like to know if Tommy Preston and Rose Parker took out life insurance on each other. And anything you can dig up on their backgrounds."

"We're on it. But where are you going? Want us to tag along?"

"No let's divide and conquer. Caity and I are heading back to Dolphin Beach. It seems there's been more trouble. Not sure just what, but Inspector Brousseau says it's urgent."

Chapter 14

Wednesday
Near Plage Des Dauphins
Tahiti Nui

"COME ON OUT now, Rose, my love." The door to the barn rattled shut behind Tommy. She probably thought he couldn't see her lurking in the shadows, crouching behind the waist-high fence of an empty pen. He could charge in there and drag her out, but he'd rather not wade through the bucket of slop she'd apparently kicked over in her haste.

"Let's talk this over and see what we can work out," he said. What was her game? Did she really think she could outwit him?

No answer.

He glanced at his watch.

Wait another minute.

Let her think she's well hidden.

He had the upper hand, and he was enjoying it. "I'll make you a deal, babe. You give me what I want, and I'll tell the cops this was all a misunderstanding."

From his vantage point he saw her lurch forward. As though she was actually considering taking him up on the offer. Maybe if he sweetened the pot. "You and Lilly can go home, and I'll never interfere with either of you again."

Rose climbed to her feet.

He stuck his pistol out front and watched, slack-jawed, as she came out of her corner. She marched right up to the wall of the pen and stood in front of him with her hands on her hips, bold as brass.

She would've made a damn fine wife.

"What is it that you want?"

Oh really? She didn't know? He was the one with a concussion. "Don't play games with me. I want the thumb drive."

"And in exchange I get what?"

"I told you. I'll tell the cops it was nothing—an accident. That I don't want them to bring charges."

"How generous of you, considering *you're* the one who tried to murder *me*."

"That's not how I remember it." She was probably lying, trying to confuse him. He couldn't remember anything but bits and pieces about what happened in the water. Flashes of Rose with a pistol in her hand, swimming through blood, that mammoth of an FBI agent locking an elbow across his chest. What he did remember however was what happened *before*.

On the morning of their wedding, he'd caught her red-handed copying files from his computer. Until he'd seen her stick a thumb drive in her pocket, until he'd seen the reflection of his laptop's screen in the mirror flashing *SADIE*. Until she'd slammed down the cover of that laptop to hide her treachery, he'd planned on making her not only his wife, but his true companion.

She could've had it all.

But she hadn't wanted it all.

She hadn't wanted *him*.

And that was the one thing he could *never* forgive. When she'd rejected him, she'd signed her death warrant . . . and Lilly's, too, of course. Because Rose loved Lilly, but she didn't love him, and he couldn't have that. "Give me back the SADIE file and all is forgiven."

"I don't have it on me." A visible shiver traveled the length of her body. He noticed her shirt was sweat soaked. She might have the chills from all that running and climbing and rolling down hills.

He had a sudden urge to wrap her in his arms . . . and strangle her.

His nose itched from all the hay lying around and it gave him an idea.

Keeping his pistol trained on Rose he sidestepped over to a pile of tools propped against the wall and grabbed a pitchfork.

Boom.

He banged the pitchfork's handle on the floor. "Don't make me do something we'll both regret. There's no way out of this. I've got a gun, and this interesting pitchfork here, and you've got something that is useless to you but valuable to me."

"You wouldn't be threatening me if SADIE didn't have the power to destroy you."

It did, indeed. But it almost sounded as though Rose didn't understand what she had. And if that was the case, how would she know to seek it out in the first place? But those weren't the questions that mattered to him most. He craved the answer to a different query before he watched her die. "Why are you bent on destroying me, Rose? What have I ever done to you?"

She rubbed a spot of sunlight on her arm, and then looked up.

He followed the path of her gaze.

A rope hung from the roof—a swing for the kiddies.

He dropped the pitchfork and gripped the pistol with both hands. But he couldn't shoot her until he had that file. "Don't—"

The floor creaked.

Rose sprang, arms extended, reaching for the rope.

Too late, Tommy ducked. She came soaring over the stalls, feetfirst. A crushing blow to his chest sent him flying back. He landed against the far wall and crumpled to the floor as his gun went spinning across the floor.

Rose lunged for his Glock.

Tommy leaped, knocking her flat, before she reached the gun. He pinned her with his weight and twisted her arm behind her back. "You just signed your sister's death warrant." He put his mouth close enough to hers to take her breath into his lungs—one last time. "You're *both* dead. I want you to know that, before I—"

Shouts and footfalls interrupted his promise.

"Hell." He jumped off of her, grabbed his gun, and backed away.

A wild grin spread across her face, and she got into a crouch as if ready to spring again.

His heart raged in his chest.

If she stood her ground, he'd either have to shoot an unarmed woman in front of witnesses, or allow her to surrender and go back to the safety of a jail cell—he couldn't touch her there. And he didn't yet know what she'd done with SADIE.

Where is SADIE?

This crazy bitch might have the power to destroy him from beyond her grave.

"Run, Rosy. Run! Now, Rose!" His throat closed, and with a rage that flowed like poison through his blood he vowed that he would take from her the one thing she loved the most. "Run for your life if you ever want to see your sister again."

A flash of anger sparked in her green eyes, like lightning on a stormy sea. "You forget I have SADIE. Touch one hair on Lilly's head, and I give you my word, I will destroy you."

Chapter 15

A LITTLE IMPROMPTU task force, consisting of Caitlin, Spense, Gretchen, and Dutch had gathered in their hotel suite bright and early. As far as wrapping this case up went, yesterday had been a total bust. Rose Parker had escaped from her Papeete holding cell before they could interview her and allow her to *explain everything*, and then later, after being spotted at Dolphin Beach, she'd slipped through the police's fingers yet again, reportedly making off with cash, clothing, and makeup she'd swiped from some tourists. Inspector Brousseau had summoned Caitlin and Spense to assist in the mess, but by the time they got there, there was little to be done.

Over Brousseau's protest that it was not her responsibility, Caitlin had reimbursed an irate food vendor for the cost of a stolen burger. The American family had declined her offer to make good on what Rose had pilfered from them. Then Caitlin, Spense, and Brousseau had spent the afternoon taking witness statements—including one account claiming that a man matching Tommy Preston's description had chased Rose down the beach.

Tommy had, in fact, been released from the hospital early that same morning, but when a gendarme tracked him down, he was napping in his hotel suite and denied any knowledge of the incident, stating that he'd like to be updated in the event Rose was apprehended.

There had also been a report of a disturbance at a nearby property where a farmer and his wife spotted a woman about Rose's size and build fleeing from the barn. The police had yet to confirm the veracity of that story, but there was no reason to doubt the farmer's word. And finally, in the minor news department, Spense had missed his tuxedo fitting.

But today was a new day, and Caitlin had a feeling something was about to break.

Yesterday, at the cake tasting, they'd come up with some questions—today was about getting answers. While she and Spense had been chasing wild geese, Dutch and Gretchen had been gathering vital information.

"Okay, first up, we have a wedding dress report." Gretchen fanned a set of photographs out on the desk. Different shots of Rose Parker Preston's bloodied and torn gown. "Right off the bat, Brousseau's team noted it appeared to be torn in the back, with multiple buttons missing. Which might mean it was ripped in the struggle in the water with her husband, or that she deliberately tore it off to make a faster getaway."

"Or both," Caitlin said. "If the gown was torn during a struggle, it would've been easier for Rose to shed. I can't imagine how she could've gotten out of a wedding gown so fast and made her getaway otherwise. Have you ever tried to undo one of those things?"

"No, but I'm looking forward to it." Spense grinned and put his hands behind his head.

She flushed. She'd walked right into that one. "But a struggle still doesn't tell us who the aggressor was. Either party could've initiated a physical battle underwater. What else did you find?"

"After we spoke with the French state police, they inspected the gown again and made note of this." Gretchen held up a photo of the bodice of the wedding gown.

"I remember I could see that beadwork all the way down the beach," Spense said.

"Because there's a lot of it, and underneath, in the lining is a pouch, just big enough to conceal a Ruger LCP II. It closes with Velcro. We contacted the dressmaker and were told it was a special customer request. The extra beading was added to disguise the concealed pouch."

"So Rose Parker had a pouch sewn into her wedding gown to conceal a pistol." Spense whistled.

"Sure looks that way. Although she didn't specify to the dressmaker the purpose of the pouch. The seamstress thought it might be for carrying a wallet. But there are faint perspiration stains under the beadwork in a pattern consistent with the muzzle of an LCP. It looks a lot like premeditation. But it doesn't explain why Rose would attempt to kill her husband in an underwater shooting."

"I like the moms' idea that she planned to do it later, at the hotel. And I've got motive right here." Dutch tossed a manila envelope onto the coffee table. "An insurance agent from Riverbend, Texas, faxed these over this morning."

"I'm surprised the agent just handed over the policies without a warrant." As Caitlin smiled her appreciation at Dutch, she couldn't help noticing he was sitting just a skosh closer to Gretchen than usual.

"If you want to get your money's worth out of Dutch and me, you've got to give us a tougher assignment than convincing a small-town insurance man to give up the goods," Gretchen said. "So no, we didn't have any trouble persuading him. We Skyped him, flashed our Bureau creds, and he caved. Dutch was going to offer him tickets to a Cowboys' game, but it wasn't necessary."

"Maybe you two should go to the game instead," Spense suggested. "Gretchen could make a side trip to Dallas for the weekend."

"I'm in if Dutch is in. Which one of these three-million-dollar life insurance policies were you interested in?"

Caitlin caught the sparkle in Gretchen's eye.

Gretchen was dribbling out information to make things more interesting. But Caitlin didn't mind playing along. "There's more than one?"

Spense swept the envelope off the table and dumped its contents. "We're interested in any life insurance policy that Tommy Preston holds on the Parker woman or her on him."

"Yes, but which one?" Dutch asked.

Caitlin had to admit, this game was getting more interesting by the minute. "Which policy?"

"Which Parker sister?" Dutch exchanged a knowing glance with Gretchen.

Spense, who'd been shuffling through the papers, jerked his chin up. "Are you saying Tommy Preston has more than one life insurance policy on Rose?"

"Pay attention." Dutch grinned at his brother. "Get your Rubik's cube out if you need to, because you should focus on what I'm telling you. Gretch and I brought you an actual clue."

"We don't know what it means, but it means something," Gretchen said. "Not only did Rose Parker and Tommy Preston hold life insurance policies on each other, but Lilly Parker and Tommy Preston have policies on each other, too."

"So there are four life insurance policies?" Caitlin couldn't pretend she'd been clever enough to foresee that.

Spense tilted back in his chair and, following his brother's advice, reached for his cube, solved it, and smiled.

Everyone waited expectantly.

"Well, are you going to let the rest of us in on your epiphany or not?" Caitlin asked.

"No epiphany. I'm just trying to wrap my head around a good reason for Tommy and Lilly to hold policies on each other. Because without one, the insurance company would have refused to issue them."

Spense was right. It wasn't as if anyone could take life insurance out on another person simply because he wanted to. You needed the other person's consent and not only that—the policy owner would have to demonstrate that the insured person's death would result in a significant financial loss to himself. In the case of Rose and Tommy, it was a no-brainer. Insurance companies generally treated engaged couples the same as married couples. But on the flip side . . . "As far as we know there is no valid reason that would satisfy an insurance agency and allow Lilly and Tommy to take out life insurance on each other," Caitlin said.

"As far as we know." Spense put his cube away. "But the policies do exist. Therefore, there's something about Tommy Preston's relationship to the Parker sisters that we don't yet know. We need to learn more about their history to sort this thing out."

"Tommy was released from the hospital yesterday morning. He's staying here, in this hotel," Caitlin said. "Or we could start with Lilly. Brousseau said she's rented a town home in Papeete. We should update him about the policies, too."

"You two take Preston, and Gretchen and I will track down Lilly Parker." Dutch got to his feet.

Spense shook his head. "You volunteered for whatever duty, right?"

"That's what I'm saying. Yes. Anything you need."

Caitlin smiled. The truth was she wanted to interview both Tommy and Lilly. And if she was a poor delegator, Spense was even worse. She knew he'd want the chance to see both parties face to face and gauge not only their words, but their body language as well. "Then it would be great if you could contact the inspector, introduce yourselves, and tell him what you've learned about the life insurance policies. Spense and I will interview Tommy and Lilly."

"But—" Gretchen started to protest.

"And if you don't mind," Spense said . . . "I missed my tux fitting. It's Papeete Formal Wear. They open at nine a.m."

Dutch dragged a hand through his hair, and Caitlin could tell by his expression he wanted to dive into the case, not stand in for his brother at a tux fitting. But they had almost identical builds, and it was a stroke of genius on the part of Spense, whom she was certain wanted to spend as little time in any type of formal wear as possible. And it gave her a genius idea of her own.

Gretchen touched Dutch's sleeve. "You did say anything."

"Fine," Dutch conceded, with only a slight edge to his tone.

"Thanks." Caitlin smiled. "And there is one other thing . . . after the fitting . . . could you guys hang out with the moms? We promised to take them on a submarine tour."

"I've been dying to go on one of those." Gretchen's smile was big and genuine. "Where will you head first?"

"To Lilly's place," Caitlin said. The Parker twins were a fascinoma, and she was itching to hear Lilly's explanation for the insurance policies.

Chapter 16

Thursday
Heritage Townhomes
Papeete
Tahiti-Nui

EXHAUSTED AND YET somehow energized from his encounter with Rose, yesterday, Tommy steered his car into the Heritage Townhomes complex. Back at the barn, after hearing shouts, Tommy had hidden himself behind a nearby shed and watched as a man dressed in overalls and a woman in an apron charged across a green pasture after Rose. The aproned woman fell and the farmer stopped to help her, settling for cursing at Rose as she disappeared over the top of the hill.

Tommy had never even considered showing himself to the couple. The last thing he wanted was to help the cops catch Rose. He couldn't get to her if she were behind bars, and with Cassidy and Spenser around, a lot could go wrong. Maybe Rose didn't trust cops, but he couldn't count on her not to use SADIE to make a deal.

On the run was exactly where he wanted Rose.

There was no need to hunt her down.

Because he knew where Lilly lived.

And if he had Lilly, Rose would come to him.

He'd never met a woman more obsessed with her sister than Rose Parker.

His wooing Lilly would drive Rose to madness . . . and give him complete control of both women.

And control was what he needed in order to get his hands on that thumb drive.

After, he'd give Rose a front row seat to her sister's death.

He parked his rented Porsche a few spots down from Lilly's townhome in a covered space that would protect the car from the hazards of the sun. This might not be his own vehicle, but he wasn't a cad. He liked to treat a fine automobile with the care it deserved.

He killed the engine, and then groaned.

From around a corner, Cassidy and Spenser appeared. They looked to be heading for Lilly's place.

He pressed the starter button. His engine ignited and so did his heart.

He whipped his Porsche out of the parking lot and sped down the streets of Papeete, heading for the seedy side of town.

He had an important purchase to make.

WHEN LILLY PARKER opened the door to her townhome, Spense had to wipe his eyes. Whiskey fumes floated off her skin like she'd taken a bath in the stuff.

"Nice place," Caity said.

Heritage Townhomes provided modest housing to locals and tourists alike, and from what Deputy Pierre Brousseau had told them, this was the same complex George Parker liked to stay in when he summered in Papeete with his family. The freestanding frame houses were small but not crowded too close together. Lilly's unit was painted bright blue with a tall tiki totem pole and several potted pink hibiscus trees flanking the front door.

Without warning, Lilly rocked back on her heels.

Spense had to move quickly to break her fall. "May we come in?" he asked, though he was already inside, propping her up.

A bleary-eyed Lilly nodded, and Caity entered, closing the door behind her.

"You found Rose. Please tell me she's okay."

Dammit.

He regretted getting Lilly's hopes up. He'd meant to tell her straight away why they were here, but her stumble had distracted him.

Caity lightly touched Lilly's shoulder. "I'm sorry, but no, we haven't found her yet. We're here because we have a few more questions for you—if you don't mind."

They'd agreed it was best not to mention the beach incident and Rose's barnyard escape to Lilly. They wanted to know what she knew. It was possible her sister had contacted her for help, and she hadn't told the authorities. But judging by the look on Lilly Parker's face, she was either worried as hell about her sister or she was a consummate actress.

"Have we come at a bad time?" Caity asked, probably noting, like him, that Lilly was wearing the same yellow blouse as yesterday. All-over wrinkled, as though she'd slept in it.

He could see the kitchen through an open door. Green walls. An empty bottle lying on its side on a white tile countertop.

Caity helped Lilly to the sofa, with Lilly walking very slowly, and a little off balance. She hadn't quite slept it off, or maybe she hadn't slept at all.

"We can come back in a few hours," he said. No reason not to start with Tommy and give Lilly a chance to get it together.

"No." She gripped the arm of the sofa. "That's not necessary. I can guess what you think, but I'm not drunk, just a little hung over and dead tired. You're police. You should know that fatigue can mimic alcohol intoxication."

Just the fact that she could articulate her point so well made Spense believe her.

"I don't want to delay. If you think it will help find my sister, let's do this now."

"I'll make coffee then," Spense said, and left Caity to tend to Lilly without waiting for permission. When he returned from the kitchen, Lilly gratefully accepted the cup he gave her. She took a sip and wrinkled her nose. "Cold."

Given the likelihood that she'd slosh hot coffee on herself, Spense had taken the liberty of putting ice cubes in the cup. "It's a warm day. I thought you'd prefer it that way."

"You thought I'd burn myself. I've already told you, I'm hung over, but I'm not drunk. I'm simply exhausted and . . . sad."

"And that makes you every bit as likely to spill your coffee." Caity gave Lilly's prior argument, about fatigue mimicking drunkenness, back to her just in time for brown liquid to gush from the cup and onto her blouse.

Lilly poked at the stain. "Maybe I should've just said *thank you*." Then she gulped the cold brew in a few seconds, and after, put her hand on her forehead like she was taking her own temperature. "I think I'm entitled to go a little nuts under the circumstances. My sister's accused of the attempted murder of her husband. I may never see her again, and she thinks I hate her."

"Why would she think that?"

"My brain is pounding like the devil. I need an aspirin." Lilly made a move to get up, and Caity motioned her back down.

"I'll get it," Spense said. It only took a moment to locate the container that was already open on the counter near the empty whiskey bottle. He noted with some relief that the medicine bottle appeared full.

He brought back two tablets and a glass of water.

Lilly swallowed the aspirin and said, "Thanks. I never drank half a bottle of whiskey by myself before."

Caity raised an eyebrow. "Only half?"

"Yes. I drank the rest on the morning of the wedding."

Spense refrained from pointing out that that meant she had indeed drunk half a bottle of booze by herself before, because he did get her point. She meant she wasn't a drinker. And maybe that was true, current evidence to the contrary.

"You were drinking on the morning of your sister's wedding? But wasn't the ceremony on the beach around sunset?"

Lilly nodded.

"So you were celebrating early?" Caity prompted.

Lilly scoffed. "Celebrating? Hardly."

"You didn't want your sister to marry Tommy Preston," Spense said.

"You guys are a couple of geniuses."

Spense pulled up a cane-back chair and sat down. It felt too unstable for his big frame so he stood back up. This was good. Lilly wasn't bothering with social graces. Maybe they'd get the truth out of her. A rare event on a first—make that second—interview. "Sounds like you don't much like Tommy Preston."

Lilly shook her head *no*, then seemed to change her mind and nodded *yes*. "I don't know," she said after a moment. Like she had to really think hard about the question. Which seemed more than a little strange. Surely she knew her own opinion of the man. Spense opened his mouth and closed it again. For now, he'd let it go.

Caity waved her hand to include Spense and said, "Agent Spenser and I want you to know that we're taking what you said yesterday seriously."

"Which part?"

"All of it. But especially the theory that Rose might have been provoked into shooting Tommy. You say she's never been violent before."

"Never."

"What about Tommy? Has he ever been violent?"

"That I know of firsthand?"

Spense's radar went up. "Just answer the question."

"I don't know."

Just like she didn't know whether she liked him or not.

"But I do know Rose. And she isn't—violent. So thank you for listening, because that inspector seems to think that since Rose fired the gun that it was all planned out. And that she wouldn't have run away if she weren't guilty. But one thing life with my papa has taught me is that things aren't always what they seem."

Ah yes, *life with Papa*. Another point to circle back to.

"You know Rose better than anyone," Spense said. "So if you say she's not prone to violence, then either you're lying or you're correct that things aren't as they seem. She wouldn't have shot anyone unprovoked."

"*I'm* not lying."

"Okay. Let's assume not. You know any reason that would make Rose shoot Tommy?"

"All I can think of is self-defense."

Caity brought her fist under her chin. "That's what I'm thinking, too. So let's take that a step further. My next question is do you know any reason why Tommy would try to hurt Rose?"

A tear slid down her cheek. "I—I really don't know who to believe in this situation." She exhaled audibly. "I don't think Rose would hurt Tommy, and I also don't think Tommy would hurt Rose. But I—I must be wrong about one of them, because everyone is saying she shot him. Why would she do that?"

"That's what we're trying to figure out. There are some common motives for murder. Revenge, money, jealousy." Caity lifted one shoulder.

Clever how Caity had stuck *money* in the middle, as if it were of little significance. And yet Lilly's posture had gone rigid at the word. Spense made a mental note and asked, "Do you happen to know if Rose or Tommy carried life insurance on each other?"

Lilly's lips quivered almost imperceptibly, but enough to let Spense know he'd touched on an area she hadn't expected. "Are you aware of any life insurance policies Tommy and your sister, Rose, may own?" he rephrased.

Lilly folded her hands tightly in her lap. She waited a few beats. Looked to Caity, though Spense had asked the question. "Not on each other. Not that she told me about. But we weren't on good terms of late." She unfolded her hands and tucked a piece of long blond hair behind her ear. "How I wish I could go back in time and tell her how much I love her."

She seemed to need a minute, so they gave her one.

Eventually, without prompting, she continued. "I should mention that Rose and I have insurance on each other—we plan—that is we planned—to open a yoga studio together in California—that was before Tommy. And, um, Tommy and I have life insurance policies on each other, too. At least I assume he hasn't canceled anything since the premiums are paid up for a year." Her face drained of color. "You think Tommy might have tried to murder Rose for insurance money?"

It was a good sign she'd volunteered the information that she and Tommy had policies on each other. Spense had expected he'd have to drag it out of her. "We should at least consider the possibility."

Her hand trembled as she reached for her water glass. "Then what's to stop him from coming after me next?"

"That's a big leap, Lilly," Spense said. Though not an unthinkable one. They needed to determine quickly if Tommy Preston was an innocent victim or something worse. At the moment they had no indication, other than Lilly's assertion that her sister wasn't violent, to implicate Preston in anything. "Let's back up and start by having you explain why you agreed to let Tommy take out a policy on you in the first place. You must've given your consent."

"I did."

"And you would've had to have some sort of financial interest in one another, too. Were you . . . are you and Tommy Preston business partners?"

Her face flushed. "Of course not."

To Spense, Lilly seemed oddly offended by the suggestion.

Caity shot him a questioning look, picking up on the sudden increase in tension in the air.

He shifted in his seat before continuing. "Okay. Not business partners. Then what exactly is your connection to Tommy Preston? Besides the fact that he's married to your sister."

Lilly took another sip of coffee and dropped her head into her hands, obviously distressed by the question. He checked his watch. A full three minutes went by before she looked up again.

She yanked a tissue from a box on the coffee table and blew her nose, then pulled in a shaky breath. "I met Tommy Preston at a department store. I was working at the jewelry counter. He bought a few pieces, very lovely, very expensive ones. I assumed they were for a girlfriend, but he volunteered that the jewelry was for his mother. Do you believe that?"

Spense didn't know if he did or not. "Was it?"

"Absolutely. His mother is here in Tahiti for the wedding. You should talk to her, too. Maybe she can shed some light on things."

"We'll do that," Caity said. "But you were saying you were working as a saleswoman when you met Tommy."

"Yes. We got to talking, and we hit it off. He kept coming back every day. And he always bought something."

"That's a lot of jewelry."

"It is. Anyway, he's very charming, as I'm sure you'll find out. And obviously, he's very good-looking."

Spense shrugged.

"He is," Caity agreed. "And that must've been a nice commission for you."

She flushed again. "Well, yes. You can see how a girl would be swept off her feet."

Spense didn't see that. A man buying a lot of jewelry for some-one else would've made him suspicious, not goo-goo eyed. But Caity nodded vigorously, so there must be something to Lilly's point.

"And it wasn't just his charm. I'd recently lost my papa and Tommy was so very, very kind to me. But after a few weeks, he said he couldn't afford to keep buying his mother jewelry, and could we go for coffee. Of course, I said yes. We wound up dating, and eventually we talked about moving in together. Naturally, I wanted Rose to meet him first."

"She hadn't met him before then?"

Lilly looked down at her hands. "No. I guess I wanted to keep him all to myself for a little while. You see, since we were little girls, we've always shared everything. Twins and all—we're not identical, but still. And our mother wasn't around—she died giving birth to us. Honestly, Rose and I are almost too close. She's incredibly protective of me, and I suppose I wanted some sort of boundary. A little bit of independence."

"From Rose?"

"And from Papa. I know it sounds weird because he was al-ready dead, but my whole life I've never had any freedom to go my own way. Rose and I always had to be so cautious around everyone because of Papa's business—he called it *the life*—and when I was with Tommy, it was the first time I didn't have to be careful about what I said or did. I felt like I could be my own person. Just myself, *Lilly*. Not Lilly Parker, George's daughter and Rose's sister."

Even though he and Caity kept up their most effective inter-rogation technique—silence—Lilly stopped talking. She just sat there, a blank look in her eyes that made him want to snap his fingers to bring her out of her trance. When it became crystal clear she wouldn't continue on her own, Spense filled in the gaps for her.

"And when you finally did introduce Rose to Tommy, she stole your boyfriend. That's why she thinks you hate her, and that's why you didn't want them to get married."

Lilly brought her fist to her mouth and bit it. A muffled sob came out of her throat. "Rose didn't steal my boyfriend. She stole my fiancé. *I* was the one who was supposed to marry Tommy."

That explained the life insurance policies. Tommy and Lilly had obtained policies on each other during the time they were engaged. Then Tommy switched sisters and took insurance out on Rose, too. The premiums were paid up for a while. Lilly had mentioned that earlier, so Tommy still held policies on both women.

Could all be totally innocent . . . or a hell of a motive for murder. But for whom?

This *could* support Lilly's theory that Rose shot Tommy in self-defense, but it didn't explain why Rose had a gun on her person on her wedding day. If Spense ignored his gut, and stuck strictly to logic, the facts pointed to premeditation on Rose's part. She married a rich guy and planned to murder him, collect his entire estate and a fat life insurance policy to boot. And Lilly would get a nice windfall, too, from the policy she held on Preston. A big win for *both* Parker sisters . . . if Rose could pull it off.

"That must have been devastating for you," Caity said.

"I've never felt more betrayed. More alone in the world. And it wasn't just that she took him from me. It was that she lied to me—her own sister. I love Rose unconditionally, and you would think that if she fell in love with Tommy she would've simply said so. But instead, she came to me with a horrible, horrible story, trying to get me to break up with him. My own sister tried to *con* me out of my fiancé."

A connection pinged back in Spense's head to something Lilly had said earlier. "Is that what you meant when you mentioned you didn't know *firsthand* of any violence Tommy had committed?"

Lilly nodded. Now that she was rolling, she seemed ready to tell them everything. "Yes. Rose came to me, about six months ago, and told me I had to get away from Tommy. She claimed she'd met a woman—a prostitute named Pamela Jean—and this woman had information on Tommy that could destroy everything he'd worked to build. His business, his reputation in the community, everything. Rose said Tommy had beaten Pamela Jean to keep her quiet." Her face took on a ghostly pallor. "Rose said this prostitute had later died from her injuries. She begged me to leave Tommy, and to go with her right then and there to California."

"To start the yoga studio?"

"Yes."

Spense had to wonder where the Parker sisters had thought they'd get the money for that studio. If Lilly was working at a department store, it didn't suggest wealth. But maybe they were due an inheritance from their father.

"When I refused, Rose pleaded with me over and over again. She just wouldn't let up about Tommy beating this Pamela Jean person to death."

Caity leaned forward and held Lilly's gaze. "If your sister, with whom you're incredibly close, warned you so adamantly about your fiancé, I'm truly surprised you didn't listen to her. Why didn't you heed her warning?"

"I loved him. And I didn't believe her. I'm telling you she lies all the time."

"But didn't you at least look into the matter?" Spense asked.

"I looked through the newspapers, and I didn't find any stories about a woman beaten to death. Riverbend is a small town. Surely there would've been some report of it. I called the police, too. I didn't mention Tommy of course but I asked about a woman being beaten."

"And what did they say?"

She let out a hard breath and blinked back tears. "They said women are beaten all the time by their husbands and boyfriends. That it doesn't usually make the papers, and that they couldn't give me any specifics about any cases. I wasn't entitled unless I was family. But one officer seemed to want to ease my mind, and he told me he would say that he was unaware of any case involving someone named Pamela Jean."

"Maybe that wasn't her real name," Caity said softly.

"Maybe Rose made the whole thing up." Lilly raised her chin. "Tommy never laid a hand on me. He was nothing but wonderful, always treated me with respect."

"Until he threw you over for your sister," Spense said.

"Well, yes. But there you have it. Rose's reason for lying. If this whole Pamela Jean story were anything but a complete fabrication she would never have dated Tommy, much less *married* him. She made the whole thing up to cause a rift between us because she wanted him for herself."

Spense was beginning to think Rose might be a lot more diabolical than they'd given her credit for. "Let me get this straight. I'm going to review what I heard you say, and you correct me if I get anything wrong."

Caity pulled out a pen and pad.

Spense watched Lilly's face as he spoke. "You met and became engaged to Tommy Preston. He never hurt you in any way. After you introduced him to Rose, she told you that she had information that he had beaten a prostitute to death in order to cover up information that could ruin him. You made some efforts to check the story and concluded it was false. Then Rose started dating Tommy and eventually became engaged to him and married to him. That doesn't speak well of your sister—that she would lie like that, and steal your fiancé."

Lilly began to cry. A few tears at first, and then in earnest. When she finally regained control of her emotions, she said, "Rose isn't a bad person. She doesn't usually lie to *me*. It's other people she lies to, and that isn't so terrible."

Caity put down her pen. "What do you mean?"

"She lies because of *the life*. It's the way Papa raised us. Papa made a living off of confidence schemes, and when he'd finish one, we'd have to pull up roots. Change towns and schools. Even our hair color."

"Did your father use you and Rose in his con games?"

"Not until we were seven or eight. But yes. And who can blame him? No one ever suspected two little girls of doing anything illegal. But we did. And we lied a lot. But *never* to each other. That was part of our code. *Family first.* Lying isn't a sin. It's only a tool to make a con game work."

"You mentioned a code. What else was in the code?"

"We never hurt anyone. Physically, that is. We didn't involve ourselves with drugs or rob banks."

"So white collar crime."

"Yes. And Papa chose his marks from those who could afford to spare it. And from the greedy. Papa always said he didn't bring anyone down. It was their own greed that did that."

"Honor among thieves. That kind of thing," Spense said. But it seemed like bull to him. Just a way to excuse dishonest behavior and keep his girls' good opinion.

"Yes. So you see, even if my sister lies sometimes, it doesn't make her a bad person. It doesn't make her a *murderer*."

"But Rose broke the family code when she lied to *you*." By Lilly's own report, she and her sister had fallen out over Tommy. Their close relationship would only have amplified Lilly's sense of having been betrayed. Spense had to admit that Lilly's concern for her sister, in spite of everything Rose had done to her, made him want to stick this thing out and get to the truth more than ever.

By the rapt look of attention on Caity's face, she was in this for the duration, too.

"I—I need to talk to Tommy," Lilly said as if it had only just occurred to her. "I've been avoiding it. I didn't go see him in the hospital, but his mother tells me he's back at the hotel now. I—I want to give him a chance to tell me what really happened. There's no reason to be scared of the truth, right?"

Sometimes there was, but Spense didn't see the benefit to anyone in saying so.

"I just have one more question for you." Caity's voice was soft and low. As she spoke, she seemed to be searching Lilly's eyes, as though this were going to be the most important question she'd put to the woman all morning. "Are you still in love with Tommy Preston?"

Chapter 17

Thursday
Hôtel De Plage Dauphin
Tahiti Nui

TOMMY PULLED THE baggie of heroin out of his pants pocket and slid it into Rose's drawer in between her silk nighties. In case it was discovered, he'd shift the blame onto her.

He moved into the sitting area of his bungalow, plunked down on the sofa and removed his shoes. Even without an established contact, the H had been easy to obtain. It'd taken him little more than an hour to find it, procure it, and get back to his bungalow.

Good thing.

Because Inspector Brousseau had just requested another interview, and . . . Lilly, it seemed, was coming to him.

What a lovely surprise.

Through the immaculate front window, he recognized her upturned nose, her shimmering blond hair, and the elegant way she carried herself: shoulders back, chin high, and a fluidity in her movements that came from years of contorting her limbs into yoga positions.

Showtime.

He worked the smile on his face into a pained grimace, grabbed his chest and doubled over. If he could see Lilly, by extension, Lilly could see him. Pivoting in his chair, he flashed her a good view of his rugged profile, waited until he heard the sound of her shoes flip-flopping up the steps, and then moaned loudly, because the same principle applied—if he could hear her, she could hear him.

Once she'd moved away from the window, he gritted his teeth, and then, bearing down with a clamped jaw, he pumped his fists, fast and hard, knowing all of this would raise his blood pressure, redden his face, and bulk up the vein that bisected his forehead. By the time he went to answer Lilly's soft knock, sweat moistened his hairline. He didn't need a mirror to know he looked like a man in sheer agony.

Poor Tommy.

He flung open the door.

"Oh, no." Lilly's stunner green eyes went wide, and her pupils enlarged sexily, but he had to admit she looked less appealing than he was accustomed to due to the puffiness in her face and the red splotches on her usually flawless complexion. She'd been crying— probably all night long.

Awesome.

He mentally rubbed his hands together in glee, which was a little trick he'd learned as a boy. Permitting himself inward gestures of genuine self-expression made it a lot easier to conform outwardly to what was expected and expedient.

Wordlessly he motioned her inside, biding his time, waiting for her cue before deciding on his stance. Lilly was hopelessly in love with him, he knew that for a fact, and she'd been terribly angry when her sister had seduced him out from under her—he imagined raising a champagne glass to toast his delightful pun. Then he put the self-congratulations away in order to focus on Lilly and get a good read on her.

Her fate was sealed, but his method and timing were not yet set.

How long Lilly lived would depend upon how well and how long he could use her.

Would she take his side or Rose's?

Even bad blood is thicker than water, as evidenced by Lilly's attendance at the wedding despite her crushed feelings. And Lilly and Rose were *twins*, albeit fraternal ones. Their connection was undeniable, powerful. But would it trump the spell he'd cast over Lilly from the moment he'd discovered her working her nubile fingers to the bone convincing powerful men to buy diamonds for other women?

Between him and Rose it was probably a toss-up.

Lucky for him, he had the advantage of being physically present, whereas Rose would have to exert her influence by acting only in Lilly's memory.

He made a show of walking with difficulty as he returned to the sofa.

Lilly reached one hand out, nearly touching his cheek, but then abruptly withdrew the offer. "Are you hurt very badly?"

"Is that why you've come? To check on my well-being?"

"Y-yes. And to find out what happened between you and my sister."

A good con woman would've left it at *yes*. Then again Lilly never was good at lies—unlike her sister, whose acumen for deception he'd grown to admire.

"I'll live," he said, permitting what he considered to be an expected amount of resentment to seep into his voice. And no need to feign that. How dare Rose think she could get the better of him.

At first he hadn't seen her game because Rose was good at making people believe anything she said, and he had so much to offer a woman it wasn't logical for Rose *not* to want him and all that went along with being *Mrs. Tommy Preston*. Naturally he'd believed she'd wanted to marry him.

What woman wouldn't?

And naturally he'd believed she'd felt rivalry with Lilly and had wanted to come out the winner in the husband game.

What sister wouldn't?

It had come as a complete surprise to him to learn of Rose's nefarious intent to ruin him. But now, after a couple of days' recuperation and a good sleep last night, he thought he'd figured it out.

Rose loved Lilly above all else, and he had come between her and her sister.

That had to be the reason.

His engagement to Lilly had killed the precious plan to open a ridiculous enterprise in Santa Monica—a posh yoga studio for the rich and bored. To Rose, that damn studio represented some kind of fantasy life that she called "normal."

What Rose didn't understand was that "normal" was a unicorn.

"Let's sit down. You look like you're in pain," Lilly said.

She was being solicitous, but not overly so.

He surveyed Lilly through narrowed eyes. He'd underestimated one Parker sister already, and he didn't intend to make the same mistake twice. It wasn't entirely outside the realm of possibility that Lilly was somehow in cahoots with her sister. After all, they were both cons—even if one sister was better at it than the other.

Then he chuckled inwardly at his own foolishness.

Lilly couldn't be in on Rose's plan to destroy him because: A. She had no reason and B. She had no gumption.

He touched his finger beneath Lilly's chin, raising her gaze to his, simultaneously exposing her long slender neck to his scrutiny.

He counted her delicate tracheal rings, calculating how much force it would take to crush them should he decide to wind his fingers around her neck.

"Tommy . . ." Her throat worked in a long swallow, her body canting toward him like he was pulling her by a magician's scarf.

He stepped farther away, teasing his little mouse.

No. She wasn't in on it.

Lilly was as much a victim in Rose's scheme as he. More so, because not only had Rose stolen from Lilly a rich and attentive (if not faithful) potential husband, but now, Rose's actions were going to cost Lilly her life.

Maybe sooner. Maybe later.

How the game played out would determine the timing of Lilly's demise—unless of course he lost patience with her.

Too bad she wasn't as worthy an opponent as her twin.

"I'm so sorry, Tommy. I don't understand Rose at all. She hasn't been acting like herself for months. I think maybe Papa's death—" Her voice broke.

"Poor Lilly." Inward glee. "It's not your fault. You mustn't think I hold you responsible for your sister's actions."

Lilly might be no Rose—another great pun—he raised his mental champagne glass—but there could be no con without a mark and Lilly would do for his current purposes. Besides, she was more enthusiastic when it came to applying her yoga techniques to her lovemaking, and while both sisters knew their way around a man, Lilly was better at optimizing the use of her mouth. Both women were beautiful, each had her own appeal, and he didn't care that much which Parker sister occupied his time.

He heard himself sigh as he realized his self-deception. Against all reason, he preferred Rose—the woman who'd plotted his downfall, and shot him . . . not to mention kicked him in the chest. That'd hurt like hell on top of his already bruised ribs.

Rose.

"Dear sweet Lilly." He eased down onto the couch. "I do not forgive Rose, but you, I must."

One eyebrow lifted. "Forgive *me*? For what? You chucked me for my sister, and now, thanks to you, she's in terrible trouble. Don't think I don't know you must have done something to her. Rose wouldn't swat a fly, even if it were already dead."

A tiny bit of gumption then, but only a portion of what Rose could muster. To him, looking at Lilly was like viewing a forgery of a Gauguin. The brushstrokes and color were there, but only the original possessed true magic. Rose was an original.

He indicated that Lilly could sit next to him.

She settled in slowly, as if she didn't want to bounce the couch lest the movement cause him pain.

"Apparently neither of us knows your sister as well as we thought. Because Rose is quite capable of mayhem of the worst sort. What part of *she shot me and I almost drowned* don't you understand?"

"The reason why part."

"Me either." And that wasn't a total lie. If she was planning to blackmail him or destroy his empire via SADIE, she hardly needed to shoot him, too. Either ruin his life or kill him—one or the other made sense, but really, he couldn't see the reason for *both*. Yet Rose had brought a gun to their wedding. So she must've been planning to do away with him for a very long time. "I think she might be crazy."

"But she isn't," Lilly protested.

"Are you sure? Look at the facts. She shot me not more than an hour after promising to love me forever, unless you're going to try and tell me *Anna* did it . . . no . . . that would be even more proof that Rose is crazy."

"You know about Anna?" Lilly's body went still. Like a clock with a dead battery, she suddenly just stopped ticking.

"Rose explained the whole game to me. It was terrible of your father to use her like that. I think maybe she finally cracked."

Lilly started to breathe again. "It's not what you think. *Anna* isn't a split personality or anything. It's just a game Papa taught us. I played it, too. Do you think *I'm* crazy?"

Beside him her back was straight and stiff. Her body faced forward . . . but her knees angled toward him. He surmised she was torn between her loyalty to her sibling and her attraction to him. Time to tip the scales in his favor.

"I think you're anything but. I think you're too good for me. That's what you are." He slid his hand into the space between them, inching his fingers toward hers.

She made a little gulping sound as she took his hand and turned to fully face him.

A beam of sunlight fell on her cheeks, highlighting the faintest tracks of her tears.

He made direct, probing eye contact.

Lilly loved him, still.

He could see that clearly, but a squiggle of mistrust made his skin itch. Made him wonder if he should simply kill her now.

Rose might be crazy, and a liar, but he believed her on one count.

According to Rose, George Parker had a nice fat bank account, here in Tahiti, waiting for his daughters to claim it. Rose had promised to share the wealth with Tommy to feather their marital bed. But sweet, smitten Lilly had never once mentioned her inheritance to him.

His eyes swept over her from head to toe. He didn't like the fact she'd kept a secret from him.

It wasn't that he cared about the money.

A million dollars—that was what was in the account—didn't mean much to him.

But *loyalty* was something he required in a wife.

Both women had told him about their father's line of work. And Tommy had considered that a plus. They'd loved their papa in spite of his transgressions, and they'd done his bidding all of their lives. Neither woman thought less of her father for his skirmishes with the law. So Tommy had had every reason to believe whichever Parker sister he chose would look the other way regarding his own business dealings, should she happen to stumble across something unsavory.

Not that he'd planned on confiding his sins to them. His business schemes were on a much higher level than their father's had been. Tommy wasn't a two-bit con man, and he hardly needed a shill.

What Tommy needed was a wife.

A respectable piece of arm candy for the charity balls. A woman who enjoyed singing a hymn in church on Sunday, but who knew how to have a good time when the preacher wasn't watching.

Tommy had worked hard to build a respectable life, and he wanted the family he'd never had. He was human, after all. Even an independent man such as himself yearned to be the center of another person's world.

Rose's childhood had been almost as chaotic as his. He'd thought she'd wanted a family, too.

But it turned out *Lilly* was all the family Rose wanted.

He squeezed Lilly's hand and sidled closer until his thigh touched hers. Her face flushed prettily, and her lips parted.

He had this in the bag.

The only question was where did Lilly's true loyalty lie?

Lilly wasn't good at deception in general, but she hadn't been truthful about George Parker's Tahitian bank account. And to Tommy that indicated Lilly made more of an effort when it came to keeping *family* secrets. So Lilly just *might* be lying to him about Rose. For all he knew she could've aided and abetted Rose's escape from jail. She could be in contact with Rose right now.

Which, come to think of it, wouldn't be a bad thing.

If Lilly could get in touch with Rose, that opened up an avenue of communication for Tommy.

"Darling, your eyes." With his fingers he gently grazed the corner of one, then trailed the side of his hand down her cheek, enjoying the way her bottom lip trembled at his touch.

"Wh-what about my eyes?" she managed.

"They're scaring me." He lifted her hand and pressed it to his lips. "You've never looked at me like this before."

She glanced away quickly. "I don't know what you mean."

"As if you don't trust me."

"I'm not sure how I can. After everything that's happened."

"And it's more than that. You look frightened of me."

She drew her lower lip between her teeth. "Don't be ridiculous. You don't scare me."

He rested his hands on her shoulders and slowly shook his head. "Believe me, Lilly. I'd never hurt you."

"You already have." She sighed. "But I didn't come here to talk about ancient history. That doesn't matter to me anymore."

Oh yes it did. He could see the pitiful way hope was seeping in, brightening her eyes from cold jade to warm emerald.

Too easy.

And that was exactly the problem with Lilly.

Where was her pride?

Holding her gaze, he lowered his voice to its softest, deepest pitch. "I made a terrible mistake. I chose the wrong sister, Lilly. You're absolutely right. It's me who should apologize to you. Will you forgive me?"

Her head snapped back, and he felt tension rising to her shoulders. "I'm truly sorry that Rose shot you. But I—I . . ."

Lilly sometimes developed a slight stutter when she was rattled. It was one of her tells.

"What I'm trying to say is I'm sorry Rose shot you *if* you did nothing to provoke her." She pressed a hand to her forehead. "But I don't know if you're telling the truth."

"I did nothing to deserve this."

"Why would Rose hurt you? She wanted to marry you. Maybe you . . ."

"What?"

"I—I d-don't know." She brushed his hands off her shoulders. "Maybe you hit her."

"I've never hit a woman in my life."

"Never?"

"Never."

"Then none of it makes sense. Where did the gun come from?"

"My understanding," he tried to make his voice comforting, "is that Rose had the gun on her. The police say there was a pouch sewn into the bodice of her wedding gown. I learned this only today."

Lilly's hands started to shake. He clasped both of them between his palms. "I realize it's hard to believe. Imagine how I feel, knowing she planned this months ago, when she was having the dress altered."

The look on her face might've softened him up in the past, but now he was immune to her innocence. He wanted to slap her for being so naïve.

"But that's premeditation. Rose would never . . ."

"She *did*. But I promise you this can still turn out okay."

She sniffled into her sleeve. "Rose shot you. Things are never going to be okay again. When they find her, she'll be arrested again. She could spend the rest of her life in prison."

He reached his arm around her, and when she didn't protest, he pulled her into his body. "Thank goodness the bullet lost velocity. I'm not hurt—not badly anyway. I think I know a way out of this for Rose."

She burrowed her head into his shoulder. "I don't understand."

He petted her hair. "I'm a man of influence, Lilly. I believe I can fix this whole thing up."

"Are you saying you'll drop the charges against Rose?"

"That's not up to me. But I could encourage the police to drop the matter. Tell them I won't testify against Rose. She's my wife, and I don't think they can make me. I'll have to mull it over. For your sake, I want to make this go away, but I need to be sure Rose won't try to hurt someone else."

A blank look came over Lilly's face. "How would you do that?"

He waited.

"You mean you want to talk to her first?"

"I'd have to. And there's also the matter of your sister's jail-break, so even if I decide to turn the other cheek, Rose will probably have to answer for that."

Lilly looked up, big eyed. "Well, *maybe* that would be fair. If you get the police to forget the attempted murder charge and she's only charged with breaking out of jail. I mean she should pay some price for all she's put you through—but I do *not* want to see her go to prison for attempted murder."

He patted her head.

All was well. Lilly wouldn't mind letting Rose spend just a little time behind bars.

A chink in the family armor.

No matter how much Lilly loved Rose, she was definitely pissed at her.

And she was still in love with him. So he could take at least some time to chart his course. He had procured all he needed to act on a moment's notice, but there was simply no need to scramble around like a fool. As long as Lilly was under his spell he could take the time he needed.

"Lilly, I don't want to offend you. I realize I'm in no position to say this, but . . . I've missed you."

She buried her face into his shoulder again, and her tears seeped irritatingly through his shirt. "You're married to my *sister*."

"But she shot me, and I'd say that gives me some wiggle room. So if you and I . . . if you still have feelings . . ."

"I'm not talking about what you'd be doing to Rose. I'm talking about what you did to me. You broke my heart."

"I made a mistake."

Lilly didn't have that hopeful look on her face any longer.

He needed to turn this around and fast. "I realized, almost right away, that I had made the wrong decision. It became crystal clear that I was only attracted to Rose because of how much she reminded me of you."

"Apparently more than *I* reminded you of me."

"I'm just being honest, Lilly. And for the sake of full disclosure, I'll own that I have something of a sexual appetite." He didn't look away. "*Twins.* The thrill of having you both was a lot to resist. But I should have. Unfortunately, by the time I fully understood the depth of my feelings for you, and that I'd made a horrible mistake, it was too late."

"How do you figure?"

He dragged a hand across his face to hide his sneer. Groveling to a woman he didn't respect was getting old quick. "I didn't think you'd take me back."

"You were right."

He could handle it a little longer, if it meant getting control of Lilly back and thus being able to reel in Rose. He gave Lilly the plaintive, misunderstood eyes.

She sighed.

Waterworks again.

"There, there. Go ahead and cry. Get it all out." The shirt was already ruined, and her breasts pressing into his arm felt nice. He pulled her onto his lap, and she adjusted her bottom a few times.

Just enough to give him a chubby.

He slid his hand behind her and stroked the nape of her neck. "It's okay, my darling. It's going to be all right."

She gurgled some response, and he didn't care that he couldn't make out her words. They simply didn't matter.

Allowing his hand to drift to the front of her throat, he palmed her tracheal rings, then trailed his fingers into the soft cleft between her breasts. They were big, soft, and natural. God, these Parker girls had great bodies. Venturing lower he encountered a nipple and tweaked it until it was hard and hot, like him.

She made that noise in her throat that women make when they can't help themselves. When they can't stop you from doing what you want because what you're doing to them feels *that* good.

He maneuvered her until she was straddling him, face to face.

Lilly was so easy to manipulate.

He started deflating quickly.

Heaving out a big breath, he kissed the tip of her nose and lifted her off of him, but not without giving her a bit of a grind first. "We should stop," he said. "I'm still married to Rose. And whether she deserves it or not, I know how devoted you are to her. If I led you into something today that you might regret tomorrow, just for my own pleasure, even if you forgave me, I could never forgive myself."

Lilly looked away, confused. "You're right." She leaned far away from him, as if he'd trapped her in a force field and she had to break free. "But I'm not leaving here until you promise me you'll tell the police you won't testify against Rose."

"I need to talk to her directly. I need her to promise me that she won't come after *either* of us again. Not even if you and I . . ."

Let Lilly fill in the blank.

Dangling an unspoken promise of reconciliation was more powerful than words.

"It's impossible. No one knows where she is."

"Not even you?"

She got up abruptly. "I don't. But if she thinks it's safe, I'll be the first one she'll call."

He was absolutely certain that was true.

Lilly moved to the door, then turned and sent him a last look, her eyes still brimming with tears.

"What is it, dear? How can I set your mind at ease?"

She puffed out her cheeks. Glanced around the room. Put her hands in her pockets, pulled them out, and waved them in the air. "Tell me the truth, Tommy. Do you or don't you know a woman named Pamela Jean?"

Chapter 18

"I'M JACQUES BROUSSEAU." The inspector introduced himself to a woman who, to Caitlin's eye, didn't seem old enough to be Tommy Preston's mother. Preston was thirty-six years old, and the woman Brousseau addressed didn't appear a day over thirty-five. Factor in money, Botox, and fillers and Caitlin would put her at fifty, max.

But there she lounged, at the Grotto bar, wearing, as advertised, a turquoise sarong and hanging onto a gold weave beach bag emblazoned with the words *Preston Enterprises* in raised red letters.

After Caitlin and Spense had reported back to the inspector on their meeting with Lilly Parker, he'd hustled up a joint interview at the hotel bar with Tommy and his mother. Caitlin scanned the area, but didn't see Tommy. Hopefully he wouldn't be a no show, because she was eager to see his reaction when they dropped the name *Pamela Jean*. Another quick glance around, and she turned her attention to those people actually present.

"You're Heather Preston?" Brousseau's jaw dropped as if preparing to catch a raindrop. It could happen—the hotel lobby was open air.

"I am." Heather showed a set of sparkling white, perfectly straight teeth and no inclination to apologize for looking young and beautiful. "Tommy texted he's running late, but he'll be joining us soon."

"I'm Agent Spenser and this is Dr. Caitlin Cassidy," Spense said.

Mrs. Preston's bag hit the ground with a thunk as she wrestled back her chair and climbed to her feet, arms outstretched like an aunt greeting her favorite nephew at Thanksgiving.

Spense stuck his hand out for a shake and she pulled him in for an awkward hug, a little too familiar, but hard to avoid without appearing rude.

Caitlin decided to rescue Spense by offering Mrs. Preston her hand . . . backfiring into an even more awkward three-person huddle, complete with air kisses. When Heather finally stepped back to view them at arm's length, Caitlin sighed with relief.

"You saved my son's life." Heather collapsed back into her seat. "I would say thank you, but that seems so inadequate."

To be fair, now that Caitlin thought about it, the woman's reaction wasn't out of line. Her son had nearly drowned and she and Spense—mostly Spense—had pulled him out of the ocean.

"Just happened to be in the right place at the right time. No big deal." Spense pulled up a chair next to her, and Caitlin and Brousseau followed suit. "Thank you for agreeing to meet with us. I know this trip hasn't turned out like you planned."

"It's not a problem at all. I'm grateful to you and Dr. Cassidy, and if the police think I can be of help in tracking down . . ." Her voice fell off and her face puckered as if she were fighting off a cry. She took a deep breath. "Rose . . . I'd like to do what I can. Which I'm afraid isn't much because even though I thought I knew that woman, clearly I don't have a clue as to what's going on in her head. But ask me anything you like about her."

Brousseau cleared his throat. "Actually, we're more interested in talking to you about Tommy. Shall we wait for him?"

"We can begin. If there's something I can't answer he can fill it in once he arrives. I know your time is valuable." She looked at Caitlin. "I hear you're getting married."

"We are." Caitlin shot the inspector—the obvious source of the leak—a look. Then she turned back to Heather Preston. "But don't worry about our time."

It was really quite thoughtful of her to consider it, though. Most people only thought about their own convenience when it came to police interviews.

Nice lady.

"Forgive me asking but how old are you?" Brousseau opened with a bang.

Mrs. Preston's hand fluttered to her throat as if surprised, but she didn't look put off. "Fifty-one."

"So you had Tommy when you were only fifteen?"

"I'm not sure how this is relevant to the case, but no, Inspector. I was not a teen mom. I was twenty-three and happily married when an absolutely precious, eight-year-old boy was placed in my home for foster care. Three years later, we adopted him. I lost my husband in a car accident shortly after, and I cannot tell you what a blessing it was that Tommy and I had each other. He's been the best son any mother could wish for." She leaned back in her lounge chair and motioned the waiter over.

A gentleman wearing khaki shorts and a tropical shirt arrived. "Can I get you another mimosa?"

"I'm fine, thank you. But perhaps my guests would like a drink." When she smiled, her brown eyes warmed you. Tommy had gotten lucky in the mom department—at least as far as his adopted mother went.

Brousseau shook his head. "We're on duty."

"Lunch then. Order anything you like."

The hotel was pricey to say the least.

"That's generous of you, but no thanks." The server retreated, but continued to hover around the area. Caitlin wondered about Mrs. Preston's finances. Everything from her perfect skin to her tastefully highlighted hair to her beautiful resort wear suggested Robin Leach had her in his Rolodex. Did her money come from Tommy or did she have wealth of her own? If the former, it indicated that Tommy Preston took very good care of his mother. Caitlin noted the diamond studs in the woman's ears, a diamond tennis bracelet on one wrist, and a large emerald on the other hand. Maybe the jewelry Tommy had purchased from Lilly really had been for his mother. "Pardon me for being so direct but are those lovely earrings from Tommy?"

"Yes. The bracelet and ring, too. *Everything* is from him." A shadow of an indentation that likely represented a paralyzed frown muscle appeared between her brows. "Tommy is my *son*. And he loves the fact that he's able to provide a certain lifestyle for me. Enough to get by has always been plenty for me. But Tommy had a hard time of it in the early days, and now he's made a success of himself. He takes pride in that. And I take pride in him. So if you're thinking anything else about my relationship with Tommy, you're out of line. Do I make myself clear?"

"Crystal," Caitlin said. "I apologize if I came across as . . ."

"Judgmental," Brousseau offered.

"Intrusive," Caitlin finished her thought in her own words. "I'm simply trying to get an accurate picture of Tommy's family situation. And Lilly Parker told us when she first met Tommy he was buying gifts for his mother."

"I get it. You're trying to verify her story. Sorry if I seemed defensive, it's just that people can make cruel assumptions, and I don't allow cruel—especially not when it comes to Tommy. I've made it my job to see to it that that part of his life is over. His past doesn't define him, but neither of us has forgotten it. If you want the whole story, I should tell you before he gets here. The sad parts are difficult for him to hear, and the good parts might embarrass him. Tommy is a very humble man, and he doesn't like to brag."

Caitlin had a feeling Tommy didn't mind his mother gushing over him, but kept that thought to herself. "That would be helpful. Just tell us in your own words."

"I admire my son for so many reasons." Mrs. Preston fished around in her Preston Enterprises beach bag for a tissue. "I might need this if I'm going to tell the Tommy saga."

Brousseau picked up a leather-bound menu and waved the server back. "Maybe I'll have something after all. What's your fish and chips?"

"Mahi mahi. An excellent choice."

"I'll take that."

"And for the ladies?"

Mrs. Preston gestured a *no thanks*, and Caitlin did the same.

"I'll have the tofu and beet salad and a glass of still water," Spense said.

The Inspector smiled and added, "I'll have chocolate milk."

Okay, then everybody was ordered up. Time to get Mrs. Preston talking before Tommy made his entrance.

"So this is a three hankie kind of a story," Caitlin paraphrased the woman's words.

"I'm afraid so. I might need an entire packet of tissue, in fact."

Spense leaned forward, giving her his full attention. The inspector pulled out his phone. "Mind if I record?"

"Feel free." Mrs. Preston dabbed a dry eye, perhaps warding off an impending tear. "Tommy's biological mother, Sadie Packard, was a good woman. To have given birth to a boy like him, she must have been. I believe in my heart she was one of God's tortured angels—and I've always told Tommy the same. We have to look at her with forgiveness in our hearts and understand that she was afflicted with a wrong mind."

The inspector scratched his head. "My English isn't perfect. What is a wrong mind, please?"

"I don't know how to explain it any better than this. She wasn't exactly delusional, but she didn't seem to be in touch with reality at all times. I think the drugs had her mind all twisted up. If she'd been able to think clearly, I know she never would've hurt Tommy. I'm one hundred percent sure Tommy's mother loved him."

"Why are you so sure of that?" Spense asked.

"Because what mother wouldn't love an innocent boy?"

A thoughtful look came over Spense's face. "I wish all parents were capable of loving their children, innocent or not, but I have to tell you I don't think that's the case. You said she never would have hurt him. What did she do to Tommy?"

This time when Mrs. Preston dabbed her eyes the tissue came away wet. She discarded it and grabbed another one. Took a long breath. Checked over her shoulder as if wanting to be sure no one was nearby. "His mother was an addict. She couldn't work, because of her ... anyway ... if Tommy had a father ... well of course he must have ... but no one can say who he might be. At times, his mother would clean up, but then, she'd go right back to the H. While she was in ..." She seemed to have reached a point in the story that was quite difficult to relate.

Caitlin was about to urge her to slow down, take her time.

"Treatment." Brousseau finished her sentence for her as if he didn't have patience to allow the story to unfold.

Mrs. Preston looked at him somewhat sharply. "*Jail.* I was going to say while she was in jail. That's a poor man's rehab. The place they go to dry out. The less fortunate among us can't afford fancy hospitals like the kind the movie stars go to. So you see what an accomplishment it is that Tommy not only survived, he succeeded."

"I can see why you're so proud of him," Caitlin said. "Where was Tommy during these times, while his mother ... Sadie?"

Mrs. Preston nodded.

"While Sadie was in jail?"

"Whenever she'd get sent away for drugs or parole violations—carrying a firearm, soliciting, and so on, Tommy would be placed in foster care. Then once she came home, she'd be clean. Child services is big on family reunification, and they'd send him back to her. It's not easy to place little boys, you know. But the last go round, she simply couldn't pull herself together."

"She wasn't sober?" Spense asked.

"I'm not sure. What I do know is that the social worker found her crying every day. The place was filthy—even worse than usual. Tommy was caught stealing food to bring home to his mother. I suppose if he hadn't taken the initiative, they both would've starved to death."

"Why didn't they find him someplace else to live? There are orphanages in the United States, I believe." Brousseau seemed moved, judging by his low, gentle tone.

"They planned to take him away from her again." Mrs. Preston gulped and waved her hand in the air. "I'll have another mimosa, please."

She sat stiff-backed while she waited for her liquid courage. Caitlin, Spense, and Brousseau remained quiet, observing her. Her chest convulsed a time or two and Caitlin knew she was stifling sobs. The waiter came and went quickly, as if he'd already had the drink ready.

Mrs. Preston downed it in a few big swallows and then picked up her story, suddenly all self-control. "After Sadie failed to check in with her parole officer, a social worker went out to the home to take Tommy away."

A smear of blood appeared at the corner of her mouth.

She must have bitten her cheek or her tongue.

"The social worker found both Tommy and his mother near death. Sadie had shot him up with heroin—a dose so big the doctors called it a miracle when he lived. Sadie didn't make it. And as awful as it seems to say this out loud, I believe that was for the best all the way around."

"Perfectly understandable you'd feel that way," Spense said. "Doesn't make you a bad person you felt relief, knowing Tommy was out of danger."

"But he wasn't. Not then, anyway. They put Tommy in a group

home run by the state." She gestured to Brousseau. "A Texas version of an orphanage. Understand?"

Brousseau nodded.

"But Tommy ran away over and over again—he denies it, but I suspect he may have been . . . assaulted . . . in that place. He'd live on the streets for months, dodging the cops before they'd find him and take him back to the home. You can see why I look up to him. If I'd gone through what he did, I believe I would've given up and turned to a life of crime, or I would've jumped off a bridge or something. But not Tommy. That little boy took all that suffering and used it to make himself into a great man. There isn't anyone more generous than him. Just ask the people of Riverbend, Texas, if you don't believe me."

Caitlin exchanged a glance with Spense. Something for Dutch and Gretchen to follow up on along with the Pamela Jean question. Riverbend, Texas. A small town where everyone knows each other's business. No telling what could be dug up with a phone call from Dutch Langhorne, Special Agent in charge of the FBI's Dallas field office. The townspeople would probably line up to bend his ear. "I'll take your word for it. After all you know him better than anyone. But you haven't told us how he made it out of that orphanage and into your loving home."

"Sorry. I thought I mentioned before that the social worker, the one who found Tommy lying half-dead, curled up in Sadie's arms, was my college roommate. Of course her work is confidential, and she's very good about protecting the families' rights, but she was disturbed by Tommy's situation. Heartbroken, I'd say. Anyway, we went to lunch one day and she broke down and told me Tommy's story, even though it was against the rules. How no one wanted an eight-year-old boy with a penchant for stealing and running away.

His chance of finding a permanent placement was low, and she was sure that one day, the street life would do him in."

"So you agreed to take him," Spense said.

"Not at first. But when I heard what that child had been through, I wanted to meet him. My friend arranged it, and every day for a month I visited him in the orphanage. At first, I went alone, but later I brought my husband along. I needed to be sure we were a good fit. I guess that sounds selfish, but I didn't want Tommy to be disappointed. I didn't want to bring him home and then have to turn around and send him back. I needed to be sure there was a real chance of it working out."

"Seems like it did."

"Oh, yes. From the very start. I've never seen such a good helper around the house. Tommy was respectful to his new father and me. Friendly to the neighbors and everyone at church. And the biggest surprise of all was how smart, smart, smart Tommy turned out to be. Once he got settled in his new school, his grades just kept getting better. Within a year he'd been moved into the gifted program."

"I think you should give yourself some of the credit for how he's turned out," Spense said.

Mrs. Preston's cheeks colored. "Thank you, but all the credit goes to him."

No eight-year-old is that good.

Caitlin couldn't help wondering how much of his exemplary behavior was really *Tommy* and how much was a show to keep from being sent back to the home. A survival mechanism: keeping his true self hidden and replacing it with the façade of the perfect son.

What would living your life afraid to express disagreement or show any imperfection do to a person? The shrink in her couldn't help doing some quick math. A child's sense of right and wrong develops, at least according to Freud, between the ages of three and five. Trust versus mistrust long before that. Yet Tommy had been eight years old before loving parents came into his life. Up until that time he'd been scrapping on the streets to survive.

Even though in Mrs. Preston, Tommy had found someone who, by all appearances, genuinely loved him, Caitlin's training told her Tommy probably never let that love sink in. It would be difficult for him to believe the authentic Tommy could receive a mother's love—because he hadn't gotten it from the one person who ought to have loved him unconditionally—Sadie. Instead, he'd learned to present a false persona to the world. Of course this was all just educated speculation, but her gut told her that a desperate street kid still lurked beneath Tommy's surface. With enough stress and the right trigger, that kid would come out fighting.

Spense cleared his throat, and the sound snapped Caitlin back to the moment. "I'm sorry. What were you saying, Mrs. Preston?"

"Only that I believe in doing good for others, and that I tried with Tommy. But in the end, Tommy wound up doing more for me. Sometimes I feel guilty about that. I worked at a used car dealership from the time I was eighteen, and when Tommy was in high school I got laid off. It took me six months to find work again, but Tommy went and got an after-school job to help out with the bills.

"At first, I wouldn't take his money, but he said if I didn't, it meant we weren't a real family. So from then on, I didn't fuss over anything he did for me. I know it makes him feel good inside."

"And how about now? Bring us up to speed on Tommy Preston today."

"Guess who owns that used car dealership, the one that laid me off?" Mrs. Preston beamed.

"Tommy," said the inspector.

"Uh huh."

"How did that happen?" Spense asked.

"I told you he was smart. He got a full ride to the University of Texas and came home with a master's degree in marketing. Then he took out a small business loan and started up with one laundromat. That went to two. Now he's got so many businesses I can hardly keep track. He bought me a house and a car. Pays all my expenses. Like I said before, at first I felt it wasn't right for him to take care of me. But his heart is big, and it makes him so happy to do for others. He's the person you turn to if you're down on your luck. Everyone in town knows if you need a job Tommy will give you one. He's been Riverbend Man of the Year *twice*."

"That's quite an honor," Brousseau said. "Is there more he does for the town or is the award mainly due to his success in business?"

"Oh, he does a lot more." Mrs. Preston ducked her head into her bag, then whipped out what looked to be an oversized pen and handed it to Brousseau. "For instance, he sponsored one hundred of these rescue injectors for the community."

Brousseau pulled the cap off.

"Careful." Mrs. Preston touched his arm. "That's not a training pen. It has real medicine and a needle inside."

"Oh, I see. It's one of those epinephrine pens for people with allergies."

"Close, but not quite." Mrs. Preston retrieved the object and then passed it to Caitlin. "I bet Dr. Cassidy will recognize this. It's an auto-injector that contains naloxone."

Spense's brow lifted. "The opioid antagonist?"

"Yes."

"I'm afraid I'm lost." Brousseau scratched behind his ear.

Caitlin saw that Mrs. Preston was looking to her, the doctor in the group, to explain to Brousseau. "You were on the right track when you thought of an EpiPen, Jacques. This works in much the same way, only it rapidly reverses the effects of opioids instead of allergic reactions. So if you were the parent of a teen, addicted to heroin, for example, the doctor might provide you with one of these injectors. If you found your son or daughter near death due to an overdose, you could administer the naloxone and reverse the coma. It's a little more complicated—repeated doses can be needed after an hour or so—but that's the gist."

"These injectors save lives. With a prescription, they're perfectly legal. Tommy and I carry them everywhere we go." Mrs. Preston's hands flew up in an animated fashion. "We've got an epidemic of teen heroin use in our county. Tommy's very involved in a program that finds resources for these kids and their families. And he's determined that *everyone* who might someday have use for one of these rescue injectors has access to them—they're quite expensive, I'm afraid. Every cop and first responder in Riverbend knows how to use them. And if they forget, the injector actually gives verbal instructions. If you like, I'm sure Tommy would be happy to sponsor some of these for your men, Inspector. Shall I look into it?"

Brousseau had been listening intently. "I'd be very grateful."

"Consider it done. You keep that one. I've got another in my room." Mrs. Preston sat back, apparently satisfied that everyone at the table understood that Tommy Preston was the salt of the earth.

Caitlin passed the auto-injector to Brousseau who rolled it between his fingers and then pocketed it.

"Tommy sounds almost too good to be true." Spense broke the silence.

His remark caused Heather Preston's shoulders to hunch.

"Hard to believe anyone would have a grudge against him. Can you think of any reason his brand-new bride, Rose, would want to hurt him?" Spense didn't look away and neither did Mrs. Preston.

Her lips thinned, and Caitlin could see the mamma bear in her emerging. Her gentle expression clouded over, then toughened up. This woman would definitely defend her cub if she thought he was being threatened.

"None whatsoever."

"But, allegedly, Rose tried to murder him. So she must've had some reason." Caitlin inched her chair closer to the table and leaned forward. She kept her tone casual. "Is there any chance your son might have a different side to his personality?"

"Like what?"

"Has he ever hit you? Have you ever seen or heard about him hitting someone else?"

"Domestic abuse. I know that's what you think." Mrs. Preston slapped her hand on the table, making the silverware rattle. "Hell no. Tommy never laid a hand on his bride or anyone else. The only reason a person would ever want to hurt him is if they were crazy. So there's your answer. Rose Parker is a nut. And I'm done here."

"Rose may be a nut, but she's also my wife, Mother." Tommy Preston strolled into the Grotto Bar just in time to hear his mother's rousing defense.

"Not for long." Heather folded her arms across her chest.

"Sorry I'm late, but I had a surprise visit from Lilly Parker."

"How's she holding up?" Mrs. Preston asked, the storm in her expression calming somewhat with the arrival of her son.

"Not that well, I'm afraid. But I did my best to let her know I don't blame her." The server hurried over with a chair, but before they could rearrange in order to squeeze in another spot for Tommy, his mother got to her feet.

"You're too good, sweetheart. Call me when you're done. I want to go on one of those submarine rides."

"Why don't you get in touch with our concierge and have him book us a spot? But let's make it sooner rather than later. I'm afraid I'm all done in. I'll probably go to bed before sundown." Tommy embraced his mother, then took her place at the table.

Heather Preston raised her hand in a half wave, or maybe a good riddance, and made a beeline for anywhere but there.

Ask me anything she'd said.

Except whether your son beats his wife.

As for Tommy, he sat like he was balancing a book on his head. Could be his usual posture, but Caitlin guessed sore ribs were to blame.

Spense and Tommy stretched their legs at the same time, and Caitlin saw them jump when their feet met.

"Excuse me," Tommy said.

"No worries. I guess we share the curse of the tall man."

Tommy sent him a questioning look.

"Always having to make amends for kicking our table mates." Spense grinned.

Tommy grinned back. He had a friendly ease about him that made him quite likable. Maybe it wasn't fair for Caitlin to psycho-analyze him without getting to know him first. She had to admit she was suspicious primarily because his bride had shot him.

That's victim blaming.

Something she prided herself on avoiding at all costs.

But one thing was certain.

Rose shot Tommy.

So they couldn't both be innocents.

Either Lilly was covering for Rose, or Heather was covering for Tommy.

Or else either Rose or Tommy or both was very, very good at hiding his or her true self from those closest to them.

Her head was starting to swim.

Spense pulled his Rubik's cube from his pocket and set it on the table in front of him.

She almost reached for it.

"What'd I miss?" Tommy picked up the Rubik's cube, making Caitlin glad she hadn't. Playing with a puzzle might distract him and put him off his guard. For Spense it had the opposite effect. It helped him focus. But for most people . . .

"Don't tell me. My mother told you I was Superman." He flashed them that charming smile of his. "Don't believe her. I work hard, but I'm just a regular Joe doing my best to get along in the world."

"A regular Joe with businesses all over Texas and Man of the Year *twice*." Caitlin tossed her hair flirtatiously, drawing a *knock-it-off* look from Spense.

But Spense had little to worry about since Tommy only seemed interested in the cube. "I used to play around with these as a kid. I'm pretty good at it. You should time me."

"Go for it," Spense said, hitting a dial on his watch.

Tommy's fingers flew over the multicolored squares. He handed the cube back to Spense with a triumphant flourish and a seated bow. "How'd I do?"

"Thirty-five seconds. Not bad," Spense said. "And you're right, your mother gave us the scoop on Tommy Preston and his rags to riches story—not to mention his community service. I think we got most of what we need already, but do you mind if I ask a follow-up question?"

"Not at all."

"You're awfully cool and collected considering your bride shot you and then escaped from jail. I mean she must have some monster grudge against you to do that. If I were you, I'd be worried she'd turn up out of the blue and try to finish what she started. I'm surprised you declined protection."

"Is that the follow-up question?"

"I'm just saying I'd watch my back if I were you."

"Appreciate the advice, Agent Spenser. But I can take care of myself. In case my mother didn't mention it, I've been around dangerous women in the past. Now that I understand Rose's proclivity for violence, I'll be prepared. And aside from feeling a bit wrung out, I'm physically fit. My wounds are more to my ego— and my heart—of course my heart."

"Well, you're doing a great job of keeping the hurt inside." Caitlin smiled sweetly. "Guess you had a lot of practice at that."

A muscle twitched in Tommy's jaw.

Spense twirled his cube in the air. "Time me, Caity?"

She pressed the stopwatch function on her cell. Spense worked his magic and set the cube down. "Well?"

Both men looked at her.

She checked the timer.

Interesting.

Spense's personal best for solving a Rubik's cube was six point five seconds. Only on rare occasions had she seen him take more than ten. "Thirty-nine seconds," she said, narrowing her eyes at Spense.

"You win, buddy." Spense offered a handshake to Tommy.

His shoulders opened and that uptight posture of his relaxed. "It was close though."

"Sure." Spense kicked back in his chair and put his hands behind his head. "Ready for my follow-up question."

"Fire away."

"Who's this Pamela Jean everyone's talking about?"

For a split second, Tommy's smile disappeared. It returned so quickly Caitlin wondered if she'd imagined the change in his visage. He seemed calm and collected now.

His eyes moved up and to the right.

Either he was genuinely trying to place the name, or he'd been schooled in neuro linguistics and knew Spense and Caitlin probably had been, too.

He could've mastered the art of body language in business school, and he just might have a motive to pull that skill out of his tool chest now.

Caitlin didn't mind. She enjoyed a challenge.

"Funny you should ask. Lilly just posed the same question. I don't recall meeting a Pamela Jean. But then again, I meet a lot of people so it's tough to say for certain. Maybe if you tell me her last name it might ring a bell."

"Don't have a last name for you. But I think you'd known her by her first name." Spense scooped his cube up and put it back in his pocket. "The Pamela Jean in question is a prostitute. Does that help?"

"I'm not going to claim I've never been with a lady of the evening." He offered Caitlin an apologetic glance. "I was young once, which is a poor excuse. It was only one time, and I remember her name very well. I think it would be indelicate for me to reveal it, but I will say she didn't call herself Pamela Jean." Thinking on it, he tapped his chin. "Maybe she used a pseudonym. A woman in her profession might not tell me her real name. So, my answer is I don't think I know a Pamela Jean, but I can't swear to it under oath."

Spense nodded.

"Good point about the false name," Caitlin said. She had no idea if Pamela Jean was a pseudonym either. She didn't even know if there *was* a Pamela Jean. Lilly seemed convinced Rose had made the story up as a means of getting Lilly to break up with Tommy so she could have him for herself. "But we have ways to track these things down. So how about you get over the indelicacy of it all and give us the name your prostitute gave you. We'll take it from there."

"She wasn't *my* prostitute. I told you it was just the one time. Back in my college days—on a dare from my buddies. Her name was 'Austin.'" Tommy made air quotes with his fingers. "Now that I think about it, it seems likely that was a fake name, but you never know, she could've been named after the town. Maybe her parents were UT alumni or something." He turned his palms up.

Caitlin frowned.

Tommy had picked up on one of Spense's mannerisms and imitated it—which was a subtle way of winning a person over.

Might be coincidence, but more likely it was confirmation that Tommy Preston was adept at manipulation.

"I was with 'Austin' a total of about ten minutes." Air quotes again. "I paid her $100 mostly so I could fit in with the rest of the guys. The whole thing didn't really float my boat. I had trouble, excuse me for saying, getting hard, so I never went back."

Oh yeah. Tommy was good. He'd admitted, or *invented* his performance problem to make the story seem more believable, and to make himself seem like less of a creep—which only made him seem like more of one to Caitlin.

"Now it's my turn for a follow-up question," Tommy said. "Have you heard anything more about the whereabouts of my beautiful bride?"

"We'll get back to you on that." Spense turned his palms up with an exaggerated flare that told Caitlin he recognized the slick on Tommy.

"I hope you're being sincere, because I think I deserve some answers."

He might deserve a lot more than answers. But only time would tell.

Her phone vibrated. She glanced at the message.

Or maybe they'd all get their answer right now. Rose Parker Preston had just been sighted at the hotel.

Chapter 19

THEY DIDN'T HAVE to go far. Inspector Brousseau took off, under false pretenses, for the pool area, where Rose had reportedly been sighted. Spense and Caity steered Tommy in the opposite direction, then took their leave after promising to keep him updated on any new developments. Nobody wanted Preston interfering with the potential bust of his bride. Once they had Tommy safely out of the way, Spense and Caity joined Brousseau, whom they found skulking behind a newspaper at the Hibiscus Pool.

"False alarm." The inspector lowered his paper and indicated a pretty young woman with bright blond hair and brighter lipstick. A small crowd, if you can call three a crowd, had gathered around her.

Lilly.

"I should have known," Brousseau said. "We're going to be

getting a lot of false reports with Lilly running around. And I don't have the resources to track them all down."

"Lilly's cooperative," Caity said. "Why don't you just ask her nicely to keep you informed of her whereabouts. That way if someone reports a Rose sighting, you can eliminate whether or not it's Lilly without sending a man out."

"Smart lady." Brousseau checked his cell again. "But I have to go. We just had another sighting—this one's at Heritage Townhomes and it obviously can't be Lilly. Perhaps you wouldn't mind speaking to her for me?"

"No problem," Spense said. "You got a number where she can check in?"

Brousseau passed him a card. "Just have her give her itinerary to my assistant, and please, ask her to answer any calls from this number."

"Will do." Spense clapped Brousseau on the back. "Go ahead. We'll handle Lilly Parker."

Caity tugged his sleeve. "What's going *on* over there?"

A gentleman with graying hair shook his finger at Lilly, turned, and stalked away. A man and a woman moved in closer, peering at something in her hand.

"Let's just hang out and watch for a minute," Caity suggested.

Fine with him. He was still trying to get a bead on Rose's twin. He only trusted her so far, given how protective she was of her sister. They moved in close enough to eavesdrop, knowing that Lilly could see them if she turned ninety degrees. But it didn't matter. When the jig was up, it was up. Lilly had done nothing illegal as far as they knew, and they weren't here to arrest her.

"How come, if this map is real, you're willing to sell it to us?" The woman, mid-forties, gym rat, and likely an American, asked.

Lilly pulled away the item in her hand, now identified as a map, rolled it, and held it against her chest. "I'm not."

"But you just said we could have it." The man, who was approximately the same height and age as the woman and wore a matching T-shirt that read, *Leverant Family Reunion*, planted his hands on his hips.

Lilly backed up a step. "I never said this map was for sale. I said I was looking for an investor. I'm afraid I can't let you and Jill have the map under any circumstances. I never should have shown it to you, but I wanted you to have a peek, just so you'd know it was real."

Spense elbowed Caity gently. "Gauguin's Gold?"

Caity smiled. "Looks like. You up for a treasure hunt?"

He touched the Rubik's cube in his pocket and shook his head. "I should've thought of that myself, back at the jail."

"It's only a hunch," she said, then put her fingertip to her lips, indicating they should shut up and listen.

"Come on, Harold, this is nonsense." Jill frowned at Lilly then turned her back in a huff.

Harold, whom Spense surmised must be husband to Jill, reached out and caught her by the hand. "Hold on. I've been hearing stories about this gold all over town. I want to hear this young woman out."

"Well I don't. She keeps changing her tune. Sounds like a bunch of hooey to me. We're more likely to strike it rich buying a lottery ticket, and that don't cost ten thousand dollars."

Caity and Spense exchanged a glance. Lilly wasn't just selling treasure maps at five dollars a pop. This was the kind of thing that could get her in serious trouble. Maybe she was thinking ahead, trying to raise money for her sister's legal bills.

"You better go, Harold," Lilly said. "I don't think Jill wants—"

"My wife doesn't make the decisions. I'm the man of the family."

Lilly gave him a stern look. "No way."

"No way what?"

"No way I bring you on as an investor without Jill's okay. I'm a woman, and I need a business partner. And that partner needs to show respect for women. If this is how you treat your wife, it's not going to work out for us. Suppose I brought you in on this deal, and then you tried to cut me out the way you're cutting your wife out now?"

For some reason—probably her meek personality—Spense had gotten the impression Lilly wasn't good at conning people, but at the moment, she was doing a hell of a job. She'd already landed Harold. Now she was reeling Jill in one-handed. And even though she had a higher chance of being caught at the hotel than on the street, if she did get busted, the penalty would be low. This was a target rich environment, tipping the risk-reward ratio in her favor. As far as he could tell Lilly was as smooth an operator as any he'd seen.

"I'm not cutting Jill out of any deal. I only said I make the decisions," Harold retorted.

Jill, who'd been poised on the edge of the conversation, moved back into the circle. "Are you trying to cut me out of this deal, Harold?"

"No, honey. I promise."

Oh yeah. Lilly was doing her old man proud. Of course he and Caity would have to step in soon, but he was enjoying watching her in action.

"I'm going to need more than just your word you won't cut

Jill out of any profits." Lilly approached Jill and slung an arm around her. "Either you give your wife an equal cut *in writing* or there's no deal. You *both* sign on the dotted line or you both walk away."

Jill put her arm around Lilly.

Sisterly solidarity.

"We *both* sign, Harold, or we both walk away," Jill said.

"Dear, I assure you there's no need. We're married. What's mine is yours. Legally."

"I want my name on the papers just the same."

"I'll have my lawyers draw up the agreement," Lilly said. "But I'm going to need a deposit, I'm afraid I'm low on funds, and I need something for legal fees."

This, Spense suspected, was the only true thing Lilly had uttered in the entire conversation.

"Will five hundred dollars be enough?" Harold pulled out his wallet.

"Better make it a thousand to be safe."

Jill suddenly paled. "We don't even have the papers, yet, honey. Maybe we should think about it some more."

"I only have five hundred in cash." Harold extended his hand.

Lilly took the money from him. "There's an ATM in the lobby."

Spense raised two hands over his head and waved vigorously, catching Jill's attention.

"Do you know that man?" Jill asked Lilly.

Lilly turned and made eye contact with Spense. "No." She handed Harold his money back. "But the deal is off."

"But why?" Harold rocked back on his heels. "I'll go get the rest of the money right now while Jill waits here."

"I don't need a hostage, Harold. And I said the deal is off. It's too late. I can tell from all your shenanigans you wouldn't make a good partner."

Lilly pushed the couple aside and headed toward Spense and Caity.

Harold patted Jill on the back. "Sorry, honey, I guess that's my fault. We can buy lottery tickets for the whole family. Even your cousin, Arnie. Will that make you feel better?"

"Probably a scam anyway." Jill pecked her husband's cheek. "I think we dodged a bullet."

Lilly arrived in front of them, scorched-faced and big-eyed. "Hey there. Any word on Rose?"

Nice recovery.

"Sorry to disappoint you again," Caitlin said. "Actually, there was a bit of snafu. Someone called in a report that they'd seen a woman matching Rose's description here at the pool. So we came to check it out."

Lilly's shoulders fell. "Sorry. Guess that was me."

"Guess so." Spense held out the card Brousseau had provided. "Call that number and let him know your itinerary. If it changes, check in, and if they call you, pick up right away."

"I'll do it. I don't want the police going off in the wrong direction on my account."

"You sure about that?" Caity asked.

"Yes."

"Because it has occurred to us you might not be that anxious to see your sister go to jail."

"I'm not. But like you pointed out, no one's dead . . . yet. I know if I can only talk to her, I can get her to see reason. She's not thinking straight. I'm going to get her the best lawyers I can. That's why I was working the Gauguin's Gold scheme. I know you saw me."

Spense held out his hand. "I'd lay off if I were you. The Parker sisters are in enough trouble already."

"Mind if I take a look at the goods you were peddling?" Caity asked.

Lilly handed Caity the map. "Gauguin's Gold. You can keep the treasure map as a souvenir if you like. And just so you know my intentions were honorable."

Spense didn't buy it. She was working that con to the max. "You were going to fleece that couple blind."

"But that's on them—not me. Papa always said you can't scam anyone who isn't willing to eat their own kind for a chance at being rich. If they weren't greedy, I couldn't convince them to pay me for a map to a nonexistent treasure. And it was for a good cause. I'm going to need money for Rose's defense."

"Do you think she's still here, in Tahiti?" Caity lowered her voice.

"Of course she is," Lilly said. "Rose would never leave me here alone."

Remembering Caity's suggestion about a treasure hunt, Spense sent her a look. If Rose was still on this island, they had a pretty fair idea where to look.

Chapter 20

Thursday
Hôtel Économique
(Budget Hotel)
Papeete
Tahiti Nui

TOMMY HAD HAD just about all he could take. From the moment he'd realized Rose had betrayed him, he'd needed this. It'd been years, almost a decade, in fact, since he'd indulged his weakness. But this was the only way he knew to rid himself of the pressure building in his head. He couldn't maintain control if he didn't lift the lid and let off a little bit of steam.

And this bitch deserved everything he was about to give her.

His only regret was that he'd had to beg off dinner with his mother.

But once they got back to Texas, he'd make it up to her with a nice ruby ring or something—maybe he'd even meet his next wife at the jewelry counter.

"I'm going to need another five thousand francs," the hooker repeated for the third time.

Tommy bit his knuckles to keep from wrapping his hands around her throat. He wanted to pin her down on the bed in this dump of a motel room and watch her eyes pop while he whispered to her what her future held.

"Marie . . ." He was reasonably sure that was her name. "You can't charge me extra because I arranged for some privacy. Would you prefer I take you up against the alley wall?"

Marie didn't blink. Her bloodshot eyes remained fixed on him with hazy determination. "You asked for an hour service. I spent twenty minutes in the car and another ten waiting for you to register."

"Twenty minutes riding around in an air-conditioned Porsche instead of prowling the stinking hot streets? My heart bleeds for you."

"My time is valuable."

She might be overestimating her market worth. Her large fake breasts were her best asset. Black roots led to oily orange hair. A deeply lined forehead contrasted a garishly lipsticked mouth. His gaze whipped over the rest of her: beer belly, stretchy flesh, skinny thighs, no underwear . . . a shaved crotch. "I can see just how valuable."

She propped one hand under her outstretched elbow as if she couldn't hold it up any longer. "Fifteen thousand francs."

He inhaled a breath of mildewed carpet and air freshener, then eased down beside her. The bed creaked beneath his weight. He pressed ten thousand francs into her palm.

"This is not enough."

"It's all I've got on me." Not true, but they'd made a bargain, and he was the kind of man who stuck to his deals.

She closed her fist around the money and stood. "*Merde*. This pays for time you already had plus the time to get me back. Drive me home please. You agreed you would."

He grabbed her wrist and yanked her down. "Not so fast, Marie."

Her dull eyes flickered, telling him she was afraid.

Good.

"I don't have any more money, but I do have something else that might make up for it."

He pulled the baggie from his pocket and dangled it in front of her. "Will this do?"

"Smack?"

He nodded.

"Too cheap. You owe me five thousand francs," she said, but she couldn't take her eyes off the stuff. She was probably due for her next fix. Maybe why she was in such a hurry.

He put it away. "Sure, you're right. It's not worth enough to make up the difference. I'll take you back."

She licked her lips. "I'll give you fifteen minutes."

He pulled the baggie out and waved it again. "One hour."

She propped her back against the headboard and nodded. Bent her knees and spread them, giving him a view fit for a gynecologist.

He put one hand on her thigh, all but flattening it against the bed.

"I want to get high first. More fun that way." She pushed against his hand, trying to close her legs, but he held it firmly against the bed. Then she sighed. "You want to look at me while I get high?" Her voice sounded distant, as if coming from much farther away than the height of a headboard.

"Yes, that's exactly what I want." His palms tingled as he passed the heroin to her.

"I need my purse. I'll get up or you can . . ."

"Stay just like you are." He leaned over, lifted her soiled cloth shoulder bag off the floor and dumped its contents onto the quilted bedspread.

What a marvelous assortment of tools of the trade. Sort of a junkie-whore go bag.

As she worked in silence, he watched, lips parted, heart racing in his throat.

"Take more. Go ahead, be greedy." His voice came out dry and raspy.

With eager hands and glazed eyes, she prepared her fix. She was indeed, a very, very greedy girl.

Soon her head jerked and her body slumped. Her limbs flung aimlessly around her. Her chest heaved heavily.

One hour.

That was all the time he would take.

He would not cheat her.

He observed her breathing become shallow. When at last she seemed barely conscious, with her mouth hanging open and drool spilling down her cheek, he donned a pair of latex gloves. Next, he prepared another syringe, using all the H that remained in the baggie. "This is what you want, Marie. Remember, you asked me for it."

He did what he came to do. Then he pulled out his pocket watch, curled into a ball at the foot of the bed, and began the countdown.

Fifty-one minutes later he checked her pulse.

Thready.

From his pocket, he pulled his auto-injector. Her skin was gray and cool to the touch, but she was still breathing—barely.

There was still time to reverse the effects of the heroin.

The naloxone would keep the devil at bay at least an hour, giving Tommy plenty of time to get back to his bungalow before calling the paramedics.

Then again, the woman had tried to cheat him out of extra francs. If she hadn't, he would've been more inclined to spare her.

He slipped the rescue injector back in his pocket.

Casting a glance around the room, he realized he wasn't sure what he had touched. He was going to have to wipe this place down well . . . but not for another nine minutes.

He'd paid for the hour.

He was going to take it.

Chapter 21

CAITLIN POWERED DOWN her phone and pocketed it. She had one service bar left and she doubted that would last. Another half mile of hiking and they'd be off the grid for real. "Brousseau says for us to carry on if we like. His crew just chased down the third Rose sighting this morning, and it led to a dead end. He still thinks she's somewhere near town, but they haven't found her yet."

"What about us? Do we really think this phony treasure map is going to lead us to her secret hiding place?"

"I don't know. But somebody should check it out, and Brousseau has his hands full in Papeete—at this point Rose has been sighted more times than Elvis." Caitlin turned the map to Gauguin's Gold this way and that, squinting at the half-inked squiggly arrows that led to an unnamed trail, gave up, and checked out the area up ahead with her binoculars. "Looks like rough terrain."

"Probably intentional on George Parker's part. I doubt he wanted his marks to make it to the big red X. Anyone who can't reach the spot can't complain when he doesn't find the gold."

"Makes sense." That was likely the same reason George Parker had claimed the treasure was on Tahiti Iti—the small end of the hourglass shaped island of Tahiti. Tahiti Iti was separated from the larger Tahiti Nui by an isthmus and contained many wild coastal regions accessible only by foot or by boat.

And Parker's map was virtually impossible to decipher—clearly by design.

But he'd either overlooked something, or else he hadn't cared enough about covering up his two-bit treasure map scam to bother with complete camouflage. His map might be mostly unreadable, but it did show Mana Falls in close proximity to the buried gold. So she and Spense had simply stopped by the hotel gift shop and picked up a map to the falls. Only trouble was they'd come far enough they now needed to rely on Parker's map to guide them the rest of the way.

Spense took off his cap and swatted away a flying insect the size of a frog. "I vote *no* on going all the way to the X. From what I can tell, the spot is so remote not even a helicopter can get you there, unless you're willing to drop out of it airborne. There's no feasible place to land. Rose isn't hiding there. She can't make it that far without special equipment, and I doubt she was able to pilfer pitons and carabiners during her outing at the beach."

"Not to mention we haven't got any either." Caitlin had to laugh at Spense who seemed to think a lack of equipment would stop Rose, but *they* could make it if they chose. *They* were taking a vote. "I vote *no*, too. But it doesn't mean Rose isn't hiding out around here somewhere. I say we keep searching. There are boot prints on the trail marked *Mana Falls*."

"They look man-size to me, but they're a few days old by the looks of it, so the time frame fits. "

She looked around and inhaled deeply. The intense greenery, the luxuriant vegetation, the scent of sun and tropical flowers was a delicious feast for her senses. Surely it was better to be out among this beauty than back at the hotel planning the ceremony.

Her shoulders pinched together. "Do you feel guilty?"

The puzzled look on his face quickly morphed to understanding. "You mean because we're out here having a kick-ass time."

"Yes, and the moms are stuck back in town planning our ceremony and handling little details that are actually the responsibility of the bride."

"You mean the responsibility of the bride *and* groom." He dumped his cap back on his head. "Besides, I'm sure they're in mom heaven planning our wedding and our future. I'm sorry we're not with them today, but I don't feel guilty for taking pleasure in the hand we've been dealt."

"I suppose you're right. A wedding ceremony doesn't compare to a woman's future hanging in the balance. Three futures, really, since we have to think of the impact on Lilly and Tommy if we don't find Rose before she does something that can't be undone."

Spense tossed a branch he'd been using as a walking stick down a hill, then grabbed her and pulled her against him. "Our wedding matters."

She could feel his heart pounding in her ear. His shirt was sticky against her cheek, and he smelled like sweat, dirt, and Old

Spice. If she could stay right here, in this moment forever, she would.

"That didn't come out right." She lingered against him until he let her go to scratch an itch. "I sincerely hope when we find Rose, that somehow she'll be able to justify what she's done. Maybe she has some kind of fantastic explanation that will clear all this up and she and Lilly can go back to the States and open up their yoga studio."

"Why are you so set on Rose's actions being justified?"

"Because I have a feeling about her."

"Babe, you don't know her well enough to have a feeling, in fact you don't know her at all."

"True enough. But that night when they handcuffed her and took her off to jail, there was something in her eyes. I can't help thinking this might all be a cry for help. If we don't find her in time, and she manages to shoot someone, it's going to end any chance for her to have a normal life."

"What makes you think she wants one?"

"The yoga studio. Lilly says Rose was determined to open it with her. Think about it. *Yoga.* What better symbol of peace and change and restoration?"

"You're reading a lot into that, Caity."

Maybe she was.

"Let's keep moving," he said.

She hoped not, but Spense might have a point. Lilly and Rose had been raised by a con man. They'd lived an unsavory life on the fringes of society and mostly outside the law. According to Lilly, Rose's biggest supporter, Rose was a chronic liar. Caitlin had to admit the possibility that Rose could be dangerous, and it seemed likely she was armed.

Caitlin should be more on guard in case Rose was indeed in the area. She should be paying closer attention to her surroundings.

Suddenly, a buzzing sound caught her attention.

"What the hell?" Spense said.

The buzzing grew loud, then louder still.

He grabbed her hand.

She'd heard bees before, but not like this. "This really is the treasure map from hell. I feel awful for the poor chumps traipsing around out here in search of Gauguin's Gold."

Spense cast an exaggerated glance around. "The only chumps I see out here at the moment are us."

She frowned. "I never asked you, but I don't suppose you're allergic."

"No. Not allergic to bee stings."

"Me neither. So let's keep going. I say this is a perfect hiding spot, complete with bees to ward off intruders. They're as good as an army of archers on a hilltop in terms of protection and Rose knows this area well. We've come this far, Spense. If we give up now we really are chumps."

"Okay, but let's take it nice and easy. I don't love the sound of what's around that bend."

Sure enough when they came around the curve in the path she saw them. Hives. stacked in the trees one atop the other. She remembered reading somewhere that one hive could house up to 60,000 bees. She didn't want to do the math on how many bees this might be, and the thought stopped her dead in her tracks.

An entire nation of bees ready to swarm.

Then she inhaled slowly.

She also remembered reading that bees are generally peaceful, so she shook out her hands and walked on, careful not to jostle the hives or dislodge any rocks or branches. A moment later they'd successfully traversed the stretch of hives. She let out a long breath of relief and then she saw it: a rock tumbling down the side of the cliff, bouncing from one hive to another.

Don't panic.

"Spense," she whispered in warning.

A wave of insects flew in formation from the hives and arrowed straight for them.

Now you can panic.

"Run!" she yelled.

Spense shoved her in front of him, and she jogged as fast as she could over the rocky path. Spense could've easily outstripped her, but he kept pace behind her giving her as much cover as he could with his outstretched arms.

Her heart raced to keep up with her breathing, providing precious fuel for her flight. Behind her she saw a black cloud of angry insects chasing them. Their buzzing electrified the air like a summer lightning storm.

"Water!" Spense called out to her, as his hands steered her in a sharp left turn. She darted through a wooded area then slid, like she was stealing home base, into a muddy streambed. Spense crashed in on top of her, and she shivered in the cool water. With thousands and thousands of bees circling above them, they crawled on their bellies, panting, seeking safety in deeper water. The tail of the formation tightened its line and dove toward the stream.

She couldn't bear to look.

"Open your eyes," Spense whispered in her ear.

She forced herself to look up.

"Holy crap." She uttered the words through chattering teeth.

The bees had reversed course. They were headed back home.

"You can say that again. You okay?"

"Uh huh. You?"

"Swell. Just swell. My guess is this is the spot where everyone gives up and goes home."

"Which means Rose would hold up somewhere near here. I bet we haven't much farther to go." Caitlin got to her feet and glanced down in dismay at her torn wet jeans. Then she looked at Spense. His muddy hair stuck up in weird spikes, like a little boy who'd gotten hold of hair gel for the very first time.

She tiptoed up, wiped a smudge from his cheek, kissed him hard on the mouth then drew back. "You know what I love about hanging out with you? There's never a dull moment."

He kissed her back just as hard.

"Ditto," he said when they came up for air. "Does that mean you want to keep going?"

"I didn't do battle with those bees just to turn around now. I say if Rose hasn't fled the island, there's a good chance she's hiding somewhere remote, but where she's familiar with the terrain—like here."

"Agreed. I say we keep going, and on the way back, we need to find a detour around those hives."

"You think?" There was no way in hell she was strolling past that death trap on the return trip.

A half hour later, her legs were ready to give up. But she was determined to go a little farther. They'd covered a lot of ground already, and there was nowhere else to search except the falls. If Rose wasn't there, they'd likely guessed wrong about her holing up at the end of her father's rainbow.

Spense slowed up and motioned her over to him. "It appears

we've followed the map well." He halted and pointed. "We've reached the chutes and ladders portion of our journey. Are you up for it?"

"Of course." She could hear the roar of the nearby waterfall. *Mana Falls*.

As a girl, and even as a young woman, she'd been the careful sort. But since she'd been around Spense, she'd changed. It wasn't that she'd grown reckless, but she had begun to appreciate that with great risk there could sometimes be great reward.

According to the map, there was a cliff with a steep drop-off, and rudimentary steps to make your way down to the bottom of a canyon graced by a hidden waterfall. The locals warned tourists not to venture to this part of the island without an official guide, partly to keep it for their own enjoyment, but also to prevent injuries, if the sign at the top of the cliff was any indication.

Descendez à vos risques et perils!

Descend at your own risk!

"Looks like fun to me," Spense said.

Jutting rocks formed a semblance of steps trailing down at a nearly vertical angle. About halfway down, the "steps" became truly sketchy. Along that portion of the climb, there were only a few toeholds. Like something you'd see at a rock climbing gym—only spaced widely apart with few handholds and a really, really long way to fall. To aid hikers intrepid or foolish enough to chance the journey, a rope dangled. It was attached by a carabiner and piton buried in the rock—sort of like a broken guitar string hanging over its sound hole.

"Just exactly how old do you think that rope might be?" She looked to Spense for advice. Hard to put her trust in that weathered old thing.

He shrugged.

"We can make it even without it," she said. "Maybe we shouldn't rely on the rope to get up and down. I'm not sure it will bear our weight."

"Point taken, but it will be a lot tougher. I'll head down first, and test its strength, then you can decide whether to follow me or not."

"Oh, I'm following." That wasn't a question. "It's just do I want to grab onto that rope or take my chances without it."

"Do not follow me unless I give you the go-ahead." Spense was already clambering down. At the midsection he slowed considerably. "Just stay there until I give you the signal."

The hell with that.

She was doing this—carefully of course. Gingerly, she toed her foot onto one crumbling stone after another, until she arrived at the portion where she had to choose.

To rope or not to rope.

Spense yelled something up at her, but she couldn't make out his words above the falls. And she was afraid to look down. She'd been keeping her eyes glued to the sheer rock wall in front of her, finding her toeholds by feel.

"What did you say?"

"Pope!"

Okay, he had to have said rope. Listening above the sound of the falls was like texting with auto correct.

"Caity, look at me."

She dared a glance down.

Spense lounged at the bottom of the canyon on a big boulder, looking totally chill, like this whole ordeal hadn't even winded him. He made a hand-over-hand motion presumably to represent climbing. "The Pope is good."

She was still wary, but she trusted Spense. If he said the Pope was good, she was willing to convert. She grabbed hold of the thick hemp, with one hand at first, not daring to put her full weight on it. After a few downward steps, her confidence grew enough to use both hands and rely on the rope for support. It took her another fifteen minutes, and a few terrifying stretches across gaping rocks, but in the end, she made it down. She hadn't set any world records for speed, but she had arrived at the same boulder in the sun as Spense.

Life was good.

The day was hot.

And the falls—breathtaking.

This place reminded her of Havasupai at the bottom of the Grand Canyon—minus around a jillion tourists.

She'd love to spend a few minutes in the cool water of the falls. She was caked with mud and her knees stung from sliding on them into a gravelly stream during the great bee escape. But best not take the time. They were in pursuit of a possibly dangerous fugitive, and just as importantly, a fugitive who was proving to be her own worst enemy.

Ever since they'd hauled Rose away, Caitlin hadn't been able to shake the feeling that nothing about this case was what it seemed.

For everyone's sake, she wanted to get to the bottom of it. And that needed to happen fast, given the pressing date she had with Spense, Sunday at sunset on Dolphin Beach.

"Keep going?" Spense asked.

She was still getting her wind back after the treacherous climb into the canyon, so she gave him a thumbs-up and they pressed on in silence.

But not for long.

About the same time her breathing normalized, the path ended in a sheer vertical cliff that was twice as high as the one they'd scaled down.

"The buck stops here," Spense said.

No way to get up that without rock climbing equipment and a hell of a lot more skill than Caitlin possessed. "I don't think Rose is up there."

"Not unless she's a mountain goat."

"I guess I'm the goat. I was so sure this map would mean something to Rose. I really thought this was the place she'd feel safe. Guess I was wrong."

He stretched his arms and did a three-sixty. "*We* were wrong. But you have to admit it's been a great day."

"Bees and all." She grinned, because Spense was right. "You know what would make it even better? A swim at the bottom of the falls before we tackle the climb out."

"That sounds good to me."

The sun shining down on her skin was like a battery charge. She felt so energized she had to force herself not to race Spense back to the falls. They had a long journey home. So like a sensible person, she waited until they were a few yards away to break into a run. But he was too fast for her. His clothes were off before she could suggest a skinny dip.

Great minds.

She quickly wriggled out of her clothes and scrambled up onto some boulders.

The pool beneath the falls was too shallow for diving, but it seemed deep enough to jump in feetfirst. Caitlin landed with a magnificent splash that hid Spense from her view. A second later he popped up next to her. She ducked, anticipating a revenge splash, and then a chase, but Spense had other ideas. He was all business as he took her in his arms.

"Life is short," he said. Though it was said lightheartedly they both knew it was true. "Let's honeymoon first."

SPENSE LAY BESIDE Caity on the rocks with their clothes beneath them for towels. His body felt boneless, his skin warm, and his heart full. Caity satisfied every appetite he had and cultivated ones he hadn't known before her. He'd never minded spooning for example, but after-sex banter had never been his thing. With every other woman, he'd been uncontrollably sleepy after making love. With Caity, he didn't want to fall asleep.

He just wanted more.

More touching.

More *time*.

Reaching out, he took her hand.

He let his gaze drift over her naked body.

More beauty.

And yes . . . more talking.

Even if it was shoptalk. In fact shoptalk was what interested him most. He loved this job. The intellectual high he got from solving a complicated puzzle, the thrill of the chase, the swell of righteous pride when they got the bad guy—or gal—off the street.

So when Caity said, "You think Rose is still on the island?"

He propped himself on one elbow and willingly chimed in. "I think if she is, we better find her fast."

"I couldn't agree more. Either she's gone, or she's not done."

"Tahiti has such a small police force, and it's surrounded by water. Rose has shown herself capable of making an escape by sea. And any woman who can con her way out of police custody could've found her way off this island by now. It's not like the French police have an entire task force out looking for her."

"Of course she might be long gone by now. But if Lilly is right, and Rose is still around, what do you think her agenda is? Make amends with Lilly? Finish off Tommy?" Caity asked.

"My guess would be both."

I can explain everything.

"Too bad the cops took her away before she had the chance to say her piece." Spense knew that had been bugging Caity, too. "If we'd had a chance to talk to her . . ."

"You think Rose would've told us the truth."

Spense lifted a shoulder. "I think she risked capture, not to mention adding additional charges, by coming into our hotel room. She *wanted* to tell us her side of the story. So whether that story was truth or an attempt to manipulate it, talking to us was of critical importance to her. Obviously she didn't want to spill her secrets in front of the police, but it's too bad she couldn't give us a clue."

Caity bolted upright. "Maybe she did. How do we know she didn't circle back to our hotel, only this time she was careful not to get caught?"

"You think she left us a secret message."

Caity picked up her jeans and started hopping into them one leg at a time. "Maybe it's wishful thinking. But if Rose wants to communicate with us, which she clearly does, I believe she can find a way."

His legs had grown stiff, and he'd had about enough of the rock that was pressing against his spine. He stretched and stood up, too. Then he pulled the most gorgeous half-naked woman he'd ever seen in for one last kiss. "Thanks for earlier."

"It was beautiful," she said.

And it was, making love to the woman of his dreams, at the base of a hidden waterfall they'd risked life and limb to reach. It wasn't the kind of thing you'd find advertised in a travelogue. It was more the kind of memory you store in your heart forever.

And forever was exactly how long he intended on keeping Caity.

He watched her scramble into the rest of her clothes with what seemed like a new sense of urgency. Rose wasn't here. It was time to get home and search for more clues. Maybe one Rose had left deliberately. Why hadn't they thought of that before?

He dressed quickly and shot Caity a grin. "Let's roll."

She pulled out Parker's map, then crumpled it up, and stuffed it in her pocket. "Guess we don't need this anymore."

They easily retraced their steps to the cliff face with the steep steps and rope. Caity should go first this time. He'd bring up the rear and steady her if needed.

"After you," he said.

She put a foot up, and dirt and gravel rained down from above. Not much, certainly not a landslide, but enough to give him pause. "This cliff seems like it wants to give way any minute," he warned. "Don't rush it. I'll be right behind you."

The first part of the climb was uneventful. Not surprising since the steps were closer together and more level toward the bottom.

But he knew trouble was waiting for them. They reached the steepest, and least defined section and his gut clenched. His training had gotten him through worse climbs than this, but Caity was a civilian. In shape, sure, but she didn't have the background or the muscle he did. At least she was rested and refreshed from the waterfall.

And she had the rope.

He knew she wasn't jazzed about relying on it, but given how long it had taken her to get down, she was going to need it to make her way back up and out. Climbing slowly behind her, he took it easy, giving her just the right amount of space. Now and then, he tugged on the rope, testing its strength.

A scraping sound came from above, followed by another gravel slide.

He spit out a mouthful of dirt.

Dammit!

Every few minutes debris trickled down onto them—strange, since they hadn't had the problem on the way down.

Another rain of pebbles.

Caity looked back at him. "Goat?"

"Maybe." There was something mucking around up there, that was for sure.

"Long as it's not bees," she shot back.

"Keep your head down and stay alert for falling rocks."

He'd like to joke back, but his nerves were on edge. A rockslide in this situation could be lethal. He would've suggested turning back and waiting for conditions to improve, but they were halfway up. The bottom was as far away as the top.

The good news was Caity seemed relaxed. She was climbing quickly and with confidence.

The bad news: Grit continued to come down, like a drizzle threatening to break into a full-fledged downpour. Every muscle in his body was screwed up tight. His gaze locked on Caity, who currently had one hand on the rope and the other on the ledge above the midsection. The large, flat area that signaled the spot where the climb leveled off. From there, secure steps led all the way to the top.

Caity leaned back against the rope and wedged one foot into a crevice as she reached out with her free hand.

His throat constricted.

You're almost there, babe.

She shifted her weight onto the face of the cliff, released the rope, and hefted herself up onto the ledge.

His chest loosened and his heart rate slowed.

She'd made it to safety.

From here on out it was all gravy.

Until it wasn't.

His foot slipped on a bit of scree, and he grappled with the rope, taking it by both hands to steady himself.

What the hell?

He could feel a certain amount of give in the rope that hadn't been there before. The muscles in his arms tightened as the rope slackened.

He kicked his feet, trying to get a toehold but couldn't find one.

Focus.

He had to get his weight off the rope, but the cliff was slippery and there was no place for him to get purchase.

With the soles of his feet pressed against the crumbling wall of dirt, he muscled his way higher, toward a possible handhold. The rope jerked, and he watched in disbelief as its anchor wobbled and slipped. The piton that secured the rope stuck out from the cliff wall. It was working its way loose.

Panic welled in his chest for a nanosecond, then sent adrenaline flooding his body, triggering his brain into safety mode.

His life didn't flash before his eyes.

Instead, he envisioned his Rubik's cube. He had seconds, no more, to solve this puzzle. There was still time before the anchor broke free.

You can do this.

To his left, he could see a potential foothold and near it, a place to grab the rock with his hand. He stretched his leg to the side, but couldn't reach.

The rope slipped another inch, making his elbows jerk.

If he lost more ground, the path to safety would be out of range.

Bend your knees.

He could use the rope to swing sideways. But the momentum would pull the anchor free.

One shot.

That was all he had. If he didn't take it, he'd never hold Caity again.

Fuck that.

Kicking off the rock with one foot he propelled his body sideways and released the rope.

Seconds expanded into a lifetime.

A gift that gave him time to envision Caity's smile.

Her sweet voice whispered in his head.

You can make it. Just take my hand.

He reached out and grabbed the rock.

As the rope plummeted past him on its journey to the bottom of the canyon, one dangling foot found purchase.

His arms felt as though they would release from their sockets any minute, like a wishbone being pulled apart by a couple of determined kids. His gut swam, but his core remained strong.

He managed to get his forward foot into place, and reached higher.

Yes!

He gripped the rock and leaned against it, allowing himself one second of rest, less than that really, and then began to hoist his weight up, one toehold at a time.

This was no rock climbing gym, and he didn't have the luxury of scouting his route so he took it one step at a time.

He found himself heading into a dead end with no more toeholds and had to back down.

Grunting, he started over again.

His chin came up.

He moved another foot up the cliff and saw a slender arm reaching over the ledge, waving around.

His heart thundered in his ears.

Caity was supposed to be safely at the top. Out of danger of falling rocks. Not leaning over a ledge trying to rescue him.

Too dangerous.

But he didn't have enough breath left to order her to get the hell back, and he knew she wouldn't listen anyway.

The only way to get her out of this safely was to go with her.

He reached for her outstretched hand and heard a terrible sound squeezed out of his chest.

Her two hands locked around his wrist.

"On three." Her voice was pure calm.

One.

Two.

He pushed. She pulled. And somehow his chest found its way

up and over the ledge. Caity dragged him the rest of the way, then she threw her arms around him. He pulled her tightly against him. "You could've been killed," he admonished her. "What if my weight had pulled you off the ledge?"

She held his hands between her face and looked him dead in the eyes. "Would you have left me to make it on my own?"

He let out a sigh. "No way."

"Then shut the hell up and take me home."

BY THE TIME they finished the hike out, the sun had set. The detour around the hives had added extra miles, and the muscles in Caitlin's legs felt as though they were attached to rubber rather than bone.

Another hour or so drive back to the hotel, and then the search for the secret message Caitlin was convinced Rose had left them began. With the help of Dutch and Gretchen, she and Spense tore the bungalow apart.

To no avail.

Spent, Caitlin dropped onto the cushionless sofa. Her spine hit the hard backboard, and she eyed the pillows on the floor surrounding her feet, but didn't have the will to get up and replace them on the couch. For that matter, she barely had the will to keep her eyes open.

"I'm not saying Rose didn't leave you a clue, but I am saying if she did, it's not in this room. I'd stake my Eagle Scout badge on that one." Dutch pounded a plush cushion and stuffed it behind Caitlin's back, which took the edge off the bad news.

Maybe it had been wishful thinking on her part—to believe Rose had returned to their hotel at some point and left them a clue to help them unravel the truth. "You're right. Of course you're right, but Rose Parker Preston did not break into our hotel room, hold us at gunpoint, and promise to explain everything for no reason."

"Maybe that reason is she's crazy." Gretchen came over and gave Caitlin a quick hug. "I know how much you want to see the good in people, but in this instance, you may be reaching. Looking for some justifiable explanation for this woman's reprehensible actions."

Dutch drew his eyebrows together. "I'm sure glad you saw the good in me, Caitlin. Things would've turned out a lot differently for me if you and Spense hadn't given me the benefit of the doubt when no one else was willing."

Caitlin's heart squeezed at the reminder that Dutch had once been the prime suspect in his wife's murder. Her shoulders lifted. Her eyes widened, and she sent her future brother-in-law a smile.

She suddenly felt a second wind coming on. "Even crazy people act on their own internal logic. There was definitely something she wanted to say to us."

"Okay, I'll play devil's advocate again." Gretchen stood with crossed arms. "Did Rose offer to explain everything before or after the gendarmes burst into the room?"

"Before." Spense took a seat next to Caitlin. "Rose had the drop on us, and after she told us to put our hands up, *that's* when she said she wanted to explain everything. It wasn't just a ploy to placate the gendarmes. I think Caity's right. She sought us out to tell us something that at least in her mind was of vital importance. Something worth risking getting caught and sent to jail for."

There was a soft knock.

"I can't help thinking if we'd just had a few more minutes alone with her."

"She might have shot you, just like she did her husband." Brousseau walked through the door Gretchen had opened for him.

"Well, yes. That's a possibility, too." Caitlin grinned. "I'm very grateful to your men, Jacques. I'd rather be alive and curious than dead and satisfied."

"Me, too." Spense got up to greet the inspector with a shake. "Thanks for coming by—we're anxious to hear all about your day."

"The interest is mutual."

"You first," Spense said. "What happened with all those Rose sightings?" He knew the police hadn't found her, but he was curious to know if there had been any real leads, or any pattern to the sightings.

"Dead ends everywhere. And a lot of it thanks to the sister. Lilly not only did not check in to let us know of her whereabouts, she didn't pick up our calls. So we were forced to try to track down every possible Rose sighting."

"You think Lilly's deliberately making the search for her sister more difficult?" Caitlin had wondered more than once why Lilly, who freely admitted she didn't trust the police, would cooperate with them.

"It's crossed my mind. But she claimed, when she finally did check in tonight, that she spent the entire day at a beach with no cell service. That doesn't explain why she didn't tell us ahead of time where she'd be, though."

"I think we should assume Lilly is trying to look out for her sister."

"Even though her sister stole her fiancé. I guess blood really is blind," Brousseau said.

"I think the saying is *love* is blind." Spense took his seat next to Caitlin again.

Funny how a little thing like feeling the warmth of him next to her could set the world right for her.

"Same idea. Anyway, we did find two patterns of interest amidst all the calls. There was a cluster of sightings around an internet café, and another near Dolphin Beach and the hotel. One witness claims he saw Rose digging up ground beneath a banyan tree. When our man got there, there was no Rose, but someone or something had dug deep beneath the roots of that tree." Brousseau touched his upper lip. A habit that made Caitlin wonder if he'd recently shaved a mustache. "But what's this I hear about bees and Spense nearly falling to his death?"

Caitlin let Spense tell it, and he did do the story justice. No false modesty for Spense. He'd made quite the leap off a dangling rope, avoiding death by a fraction of a second—and he took credit where credit was due.

One of the things she loved about him.

Actually, at the moment she couldn't think of anything she didn't love about the guy. Good thing, since they were getting married day after tomorrow.

"And you think this was sabotage. Someone trying to kill you?"

"Or at least stop us from carrying on with this investigation. To me that means we're getting close."

"Close to what? Finding Rose?"

"Or finding the truth. Whoever tossed a rock onto the hives and loosened the rope's anchor definitely doesn't want us to find out the truth."

"*If* someone did those things intentionally, I'd have to agree. I'm going to send my men out there tomorrow to look around. But I have to tell you, both of those events, as unfortunate as they were, could have been accidental. The path down the side of the cliff to Mana Falls is treacherous. And the hives have been around a long time. They weren't placed there for the purpose of harming you and Dr. Cassidy."

"Maybe we should go back with your crew, tomorrow," Spense offered.

Brousseau shook his head. "I'd prefer my men handle it. No offense, but if you hadn't gone out there in the first place, I wouldn't be losing manpower to a search that's unlikely to yield results. And besides, I'd like you to come with me tomorrow morning. If you can spare the time."

"Where to?"

"The First National Bank of Papeete. The manager reported a suspicious transaction involving George Parker's bank account."

Chapter 22

LIKE PAPEETE ITSELF, the First National Bank was full of color and vibrant people. Pineapple-yellow walls in the entry gave way to parrot green in the lobby. Each staff member they passed on the way to the bank manager's office greeted them with a *Bienvenue les amis*.

Caitlin felt her spirits inch up with every welcoming smile. But she had to admit she was still a little low. For one thing, Brousseau's frustration had rubbed off on her. Yesterday, in addition to chasing false Rose sightings, the inspector had attended a disciplinary hearing for his brother. Deputy Pierre Brousseau had been suspended without pay until he completed an alcohol rehabilitation program. After that, he might or might not be able to return to the force depending on the findings of a future committee.

Caitlin was sympathetic to Pierre, who seemed like a nice guy. But nice guys don't always make good cops. In truth, it seemed a more than fair finding to her. Trouble was the inspector had now been left both short-handed and red-faced. He'd also been given a letter of reprimand, since he was in command at the time of Rose's escape.

Caitlin returned yet another smile and tried to shake off her mood. Spense had nearly lost his life yesterday, and the whole incident had brought her anxieties to the fore. When she woke up this morning, that familiar feeling of having a bad luck charm sewn into the lining of her life was back in full force. She understood it was irrational, that her happiness hadn't made the gods jealous and caused that anchor to come loose and break off the rock. But if anything ever happened to Spense, she didn't know how she could bear it.

She pulled her cardigan tighter around her shoulders.

They'd reached the bank manager's office.

Brousseau ushered them inside. The manager, a jowly man with skin a shade more pink than tan, was seated behind a teakwood desk that boasted, appropriately enough, a banker's lamp.

"I'm delighted to present my friends of the investigation, Special Agent Atticus Spenser and Dr. Caitlin Cassidy," Brousseau said. "This is Monsieur Bertrand Fontaine."

Fontaine came out from behind his desk and greeted them, in the French style, with kisses on the cheek.

Très charmant.

"Special agent like James Bond? I didn't realize this was such an important case, Inspector."

Brousseau chuckled. "*Non, mon ami.* Bond is a British secret agent. My friends are American—FBI."

"Even more impressive. But why are they here?"

"They're getting married." Brousseau spread his arms.

Fontaine's eyebrows lifted. "Ah, now it is your turn to joke. But Tahiti is a wonderful place for lovers. On behalf of all of Papeete, I say congratulations to the happy couple."

"*Merci,*" Caitlin said.

Spense sat down on a love seat and pulled his Rubik's cube from his pocket. Tossed it in the air. Caitlin took a seat next to him and waited, tapping her fingers on her knees.

Small talk was one thing, but they had serious matters to attend.

A few more jocular phrases and pats on the back, and Fontaine and Brousseau finally took seats. Rather than return to his position behind his desk, Fontaine had chosen an armchair facing them. When he leaned forward, his knees crowded Spense's. "Now then, in all seriousness, what has the FBI got to do with this?"

"I'll take that one," Spense said. "There are American citizens involved, so we have an obvious interest. But we're not official, and you're under no obligation to talk to us."

"Not official? Well, then, Brousseau, what do you advise?"

"Talk to them. That's why I brought them along."

"Yes. Of course," Fontaine said.

A quick, silent competition for who would lead the interview took place.

Caitlin won. "We appreciate your cooperation, Monsieur Fontaine. Now, can you tell us why you reported your customer's transaction as suspicious? What about it seemed so to you?"

"I wouldn't necessarily have categorized it as worrisome. In fact, until I saw that woman's picture in the papers, I did not. Which is why it took me until yesterday to report it."

"So the transaction didn't happen yesterday. When did it occur?"

"On Monday."

Caitlin's skin prickled. That was the day before Rose allegedly attempted to murder Tommy.

"Let's back up," Spense said. They'd been given a heads-up from Brousseau that Rose had possibly received a large sum of money from her father's bank account, but that was all they knew. "A few details about the transaction would be helpful."

"*Oui.* I recognized the woman from the papers. I thought to myself, Bertrand, this must be connected. A woman shoots her husband, and then she flees from custody. I should tell my friend, the inspector, that this young lady transferred 990,000 U.S. dollars from my bank into a Cayman Islands account—after making a cash withdrawal of ten thousand dollars. Was I right to make the report?"

"Yes. Well done," Brousseau said.

"And the account was held in a similar name."

"Similar? It wasn't Rose Parker?" the inspector asked, with a hint of surprise in his tone.

"*Non.*"

"Lilly Parker?"

"*Non.*"

Caitlin could see the camaraderie between Brousseau and Fontaine, but neither of these men had narrowly escaped death yesterday like Spense had. She hated to seem humorless, but it was time to get on with things. "Are you going to keep us playing twenty questions or are you going to tell us whose name was on that bank account?"

"Forgive me. I'll try to do better with my answers in the future."

"How about starting now instead?"

Spense widened his legs so that his thigh brushed hers.

The tips of Fontaine's ears reddened. "Anna. The account of Mr. George Parker is payable upon death to his daughter, Anna Parker."

Brousseau lifted slightly from his chair. "There's a third sister?"

Spense snapped his fingers. "Could be. But I doubt it. We haven't heard anyone speak of a third sister. And don't forget George Parker was a con man."

"So you're thinking Anna Parker is an alias," Caitlin said.

Spense pulled out a photo of Lilly. "Is this the woman who closed out George Parker's account last Friday?"

"Erm." The banker pulled his chin. "May I take a closer look?"

Spense handed the photo over.

"I'm not sure. Could be. This is a good resemblance, and I do remember a *charmant* dimple, so *oui*, probably."

"But you're not entirely sure."

He shook his head.

Next, Spense passed him Rose's photograph. "How about her? Is this the woman who came to your bank?"

"*Oui.*" Fontaine nodded immediately.

"These women are sisters, and they look very much alike. How can you be sure which woman it was?" Caitlin asked.

"How do you know your own face when you look in the mirror? You've seen it before so you recognize it. *Mais non?*"

You could crack a nut on that argument. But she'd attack it anyway. "Okay. Close your eyes. Which side of the face was the *charmant* dimple on?"

Fontaine squeezed his eyes closed and then opened them. "I cannot say, Dr. Cassidy."

Good answer. This was probably a reliable ID. It was unlikely Fontaine would remember which side of the face was marked by a dimple, and he owned up to that rather than trying to blow smoke in order to shore up his credibility. He'd come forward on his own and seemed confident it'd been *Rose* Parker who'd closed out her father's old account and transferred the funds offshore.

"For my records," Brousseau said. "Since you've never met the woman how did you know she was legally entitled to the funds?"

"As I said before, the account was payable upon death to Anna Parker. I knew the father personally, and I'd heard of his passing previously. I wondered when Anna would come to collect. George opened the account over ten years ago, and he's been depositing cash in person every year. More than once, he spoke with me to be sure that upon his death the funds would go to his daughter. When the woman in question arrived on Monday, she had his death certificate and her own valid passport. Everything was in order. So I didn't hesitate to transfer the funds according to her wishes."

"I'm satisfied. Thank you, Bertrand," said Brousseau. "Did you perchance copy her passport and the death certificate?"

"*Mais oui.* Let me get you a copy, too. It won't take a minute."

After Fontaine withdrew, Brousseau rolled a pen that he'd been using for note taking between his palms. "I believe the transfer of funds shows that the attempted murder . . . pardon me, Caitlin, I meant to say the *alleged* attempted murder, was premeditated."

"Don't know about that," Spense said. "But it definitely shows Rose has the means to flee the country."

"If it was, in fact, Rose who transferred the money." Caitlin twisted a piece of her hair and then tucked it behind her ear. "We've had one Rose sighting already that turned out to be *Lilly*. And doesn't it seem odd that a father would leave the money to one of his daughters instead of dividing it between the two?"

"My guess," Spense said, "is that the funds were supposed to be split up. Since the money went to 'Anna Parker' neither Rose or Lilly would have a tax liability."

"Rose Parker is a cold one." Brousseau shivered. "Tries to kill her husband on their wedding day and steals an inheritance from her sister as well."

"There's a mountain of assumptions in that statement, Jacques," Spense said.

But if half of them were true, Caitlin had read Rose all wrong.

As promised, Fontaine returned quickly with a death certificate and a passport for Anna Parker. The passport photo was of *Rose* Parker, confirmed by the dimple in the right cheek.

They thanked him and took their leave.

Before heading back to town, Brousseau pulled Caitlin to the side. "Your theory that Rose may have acted in self-defense simply doesn't hold up anymore. Why would she empty out a bank account and move it to the Caymans unless she was planning on a shoot and run? Unless new evidence comes to light, it's time to call off the hunt."

"If you're so sure she's guilty why would you stop searching for her?" Caitlin asked.

"Because I believe Rose Parker is sitting on a beach in the Cayman Islands even as we speak. If she's no longer in Tahiti there's nothing more for us to do. And though I admit I was curious about Tommy Preston's veracity after I heard the Pamela

Jean story, I have yet to hear proof this Pamela Jean person ever existed. All the evidence supports the straightforward hypothesis that Rose Parker Preston is a criminal deviant whose motives we will never fully understand. So now, if you'll excuse me, I have to go break the news to Lilly that her sister not only made up the story about this Pamela Jean to steal her fiancé, but now she's cheated her out of her inheritance and fled the country. Unless you two would like to do the honors?"

Spense flipped his cube in the air and stepped into the conversation. "I think you should hold off on that, Brousseau. We only found out about Pamela Jean on Thursday. Dutch and Gretchen have put out feelers in Riverbend regarding the woman, but it takes time for leads to come in. And if Rose Parker is indeed sunning herself in the Caymans right now, then who the hell set a horde of bees after Caity and me and sabotaged our climbing rope?"

"Spense makes good points." Caity faced Brousseau. "But so do you. My suggestion is we keep our options and our minds open. You've already said you were going to send a team to look for evidence that someone tampered with the rope and its anchor. While they're at it, your men could take another look around for Rose in the area around Mana Falls. On our end, we can continue working the Pamela Jean angle. Because if Tommy Preston really did beat a prostitute to death, I'd say that would shine a whole different light on this investigation."

Chapter 23

Six Months and Three Days Ago
Riverbend Memorial Hospital
Riverbend, Texas

"I'M HERE TO see Pamela Jean," Rose said firmly, keeping her chin high and her gaze level with the woman in green scrubs. A practiced liar, Rose's nerves didn't usually get the better of her when presenting a fake identity in order to gain admittance somewhere she wasn't invited, but today her mouth was dry and her stomach clenched. Today, she had to work to keep the flutter from her voice—not because she felt guilty about deceiving the woman who stood before her, hands on hips, at the nurses' station on Pod 4B at Riverbend Memorial, *Jessica Prosper RN*—but because the identity Rose was currently stealing belonged to her own sister.

Which meant Rose had entered unchartered territory.

She was taking a sledgehammer to an unbreakable Parker rule.

Never lie to family.

She threw her shoulders back.

This was for Lilly's own good. Even if Lilly didn't want to know what this was about, Rose did. Lilly was love-struck blind when it came to her fiancé, but Rose had caught the distinct whiff of something rotten in Denmark the first time she'd met the man. The truth was, Tommy Preston reminded her of Papa: all charm and warm handshakes, white teeth and humble smiles. And like Papa, Tommy could carry on a conversation with your aunt Dee or the CEO of a Fortune 500 company and convince them both they were the most fascinating people in the room.

Rose had spent her entire life hanging with con artists, and she recognized a suit cut from the same cloth when she saw one. So when she had accidentally come across a cryptic message on Lilly's cell from one Pamela Jean—no last name—you don't know me but it's urgent we speak about Tommy—Rose simply could not let it go.

Lilly had brushed off the text, claiming it was likely a jilted ex who wanted to poison her against her beloved Tommy. Lilly had deleted the message, blocked the sender, and sworn her undying loyalty to the man she was about to marry. Furthermore, in a tone with more authority than Rose had ever heard her muster, Lilly had instructed Rose to stay out of her business.

Stay out of her business?

Pamela Jean had asked Lilly to visit her in the *hospital*.

Lilly was the only family Rose had left, and she'd be damned if she'd ignore a message from a sick woman regarding Lilly's too-good-to-be-true fiancé.

Tommy might look like the perfect man, but if Rose had learned one thing from Papa, it was to trust her gut over her eyes.

Things aren't always what they seem.

"Where can I find Pamela Jean?" Rose repeated confidently,

praying that Jessica Prosper would not ask her for the patient's last name.

The nurse's eyebrows, which were two shades darker than her unkempt sandy hair and suffered noticeably from too many years of amateur waxing, raised suspiciously. "Name please."

She was about to answer *I don't know* when she realized the nurse was asking for *her* name, not Pamela Jean's surname. She met Jessica's eyes. "Lilly Parker. I got a message that my friend was ill."

The woman swept her with an assessing gaze.

Rose hadn't been in too many hospitals, but when Papa was ill, she didn't remember the staff being this picky about visitors. Maybe Jessica was one of those people who had a thing for HIPAA regulations. "Would you like to see some ID?" She had one of Lilly's many driver's licenses in her purse, and she could easily pass for her sister to a stranger.

Jessica's posture shifted out of soldier mode. "That's okay. You're just as PJ described you. And I suppose if you're not you who you say you are, she'll clear it up quick."

Rose didn't see how *PJ* could clear anything up, if, as she'd claimed in her text, she and Lilly had never met. If all Pamela Jean had to go by were photos of Lilly with Tommy in the society pages, Rose had nothing to worry about. Unless PJ was discerning enough to notice which cheek was dimpled or which twin had an upturned nose, this was going to be a slam dunk.

Jessica swiped her badge on an entry pad and a set of double doors opened. She motioned for Rose to follow her through them. "I should warn you, PJ's appearance may shock you, but we're doing all we can to keep her comfortable. She might be loopy from all the pain meds. Normally, I'd say come back later, but she's been asking for you since she was brought in yesterday. She's very anxious to see you, and I'm hoping your visit will lift her spirits."

Rose made no reply.

The less conversation she had with Nurse Jessica, the less chance there'd be of the nurse realizing that Rose had no idea who Pamela Jean was, or that Rose wasn't the sister PJ wanted to see.

Jessica stopped in front of room four fourteen. Rose, taking a quick moment to evaluate her surroundings and note the location of the stairwell in the event she needed to make a speedy exit, tilted her head in puzzlement. She supposed it wasn't unusual for the desk clerk to be absent from her post, but it was eerily quiet on the pod.

"Low census. We're closing this unit and moving everyone to the east side." Jessica smiled. "We're still waiting on a room to open up on Four East for Pamela, but you'll have at least a few minutes before we have to move her. As soon as a room becomes available, though, I'm afraid you'll have to leave."

Rose wasn't sure if this was a stroke of good luck or bad. On the one hand, no one was likely to be eavesdropping on what she suspected might be a delicate conversation. On the other, they might have to cut the conversation short. "How long do you think I have before they come for her?"

"Absolutely no idea. We have to wait for a discharge on the other side. If I could predict when the doctors will show up for rounds, I'd be the most popular kid on the block." Jessica adjusted the stethoscope around her neck. "If you're worried about being alone with her, don't be. I'm right here if you need anything."

Jessica headed to a mobile desk and powered on a computer. "Don't tire her out."

"I promise I won't." On a deep breath, Rose knocked on the door of room four fourteen.

No answer.

She looked to Jessica, but the nurse's attention was lasered onto the computer screen in front of her.

Rose peeked her head in the room and saw a woman lying in bed, covers tucked beneath her chin. One eye was swollen to the size of a lemon, and bruises covered her cheek on the same side.

Rose's chest tightened.

More than a twinge of guilt assailed her.

This wasn't like lying to a greedy mark.

This woman was gravely injured.

Do it for Lilly.

Rose slipped into the room and quietly closed the door behind her. As she approached the bed, the woman opened her good eye and groaned.

Rose stepped closer. "Pamela Jean, it's me, Lilly Parker. I came as soon as I got your message. Is it all right if I'm here? Do you feel up to a visitor?"

Another groan.

Rose had no idea if the woman even realized she was in the room or not. But whatever PJ had to tell Lilly, for her to have found a way to get a message to her under these circumstances, it must be important. Rose picked up a chair that had been propped against the wall and relocated it to Pamela Jean's bedside.

Then she sat, waiting, while Pamela Jean's chest rose and fell and rose and fell.

A half hour passed, and then finally the woman opened her eyes again, though one was barely a slit. "Thirsty." Her voice was cracked and dry, as were her lips.

From a tray table, Rose poured water into a paper cup and stuck a straw in it.

Pamela lifted a black-and-blue hand with an IV attached, motioning for the cup.

"I'm going to raise the head of your bed, first, if that's okay." The last thing she wanted was for PJ to choke on a cup of water.

"P-please," Pamela Jean said.

With a light touch, Rose pressed the button to incline the bed into a sitting position. A mechanical whirring accompanied the little upward jerks of the bed.

Pamela Jean gasped.

"Oh my God. I'm so sorry. I'll get your nurse."

Pamela Jean reached out and gripped Rose by the wrist. "Is it you, Lilly? Don't go."

"Yes, it's me. I have to find your nurse right away. Just hang on. I think you need more pain medicine."

"No. Just water. The pills make me too sleepy to talk." She struggled to sit higher in the bed. "Please don't leave me."

Whatever doubts Rose had about coming here suddenly vanished, as did the sound of beeps that had only a moment before seemed like they were coming out of a loudspeaker, and the smell of antiseptic that had been so pungent it had made her nose burn. Suddenly, she could see and hear *only* Pamela Jean. "I won't leave you. Not until you say it's okay."

Pamela Jean nodded and touched her throat. "Hurts to talk."

Rose placed a pillow behind her back, and held the paper cup steady while she sipped from a straw. "Better?"

"Much."

Her eyes rolled up, and for a moment, Rose's heart stopped beating. But then Pamela Jean took another sip of water and continued in a scratchy voice, "I have something important to tell you."

"What happened to you?" Rose had to ask.

Pamela Jean looked away, and then back. Her swollen eye oozed some kind of ointment. A tear from the other eye dribbled down her cheek.

"Was it an accident? Were you in a car wreck?"

Pamela Jean shook her head, grimacing from the obvious discomfort. "No."

Rose cringed from a sympathy pain of her own. "I know I promised not to leave the room, but I really do think I should get Jessica—your nurse." She leaned over, looking for a call button.

"No this is only for you. You have to promise not to tell."

Rose nodded.

"Say you promise." Pamela strained forward. "If he finds out I told you, he'll kill me."

Rose sat down hard in the bedside chair.

"I—I promise." She wasn't sure if she could keep Pamela Jean's secret or not, but she *needed* to hear whatever the woman was so desperate to tell her—to tell Lilly rather. Afterward she could evaluate what to disclose and whether or not to drag her sister down to the hospital to meet PJ.

"Don't. Marry. Him," PJ said, emphasizing each word with surprising determination.

This was one strong-willed woman. And she'd been through a terrible ordeal, clearly. But she was heavily medicated, probably confused, and like Lilly had suggested, Pamela Jean might very well be a jilted lover with ulterior motives.

"Look." Rose lowered her voice, just in case Jessica was outside the door. "I don't know you, and you don't know me. I'm so sorry for whatever you've been through. If you need anything at all from me, all you have to do is ask. But you can't say something like *don't marry him* and leave it at that."

PJ's head dropped back onto her pillow. She looked fragile—like a deep breath could crack her ribs. Lilly kept hearing Nurse Jessica's admonishment in her head. *Don't tire her out.* "You need to rest, and I can't stay much longer. So if you can give me a good reason not to marry Tommy, you'd better do it now."

"*He* did this to me. And he said he'd kill me if I told anyone."

"*Tommy Preston?*"

She nodded.

Rose's knees turned to water. "He beat you up and said he'd kill you if you told anyone what he did?"

PJ tore at her gown. "Yes, or what I know about him. But I had to warn *you*. I can't live with myself if I don't."

Rose's head felt like a balloon on a string. She didn't have a good opinion of Tommy Preston, but this wasn't the revelation she'd expected. She'd been prepared to hear about scandals, infidelities, dirty business dealings, and such, but not *this.*

And Lilly had been dating him for months. Her sister might be naïve, but she was neither stupid nor reckless. If Tommy had ever hit her, Rose was certain Lilly would have shared that with her. She looked at the floor, and then back up at Pamela Jean's split lip and her swollen eye. Her arms tattooed with bruises. She took a deep breath. No matter how badly she felt for this woman, she wasn't going to lie. There was too much at stake. "I'm not sure I believe you."

"I *wish* I'd never seen anything. I wish I didn't know anything." More tears leaked out. "But maybe he won't hurt you. You're not a hooker so . . ."

Pamela Jean was a prostitute, not a jilted ex. Could she be telling the truth?

"I'm sorry I bothered you. But now you know." The woman shrank back against the bed, small, and defeated. "Lilly . . . ." Her voice didn't trail off so much as disappear. Her eyes rolled back and closed.

A monitor sounded a loud alarm.

The hairs on the back of Rose's neck lifted and her stomach knotted.

Jessica rushed into the room. She listened to Pamela Jean's chest with a stethoscope, then silenced the monitor by hitting a button.

"I didn't mean to . . . Is she going to be okay?" Rose asked.

Jessica looked at her sternly, but not unkindly. She lowered the head of the bed, and tucked a semiconscious Pamela Jean under the covers. "You'd better go."

Clearly. But Rose now regretted telling PJ she didn't believe her. She should have given her a chance to tell her story. A hooker wouldn't care if Tommy married another woman, and an ex-girlfriend wouldn't pretend to be a hooker. "When can I come back?"

"Tomorrow if you like. Just check in with me first. She put you on her list."

"List?" This just kept getting weirder. "You have to be on a list to see her?" Like she was the president or something.

"PJ is on *do not name, do not publish* status."

"I don't understand."

"She requested that her name not be made public—or her room number."

"You mean because she's afraid of someone."

"I mean she's *do not name, do not publish*. But you're on her approved list. I can update you on her condition if you call. Or leave me your number, and I'll have her doctor contact you if you'd prefer." She checked the monitors and then her watch. "I'll give you two minutes."

Nurse Jessica adjusted the blankets and left the room, closing the door behind her.

Pamela Jean muttered something unintelligible.

Rose clutched the side of the bed, leaning over Pamela Jean, her body shivering with a sick feeling of dread. "I'm sorry I didn't believe you."

Pamela's eyes fluttered open. Her mouth moved silently. Rose put her ear near enough to Pamela's lips to feel her wispy breath on her cheek.

"Find . . ."

"Find what?" Rose's hands ached from clutching the bed rails.

Pamela Jean's lips trembled from the effort of speech. "Find Sadie."

Chapter 24

Saturday
Heritage Townhomes
Papeete
Tahiti Nui

TOMMY STOOD, CONCEALED behind a pillar, in the parking lot outside Lilly's townhome. He rubbed a baggie between his fingertips, relishing the soft swishing sound. The high Tommy got from heroin was strictly vicarious. Not since he was a boy, not since the day Sadie overdosed them both, had the deadly dragon flowed through his system.

But he was fighting an addiction just the same.

There had been a few times in his life, and Thursday had been one of them, when the only thing that could stop the pressure building in his brain—his mental equivalent of a junkie's shakes—was the Big H—injected not into his blood but into his soul. This whole Rose debacle had triggered an urge that he hadn't indulged in many, many years. And though watching

Marie's slow death had taken the edge off, he still had a craving he couldn't explain.

Tommy dropped the baggie back in his pocket and reached for his watch.

He easily found the round object, its solid gold warmed from resting against his thigh. He depressed the ridged winder on his watch and the case sprang open.

Twelve noon.

Up until now, he'd been disgracefully disorganized.

It was high time he became proactive.

It was beneath a man of his intellect and education to run around reacting to the moves of his fugitive bride. He needed to take control. Though he hadn't yet worked out every detail of his plan, he did know Lilly was the linchpin.

Poor Lilly.

For the daughter of a hustler she was incredibly naïve. She wouldn't smell a con coming her way if it rolled around in a Dumpster. Of course he didn't have to con her at all if he didn't wish to. He could simply take her by brute force. He'd do whatever was most expedient after evaluating her comportment.

While he pondered his options, Lilly emerged from her door, dressed in a skirt and tailored blouse, low-heeled pumps.

Conservative.

And not at all her style.

Where the hell was she off to?

He could wander over and ask, but decided against it. It was quite possible Rose had contacted her. She might be headed for a secret rendezvous with her sister right this minute.

As she walked down her steps into the parking lot, Lilly rattled a set of keys in her hands.

Dammit.

He couldn't follow in his Porsche. She'd spot him for sure.

He hurried to the street and as good luck would have it, a cab was coming up.

He stuck out his hand.

The cab halted at the curb. Tommy jumped in the front seat and handed the driver a one-hundred-dollar bill. "In a moment, a green sedan will pull out of that complex. I need you to follow it."

"Is no problem."

"Discreetly."

"Is no problem."

Tommy sighed and relaxed back against the vinyl seat. Annoyingly, sweat glued his shirt to his back, and worse, the cab smelled of onions. Glancing at his feet, he noticed crumpled foil that looked to contain the remnants of a gyro. With the toe of his shoe, he edged the mess toward the corner.

Lilly's car rolled out of the drive.

"Go!"

"I go."

Good.

Lilly drove exasperatingly slowly. Tommy glanced at the speedometer. Thirty miles an hour, and they were about to overtake her.

"Back off. I don't want her to notice us."

"Is this your wife, sir?"

"Fiancée. Ex-fiancée."

"Do not worry. I follow her good."

Considering how easy this was proving to be, Tommy was beginning to regret his generosity. Any pea brain could follow a slowpoke who signaled every lane change. If Lilly was indeed going to meet Rose, she was a discredit to her family.

He sighed.

Rose knew how bad Lilly was at subterfuge, and she wouldn't risk allowing her to lead him right to her.

He'd wasted his money, but he might as well see this through.

They arrived at the Night Star—a no-tell motel, from the looks of it.

Tommy counted to one hundred and twenty, and then followed Lilly inside and concealed himself behind a wall abutting the main lobby.

Lilly rang the bell. A medium-sized man of indeterminate age appeared—his only distinguishing feature, and it was a remarkable one, was a giant hair-sprouting mole on his chin.

"Checking in?"

"Not at this time," Lilly said as if apologizing.

The clerk rubbed his hand down his cheek and said nothing.

Tommy shifted his feet. He itched for them to get on with the discussion.

"Have you seen me before?" Lilly asked.

"You should know more than me if you've been here before," the clerk answered flatly.

"I'm sorry." Ah, the apology. Meek little Lilly simply couldn't help herself.

"For what? How may I help you?"

"I meant do I look familiar? I was wondering if someone who looks like me—my sister—is a guest at this motel."

He arched an eyebrow. "*Non.*"

"Are you sure?"

"*Non.*"

"Does that mean no you're not sure, or no she's not a guest?"

"I do not think she stays here. I would remember a beautiful woman like you." He covered his mole with three fingers and lowered his gaze. "But I am not the only clerk. Perhaps the night clerk will know. Would you care to leave a photograph?"

Lilly's shoulders trembled, and Tommy had to wonder if she had some idea what a man who liked the looks of her might do with the photograph. She opened her purse and closed it again. "No. I don't have a picture. But you'll describe me to the night clerk. You can call me at this number if he's seen her." She scribbled something and passed it to him.

He took the note from her hand, touching it in the process.

She shivered and bolted for the door.

Back in the cab, Tommy told the cabbie to follow at a safe distance.

Once again, the drive was uneventful, with Lilly making her way carefully back to the townhouse. When Tommy was certain that was where they were headed, he signaled the driver to let him walk the last block, just to be sure Lilly didn't spot his tail.

Whistling beneath his breath, he entered the parking lot of Heritage Townhomes, ready to march up the steps and set a plan in motion.

He rounded the corner, and there on the front porch of Lilly's place, a young man with a bicycle helmet stood waiting. Lilly climbed the steps. Tommy was too far back to hear the exchange of words between her and the young man, but he could see the change in her posture as the messenger handed her a small, rectangular package.

The hairs on the back of his neck lifted.

Who would be sending something by bicycle messenger to Lilly?

The answer was obvious.

Rose was up to something.

What wasn't as clear was whether or not Lilly was in on that something.

But he had an idea how to find out, once and for all, whose side Lilly Parker was really on.

He rubbed the aching muscle in his tight jaw. Then he pulled his phone from his pocket and called the private concierge the hotel had assigned to him.

"Jean Claude speaking. How may I be of service, Monsieur Preston?"

"Good afternoon, Jean Claude, I hope your day is going well. Sorry for the short notice, but it seems I suddenly find myself in need of a boat."

Chapter 25

Saturday
Hôtel De Plage Dauphin
Tahiti Nui

SPENSE SET HIS stocking feet on the coffee table in the sitting area of his bungalow, and his mother, Agatha, nudged them off with her elbow.

"Can't a man relax in his own home?"

"Not in front of company," she said.

He glanced around at Dutch, Gretchen, Arlene, and Caity. "I don't see anyone here except family."

Caity reached over and squeezed his knee.

"But I don't want anyone to think you didn't raise me well so I won't put up a fight."

"That's good because I don't want to fight. I feel terrible we were out last night when you got home from your hike, and by the time we got back from our excursion, we didn't want to disturb you." His mother sighed. "But now I want to hear all about your treasure hunt. I know it was for the case, but did you two have fun at the waterfall? Did you find Gauguin's Gold?"

The question made him realize how little time they'd had with the moms. He hadn't heard about their excursion yesterday, or even the submarine tour they took two days ago.

Caity coughed into her hand and sent him a look that she needn't have bothered with. He had no intention of telling the moms about either his near-death adventure or his and Caity's al fresco lovemaking.

Although he could throw them a bone and mention skinny dipping.

They might get a kick out of that.

He touched the hole in his forehead that Caity was boring in it with her eyes and thought better of it. "Not much to tell, I'm afraid. We did outrun a couple of bees. We had to dive into a stream to get away from them. But other than that . . . no big deal."

"How was the submarine tour?" Caity asked.

That set off a round robin of *oohs* and *aahs* and descriptions of tropical fish. Arlene had purchased a book from the gift store that identified various species, and they passed that around. Spense's chest expanded as he took in the room.

It was good to have downtime.

Even better to have family.

But he was itching to make one last search of the room.

He couldn't help wondering if last night, they'd somehow overlooked a message or clue from Rose. All the evidence did seem to point to Rose having left Tahiti—the sightings had all come to nothing, and she had a fake passport and means to travel. But even if she'd run off to the Caymans, that didn't mean she didn't leave something behind. And no search is ever final until you find whatever it is you're missing.

It's always in the last place you look.

Arlene tapped his knee. "Seems like your mind is elsewhere. I thought Rose Parker was presumed gone by now. So I just assumed you two were done with the case."

Spense shrugged. "Not quite." Then he turned to Dutch. "Did you find anything more on that woman we asked you to track down?"

"Pamela Jean," Dutch said. "We made a start, but like I mentioned to you on the phone, we're still waiting for folks in Riverbend to get back to us with more information."

"But we're definitely on it," Gretchen said. "I'll make some follow-up calls. Is there anything else you want us to look into?"

"I think the list we gave you after our interview with Lilly and Mrs. Preston about covers it. But keep your eyes open for anything that seems off."

"Anything in particular?"

"A note in the seat cushions of the rental car. A message written in lipstick on a mirror." Caity laughed. "The truth is, even though we haven't found anything so far, I still think Rose might've tried to find a way to communicate with us."

Agatha sat up and grabbed Arlene by the wrist. "Hold on. Do you mean like delivering a secret message."

"Something like that, yes."

Spense reached for his ginseng tea. "We've combed over this place already with no luck though."

Arlene fidgeted in her seat.

Agatha chewed her nails.

They exchanged a glance that Spense could only describe as furtive.

"What's going on, ladies?" he asked. "You two haven't been playing amateur sleuths, have you?"

Arlene straightened her back. "Nothing like that. But earlier this morning, a package was delivered to our bungalow for Caitlin. A bicycle messenger passed it on to a bell boy, and I guess the bell boy got us confused since we have the same last name."

"Mom." Caity was on her feet. "You don't have to explain. I'm aware we have the same last name. Who sent the package?"

Arlene flushed.

"Don't tell me you didn't read the card because it's perfectly fine if you did."

"It just said from Anna with best wishes for a happy wedding day. I've got it right here in my purse. I'm sorry I looked, but when it was first delivered I didn't know the package was for you. What's wrong? Why are you looking at me like that?"

"From *Anna*?"

"Here, see for yourself." Arlene handed over a small square box along with the card.

"Do you want us to leave so you can open it?" Agatha asked.

Spense shook his head. "No. Everyone's getting excited about nothing. I'm sure it's just a wedding gift, and you two have missed out on enough."

"Do you know an Anna?" Arlene asked.

"Who doesn't?" Caity replied.

"But what if it's your clue?" Agatha tugged the hem of her blouse.

Caity went over and sat between the moms. "Then it's our clue, and you two will have been responsible for bringing it to us."

"Just open the damn thing," Dutch said.

Perfect manners as usual. But Spense didn't mind. He was just glad to have his brother here.

Someone to put his feet up on the coffee table with.

Caity untied the ribbon and set it aside carefully. Spense never understood why people did that, since they were just going to throw it out later.

Caity took her time unwrapping the box and then folded the paper, setting it beside the ribbon.

The moms smiled, and he eased back onto the sofa.

"Oh, I love Laura Mercier," Caity said, and held up a ladies' compact. "I hope it's my shade." She flipped open the case and her hand halted in midair. "Spense, take a look at this."

She passed the compact to him via Agatha.

Agatha's brow worked into a frown. "I can't say as I've seen a gift like that before."

Spense took the compact, and at first, the problem didn't register. "What am I supposed to be seeing? Looks like regular makeup to me."

"It's been used," Agatha said with a shake of her head. "See how the powder's just slightly worn down in the center. Someone sent Caitlin a used compact."

"I think you mean a *stolen* compact." Caity gave each of the moms a kiss on the cheek. "I believe you really did bring us a clue."

"We did?" Their faces brightened.

She nodded. "Remember the day of our cake tasting? We had to leave because Rose Parker was spotted on the beach. She stole a wallet and clothes and a makeup bag from some tourists. I bet that's where this compact came from. Rose Parker really is trying to tell us something."

Caity dabbed the sponge onto her wrist and smiled. "I think there's something hidden inside this sponge."

"I'll take that." Dutch held out his hand.

Caity looked to Spense.

Tomorrow was their wedding day.

Rose Parker Preston was probably in the Cayman Islands.

Brousseau's team was currently out searching the area near the hives and the collapsed rope. And so far they hadn't found evidence of tampering, suggesting it had simply been bad luck. A freak accident. There was no immediate danger to anyone—as far as they knew.

Tomorrow was their wedding day.

He shrugged. "I really don't see a compelling reason not to let Dutch handle this. If Rose really is in the Cayman Islands, and everything is cool up at the falls . . . there's no danger to anyone at the moment."

Caity opened and closed her hand around the sponge. "You're kidding, right?"

He hadn't been.

Most women wouldn't want to be chasing a case the night before their wedding. But then again, Caity wasn't most women.

"What do you mean by *if everything's cool up at the falls*?" Arlene asked.

"Nothing," he said, hoping she'd let it drop. "And yes, of course I was kidding. Let's see what's in the mystery sponge."

"Mom, can you hand me my manicure scissors? They're in that drawer next to you," Caity said.

Arlene triumphantly produced a pair of delicate nail scissors.

Caity squeezed the sponge with her fingers and carefully cut a small square from the center. Next she peeled away the foamy material to reveal a tiny black object—a chip of some kind.

Wordlessly, Dutch pulled a laptop and a thumb drive from his brief case, then placed them on the coffee table.

Caity handed Dutch the chip.

"This is a micro memory card." He narrated his actions. "I can plug it into this thumb drive, and then read it from my computer."

While Dutch's fingers flew over the keyboard, the tapping was the only sound in the room.

It seemed no one was breathing.

A moment later, the tapping stopped, and the sounds of life resumed.

"Well?" Gretchen asked.

"I could use your expertise, Gretchen." Dutch shrugged. "Spense, you and Caity should stand by, but since neither of you have any specialized cyber-crime training, you might as well spend some time with your moms. Tomorrow is your big day, and this file is password protected. I'm afraid it's going to take me some time to get into it."

Chapter 26

"ARE YOU SURE this is a good idea?" Lilly bent to slide a bare foot into a flipper.

"No, it's a brilliant idea," Tommy answered truthfully. "But don't put those on until we're ready. I don't want you slipping on the boat deck."

They were miles offshore.

There wasn't another vessel in sight.

And Lilly Parker had a test to take.

A little game of *do you trust me?*

He didn't trust *her*, not after she'd asked him about Pamela Jean and then less than an hour later the cops had asked him the same question. And certainly not after that mystery package she'd received by messenger today.

On the one hand, he smelled sisterly collusion.

On the other, Lilly *seemed* to be genuinely in love with him, despite the fact he'd thrown her over for her sister. Tonight was designed to tell him whether she truly wanted to be with him or not, and more specifically, if she trusted him.

If she did, he could manipulate her, and that meant she'd be more valuable to him alive. He could use her to reel in Rose—the big game fish he was truly after.

But if Lilly didn't trust him, the plan was too risky.

He'd have to get rid of her now and find a different way to get to Rose.

A boating trip was the perfect opportunity to disappear Lilly forever—should the need arise.

Yes.

This black water diving expedition had been nothing short of a brilliant idea.

Besides, it was supposed to be an amazing experience. Tommy had it on his bucket list. Not that he would be kicking it anytime soon. He planned to live a very long and healthy and rich life. Too bad neither of the Parker sisters would be joining him on that journey.

Their loss.

Their call.

He'd been quite willing to bring them along for the ride.

Twins raised by a con man.

So very interesting.

"If you want to back out, Lilly, I'll turn the boat around. I don't want you to do anything you're not comfortable with." Even as he made the offer, he killed the engine. "It's just that I was thinking this might bring us back—I mean—closer together."

It was hard to read her expression in the dead of night, and it was far too early to tell if she'd be making the return trip with him.

"N-no."

The telltale stutter.

Lilly was nervous.

Which was right, unless it was for the wrong reasons.

"Perfectly normal to be anxious about a black water dive. I've heard even the most experienced divers get sweaty palms their first time." He unzipped his dive suit to his waist and stuck her hand on his bare chest. "Here, feel my heart."

Such a delicate little hand.

Such crushable little bones.

His heart was roaring in his chest, feeding off the adrenaline of anticipation.

She looked at him, her eyes luminous, her lips parted. "Tommy . . ."

"You see. It's natural to be afraid. But that's the whole point, my sweet. If we're ever going to be able to move past this terrible thing that's split us apart . . ."

She jerked her hand away. "We broke up because you married my sister. That's what split us apart. And you still haven't told me the truth about the trouble between you and Rose. That's what is keeping us apart."

"Then we *must* turn around. It seems you really don't trust me at all."

"I—I'm not going to lie."

We'll see about that.

"I don't *fully* trust you. After everything that's happened I don't believe any sane woman wouldn't have her doubts. But I do want to believe in you. That's why I agreed to go through with this. You have to understand it's hard for me to trust *anyone*. Or have you forgotten I was raised by a con man?"

"No dear, I haven't."

"Do you know where that expression *con man* comes from?"

"I do. *Con* is short for *confidence*. In order for any con to succeed, the perpetrator must be able to gain the confidence, the unconditional trust, of the mark." He reached out and touched her cheek. "Are you conning me, Lilly?"

Her skin, already pale under the moonlight became almost translucent. "Are you conning me?"

He took hold of her hands. "I love you, Lilly. It's always been you. Even when I was with Rose, you were all I could think of. I'm going to ask you a question and I want you to think long and hard before you answer. Do you still love me? Did you ever love me?"

He watched her throat as she swallowed. He'd always been fascinated by her tall, slender neck.

The wind picked up, gently swaying the boat beneath them.

"I—I tried to stop loving you, for Rose's sake. But, I don't think I ever truly succeeded." Her eyes glistened with unshed tears. "Still . . . I . . ."

"You don't trust me."

"I want to." She squeezed his hand. "So badly. But I don't know how to anymore."

"Then let me help you. Let me show you exactly how safe you are in my care."

By the end of the evening, he'd know how much Rose had revealed to Lilly. If Lilly knew everything, and if she *believed* everything Rose had told her, she'd never get into the water with him. She'd be too terrified of him to put her life in his hands.

And she'd be right.

"Are you ready, darling?"

"Yes."

"Then it's time to put on those flippers."

She struggled with them, and he helped her, rubbing his hand along the inside of her thigh to remind her of the pleasure they'd shared. "I've missed you so," he whispered.

Tied into an iron rung underneath the boat was a heavy rope. He lifted it out of the water and secured it around Lilly's waist. Her whole body trembled as he pulled the rope tight, and her fear caused his blood to expand. The thought of her failing his test and what he would do to her after excited him, but he tamped his eagerness down. It would benefit him more if he could keep her alive long enough to use her to lay a trap for Rose.

We shall see.

"Are you going to be tied up, too?" He thought he could read dread in her eyes.

"Yes. We'll both be tied to the boat as a safety measure."

She looked down at the pitch black of the ocean. "It's so dark."

"That's what makes this experience so special, so beautiful."

"But shouldn't we have brought someone along to stay up top with the boat? What if the boat crashes into something while we're underwater?"

That would be the regular way to do it, yes—to have lots of watchful eyes onboard, ensuring the safety of the divers.

But this wasn't going to be a *regular* dive.

"We're in the middle of the ocean. There's nothing to crash into. It's only a short dive. I want to keep you underwater just long enough for us to regain the trust we've lost in one another. Ten minutes in the depths of the ocean. No one around but you and me. We'll have no one else to rely on but one another. Unless, you don't want us to find our way back to where we were before Rose's interference."

"What if I don't know what I want? I—I'm scared." She stepped away from the edge of the boat.

He steered her toward the ladder. "This may be your first night dive, but it's not that different from a day dive, and I know you've done those before. I've double-checked all the equipment, particularly the air cylinders. Get your mask and regulator in place."

She did.

"Ready?"

Before she had a chance to indicate yay or nay, he lifted her by the waist and tossed her overboard. He had to laugh at the way her arms flailed in terror. He observed the dial on his watch, letting her drown in her fear for a full minute. The rope sank deep in the water. There was no way she could find her way to the surface in the dark. He debated how long he could leave her and still give her a sporting chance to prove her trust.

This was too delicious, but hardly a fair test if he waited any longer. He secured his own equipment and guide rope, then climbed carefully down the ladder and let himself sink deep. With his underwater flashlight he located her tether. He tugged it, pulling her to his side. Then he shut off the light, and grabbed her hand. They were weightless, floating beneath the boat in the blackest depths of the ocean.

This was what an out-of-body experience must feel like.

It was as if he were watching himself, watching her.

Her head and her white, white neck—the only not-black things in the universe—appeared detached from her body.

As if she'd been beheaded by the night.

He signaled her with his hand and aimed his light beneath them.

Soon, bioluminescent creatures came into view. Ghostly creatures lighting up the sea, spewing forth the skeletons of the fluorescent plankton that nourished them. Some might call it creepy. But Tommy had never felt more a part of the universe than he did at this moment.

The power of life and death was in his hands.

Never had he felt more like a god.

Chapter 27

Sunday
Heritage Townhomes
Papeete
Tahiti Nui

THE ONLY WORD that fit Lilly's modest townhome, with its tiny tiled kitchen and thickly coated green walls was *quaint*. Tommy had never been fond of quaint. Though it had been a relief compared to the orphanage, he'd lived for the day he could move Heather Preston out of that "quaint" little dump of hers.

He poured two cups of coffee and settled them on a tray along with the hot buttered croissants he'd prepared. After drying his hands on a striped cotton dish towel, he tossed it into the trash. This place was beneath him and beneath Lilly, too. Which made it all the more pitiful that it was going to be her last known address.

He strode into the bedroom with his offering of croissants and coffee.

"Good morning, my love. Did you sleep well?"

She looked quite fetching with the soft rays of an early sun side-lighting her pale skin. He smiled at the memory of last night and how the skin between her legs was the fairest of all.

"Last night was wonderful." She stretched like a lazy cat.

"It was good for me, too," he said.

He sat on the edge of the bed, and lifted a croissant to her mouth. "Try this."

She shook her head. "I'm never hungry in the mornings. Did you forget?"

He let the bread drop back onto the plate and then carefully set the tray, coffee and all on the floor. Ungrateful little bitch. He was trying to make her last morning special, pampering her. Hand feeding her like a pet, and she didn't have the sense to be grateful.

Fine.

She didn't deserve it anyway.

He took her hand and brought it to his lips. "Thank you, Lilly."

"For what?" She smiled and threw her bare legs over the edge of the bed, nearly kicking over the coffee cups.

"For giving me another chance. I've been thinking all morning, while you were sleeping, about what we talked about before."

"About Rose."

"Yes." He caressed her cheek. "I think we can make the case to the police that if I'm willing to forget she shot me, they should, too."

"You really think they would?"

"Why not? The whole jail break incident makes them seem completely incompetent. I heard the deputy has been suspended from duty. I think we might even argue that Rose could sue them for sexual harassment. The officer in question took her out of the cell and plied her with liquor. He made drunken advances, and she had no choice but to flee."

"You'd do that for Rose?"

"I'd do it for *you*." He took her by the shoulders. "But only if I have Rose's word she'll stay away from us from here on out."

"She's my sister."

This argument was getting old, but it was only for show so he might as well give in.

"All right. But she has to convince me she's not dangerous, and that she won't interfere with us."

Lilly jumped out of bed. "Let's call Inspector Brousseau right now. I have his card in my purse."

He took her by the wrist. "Not so fast, Lilly. I have to speak to Rose face to face." He sighed. "If only we had some means of contacting her. We need to set up a meeting."

Her arm went limp in his grasp. He was absolutely certain that package he saw being delivered contained a message from Rose. He doubted she'd entrust Lilly with SADIE, but whatever else was in that package, along with it, he'd bet Rose had left instructions for getting in touch with her.

"Lilly, after everything we've been through together. After last night, I think I've earned your trust."

She nodded. "You're absolutely right." Then she padded, deliciously naked, from the room.

While she was gone he stroked himself into readiness. Might as well give her one last hurrah.

She returned with a cell phone and placed it in his hand.

"What's this, then?"

"You said you wanted to set up a meeting with Rose."

He continued to play dumb. "I'm afraid I still don't understand."

Lilly sat on the bed beside him. "This came by messenger yesterday, right before you called about going on a dive. The phone is programmed with her number. I'm supposed to text if I'm in trouble."

She was definitely in trouble.

He snatched it out of her hand. "I'm going to set up a meeting with Rose and then hang onto this for you."

"I'd rather text her myself."

He turned his back. "If you want me to fix this up for your sister, you're going to have to convince me you trust me. That last night wasn't just a game. For all I know you and your sister are pulling one big con on me."

"Tommy, no."

"Then I keep the phone."

She hesitated, but only a moment. "Okay, you can hold onto it for a little while. Will you set the meeting today?"

"I'll do it right now. Nature calls me, darling, but when I come back I expect you to be waiting right here." He patted the bed. "Don't put a stitch on."

She lay back on the bed and smiled. "I'll be ready."

He hustled into the bathroom and shut the door.

Powered up the prepaid cell phone and texted the only name in the contact list: Anna.

Anna it's me.
Your loving husband.
I have your sister.

If you want to see Lilly alive again, head for Tahiti Iti now.

Bring the thumb drive and any copies you've made.

I'll text you further instructions when I please.

Be prepared to move quickly.

If you don't do exactly as I say, Lilly dies.

Chapter 28

Sunday
Hôtel De Plage Dauphin
Tahiti Nui

GRETCHEN TOOK A seat on the couch next to Dutch, and her hand brushed his arm in the process. Dutch's face flushed at the accidental touch, and Gretchen smiled at Caitlin.

Gretchen and Dutch.

It was soon after his wife's death, but with time, he might be ready. Caitlin couldn't blame Gretchen for laying the groundwork while she had the chance. And frankly, there was no one more suited for Dutch than Gretchen. Tall, beautiful, brave—and as a fellow agent, she'd understand the demands of his work.

"It's six hours until the *I do's*, folks, are you sure you want to talk micro memory cards?" Gretchen asked.

Spense grinned. "I'm pretty sure six hours is a lifetime in dog years."

And that was just one of the reasons she loved him. Funny and charming and every bit as curious as she was about what was on that card. The good night's sleep she was supposed to have gotten last night had been sacrificed to wondering about the mystery clue.

"All right, then gather round," Dutch said and positioned his laptop on the coffee table to give everyone maximum viewing access.

He clicked on an untitled folder and the contents showed one file: SADIE.

Caitlin blinked at the screen trying to remember why Sadie was pinging in her head. It only took a moment before it came to her. "Sadie is the name of Tommy Preston's biological mother."

"We know," Dutch answered. "And SADIE is protected, but it only took about an hour to get in. I've got a full file on Preston from the Riverbend Sherriff's office that includes personal and professional intel. Password is Vader@RB!."

"As in Darth Vader?" Spense put his hands behind his head.

"As in Preston's dog. You gotta love a man who loves his dog." Dutch typed in the password and a jumble of numbers, letters, and symbols appeared on the screen. "But you see the problem."

"Once we got in, we encountered multiple layers of encryption," Gretchen said. "It's well protected. And it's going to take some time to extract all the data, but from what we can tell so far the information consists primarily of account numbers. Most likely tied to offshore banks and shell companies."

"Looks like you handed us a doozie of a case for the financial crimes squad. My guys and dolls in Dallas are on it already," Dutch said.

Dallas was the nearest field office to Riverbend, so the ball was in Dutch's court now. This was no longer simply a case of a bride shooting her groom. This appeared to be a potentially major case, falling under Dutch's jurisdiction. It was up to him if he wanted to share any more information with them from here on out.

"Wait a minute," Spense said—he had that *aha* look on his face. "Heather Preston mentioned Tommy owned a number of small businesses. You got the list?"

"Yeah. Laundromats, a car dealership, campgrounds, a restaurant . . . and that's just the beginning. Anything strike you as interesting about that list?" Gretchen asked.

Caitlin had to admit it didn't, but Spense was about to come out of his seat. "Cash transactions."

She wondered if she had the same bewildered expression on her face that Spense had worn yesterday as he stared at the ladies' compact in his hand. It seemed everyone in the room knew something she didn't. "What am I missing? What's so special about cash transactions?"

"When you put them together with offshore bank accounts and shell companies? A lot. Businesses that take in a lot of cash can be quite useful to a certain segment of the population—cartels, the mob, those kinds of folks. Their dirty money can be put through a legal enterprise and then handed back to said individual or organization. Usually for a hefty fee on the part of the 'cleaner.'"

"Tommy Preston is into money laundering?" Caitlin asked.

"Google top ten money laundering businesses, and then you tell me," Dutch said.

"Is there enough here to send him away?"

"Like I said, we have to do some more digging, but from what I can tell this guy is going to go down hard. And I'm not just talking about jail time."

She didn't follow but she knew an explanation from one of the three special agents in the room would likely be forthcoming.

It was Spense who noticed her puzzled look and said, "Even if Preston isn't directly involved in organized crime, if this is what we think it is, he's cleaning cash for some bad dudes. And that means if Tommy goes down for this, his business associates are not going to want to take the chance he could bring them down, too."

"We're talking a professional hit," Gretchen said. "Let's assume Rose Parker Preston is the individual who sent me this memory card. If Tommy knows she has it, or if he simply caught her snooping around his business dealings, he'd have a solid motive for murder."

"So we're back to the self-defense theory," Spense said. "But we still have to account for the apparent premeditation—Rose had a pouch sewn into her wedding gown in order to conceal a pistol. *And* she withdrew cash and transferred a large sum to the Cayman Islands suggesting a planned escape."

"Maybe she knew Preston was dangerous so she wanted to be prepared." It could be that simple, Caitlin thought.

"But then why marry the guy? Especially when she had to steal him away from her sister to do so."

Gretchen. Always devil's advocate.

"She tried to warn Lilly away from Tommy, but Lilly wouldn't listen. So maybe Rose thought the only way to keep him away from Lilly was to hook up with him herself," Caitlin fired back.

Dutch shook his head. "You guys are overlooking the obvious flaw in that argument. If Rose knew Tommy was dangerous, and she had evidence to prove it, she could simply have called me, or someone like me."

"She didn't have to marry the creep," Spense agreed.

"Unless she didn't have the evidence she needed until now. Not to mention her family background hardly predisposes her to trust the authorities. She might've struggled with whether or not to send it to us." Caitlin was still stewing about how this fit in with the whole Pamela Jean story.

"What have you got on Pamela Jean?" Spense asked, apparently thinking along the same lines.

"Just this: There's no record on any Pamela Jean—whether that's a first and last or fist and middle name—admitted to Riverbend Memorial Hospital."

"Even if she was admitted under a *do not name, do not publish* order, that would only apply to *publicly* accessible information. Protected records would still show her hospitalization," Caitlin said. "But maybe she gave Rose a false name to add another level of protection—like those multiple layers of encryption Tommy used on his files. So the name per se is useless."

"That may well be," Dutch said. "But Riverbend is a small town and its hospital census was low. According to records, no female patient died of anything except the usual suspects in the past year—we're talking cancer, heart disease, that type of thing. Furthermore, the hospital would've reported a victim of a beating to the police and there's no record of any such report."

"In other words, Rose made the whole thing up. She simply lied to her sister to keep her away from Tommy," Gretchen said.

Caitlin shook her head. "Doesn't add up to me. Why go to all that trouble to lie about a woman who was beaten to death—and potentially be found out—rather than simply warn Lilly to keep away from Tommy because of his bad business dealings?"

"Okay, let's assume there *might* be a Pamela Jean. We haven't found her, but that doesn't mean we never will," Dutch said. "You seem to be looking for proof that Rose isn't guilty of more than self-defense and poor judgment. But what if she did plan to shoot Tommy? Lilly insists that Rose is devoted to her—to the point of smothering her. And that she was determined they open a yogurt shop in California."

"Yoga studio," Spense said.

"Your point?" Caitlin asked Dutch.

"So maybe—just hear me out—Rose steals Tommy because she's desperate to get him away from Lilly. Maybe because she's trying to protect Lilly, or maybe because she just wants to keep Lilly all to herself and carry on with their plans, or maybe *both*. She decides to murder Tommy and make it look like self-defense."

"In an underwater shootout?" Caitlin did not buy that. "Unless she plans to do it later, back at the hotel. Then Tommy catches on and tries to drown her before she can do her worst. Rose shoots him, in self-defense for real, to keep him from drowning her."

"Except if her motive was to get Tommy out of their lives, she'd have no reason at all to marry the man. She could've just killed him," Gretchen threw in.

"But then she wouldn't get the life insurance," Spense said.

Caitlin wondered if anyone else had a headache.

Spense dragged a hand through his hair. "Let's stick with what we know. A. Tommy Preston is a very bad dude, Pamela Jean or no Pamela Jean. B. Whoever sent this memory card is in grave danger if he finds out . . ."

"C," Caitlin said. "Lilly Parker is in love with Tommy and somebody, other than her sister, needs to warn her off him."

Gretchen frowned. "That someone doesn't have to be you."

"I think it does," Caitlin said. "She hasn't met either you or Dutch, and she doesn't trust the police. I'm practically a civilian."

"Five and one half hours." Dutch held up his wrist to indicate the time as they headed for the door. "And there's one other thing. We didn't find Pamela Jean, but we did find a nurse, Jessica Prosper. She filed a complaint with the Riverbend PD against one Anna Parker around six months ago. The police were unable to locate anyone by that name—no surprise there, so they didn't follow up further. We have an interview with Nurse Prosper set up by teleconference later. If anything interesting comes of it, you want me to buzz you or hold onto it?"

"What do you think?" Spense said. "See you in five and one half hours."

"Count on it, brother."

Chapter 29

Sunday
Road to Taravao Plateau
Tahiti Iti

TOMMY PRIDED HIMSELF on being a man of his word, and it seemed he was also generous to a fault. Today was Lilly Parker's last on earth and he'd indulged her beyond reason. Not only had he pampered her during sex this morning, he'd waited nearly two hours for her to get ready for their day trip without uttering a single complaint. He'd stopped at every scenic overlook on the way and even agreed to wander down a trail dotted with wildflowers— holding hands for chrissake.

But now, the time had come to put an end to all the nonsense— and an end to both Parker sisters once and for all.

The ripped yellow vinyl of the diner's booth squeaked as Tommy scooted closer to Lilly. He wrapped his arms around her and feathered kisses from her ear down along her fascinating neck.

She leaned her forehead against his and sighed.

Her breath smelled of coffee.

Though she hadn't wanted the breakfast in bed he'd prepared earlier, by now, she'd declared herself famished. They'd stopped at the only eatery around, an unnamed mom and pop diner, which was really no diner at all.

The owners had installed three booths in a screened-in room added onto the front of their home and tacked up a cardboard sign that read "Breakfast all day. Last chance before the road ends."

Of the three paved roads in Tahiti Iti, this was one of them. That, and the fact that Lilly said it was the way to Gauguin's Gold II was about all it had to recommend it. In order to keep his marks from tripping over one another, her father had two phony treasure locations. This road was paved—up to a point—and lined with ancient trees and rolling green pastures, but Tommy preferred bustle above bucolic.

The diner's stench of stale grease made him nauseous, so he nibbled at dry toast and sipped his orange juice while Lilly gobbled fried eggs, ham, and potatoes. She'd been happy enough until a few minutes ago. Since then she'd been emitting various little grunts and groans, and he noted she'd shredded her napkin into an embarrassing mess without regard for the fact the server would have to clean it up. He was sure her father, who understood the importance of presenting yourself well at all times, would not have approved. "You seem worried. How can I help?"

"You know me so well." She went to work on *his* napkin.

He caught her by the hand to stop the madness.

"What if Rose doesn't come?"

"She will. The spot I've chosen is too out of the way for her to have to worry about being spotted by the police."

"But you did mention you were coming, too. Rose might not want to see you."

"She wants to see *you*. And I've explained I'm prepared to intervene with the authorities on her behalf and pay for a good lawyer. We just need to work out the details."

"She doesn't trust you. She thinks you're capable of . . . anything."

"Once we're face to face, and you're there to mediate, I'm sure we can work things out. I need her assurance she won't try anything crazy again. We have to clear up the misunderstanding between us. And Lilly, Rose simply must accept that you're mine."

She looked at him so earnestly he wanted to slap the stupid right out of her. "I'll make her accept it."

"I hope so." He let go of her hand. "Rose has gotten ahold of some bad information from somewhere about my character. I can't say I'm of a mind to forgive her, but I am willing to forget, only because of how much you love her, and because of how much I love you."

Her eyes watered, changing their color into the most astounding shade of green, reminding him that he'd once found her quite desirable. Too bad she and Rose had made such a mess of things and forced his hand. "I have to believe that somewhere in that mixed-up brain of Rose's she thought she was protecting you. But she mustn't try to interfere with us anymore."

"Not interfere, sure. In fact, I think it would be a good idea for Rose and me to see a counselor—do you think we're co-dependent?"

He clamped his teeth to keep from bursting out laughing. Co-dependence was an understatement. From the womb on there'd been no boundaries between Rose and Lilly. When they weren't fighting like cats and dogs they were braiding each other's hair and up in each other business like nine-year-old girls at a slumber party. "Not in the least. You're the sanest woman I know."

"So you don't think I need therapy. What about Rose? I want you to be comfortable around her."

"Perhaps." Lilly was too foolish to be borne. Not only did she believe that he'd be willing to overlook the fact Rose had tried to kill him, she seemed to think he'd be open to having her over for Christmas dinner after a few therapy sessions. "But don't worry. We'll work it out . . . somehow."

In fact, he had things worked out nicely already.

While Lilly had gone to wash up, he'd dosed her orange juice with enough heroin to kill a horse. He'd used a very generous amount, since the drug is absorbed slowly when ingested by mouth. The heroin would be converted to morphine in the body and then cross the blood-brain barrier. The onset would be slow but sure and missing the euphoria of the usual methods of administration. But he needed Lilly awake and cooperative, at least until he could get her to the meeting spot. If it turned out he hadn't given her enough dope, though he was quite certain he had, there was plenty more where that came from. He wasn't taking any chances with his plan.

He needed both women under his control in a remote location. Because neither of them was going to walk out alive.

"Excuse me, love. But I need a refill on my coffee. I'm going to hunt down our waitress. Want anything while I'm up?"

Lilly shook her head.

"Drink your juice, dear. You need your vitamins."

"I'll be peeing all day."

"Won't we both?" He motioned to her juice.

She lifted her glass, then mouthed a *cheers*.

He turned away with a smile and headed for the next room where he found the waitress lounging with propped feet. "More coffee please."

She jumped to attention and he held up his hand. "Please, take your time. And may I ask a favor?"

"Yes. I'm happy to help my customers if I can."

"A friend of mine is coming by, but she won't arrive for a while. She's a diabetic and she needs her medicine. Will you be sure she gets this? Her name is Anna." He passed the server a small package he'd pulled from his pocket along with a one-hundred-dollar bill.

"I'll give your friend her medicine. There's no need for such a generous tip." She took the box and waved off the money.

He pressed the bill back into her hand.

"I understand. You're a good person. But allow me to thank you for such a lovely meal. Really, I insist. It's very important."

She looked at the bill, then back at him, and smiled. "*Merci beaucoup.* You are too generous."

He knew that already. But what could he do? It was simply his nature.

"And more coffee please, when you get the chance." He couldn't forget the supposed reason for his venture to the back room.

The woman nodded again, still staring down at her hand and her unexpected good fortune, her blue eyes wide and moist.

It warmed him inside to see her happiness.

Virtue is indeed its own reward, he thought as he walked back into the dining room—such as it was.

When he saw Lilly, her back to him, sipping her juice, his lips curled in anticipation of what was to come.

It had been more luck than genius on his part that he'd become engaged to *both* sisters, but to his credit the way he'd played it out showed his smarts. He still had that insurance policy on Lilly. So if he played his cards perfectly he could have his cake and eat it too—murder-suicide.

The cops already viewed Rose as certifiable.

But if he made it seem that Rose killed Lilly and then shot herself intentionally, he couldn't collect on *Rose's* life insurance—since they were still in the provisional phase. Rose's suicide so soon after obtaining the policy would render the benefits impossible to collect.

On the other hand, he and Lilly had taken out policies on one another more than six months ago—during their engagement.

In the event of *Lilly's* suicide it would still pay out.

An overdose was perfect.

As long as no one could connect him with their deaths, he could collect three million each on both Rose and Lilly. He had all the money he needed already, but a good businessman didn't squander an opportunity. And he deserved it for all the trouble these two had put him through.

But the game must play out precisely as he'd planned.

Lilly must kill Rose and then commit suicide.

It shouldn't be too difficult to make that *appear* to have happened.

Lilly, he could lead by the nose. And once the drugs took effect she'd be no problem at all. He only needed to get her to the meeting place before the heroin kicked in.

The problem, however, was Rose. She was far from the crazy lady he'd made her out to be. Somehow, she'd found out about his business dealings and copied the SADIE file. And he had no idea what she'd done with the information. Rose was smart enough to have a contingency plan in the event of a disaster.

So before he got rid of Rose, he was going to have to get that drive from her and get some kind of assurance there were no copies. The one thing he couldn't figure out was how Rose found out about SADIE in the first place. He kept his friends close and his enemies closer. Had someone tipped her off, or after living life in a family of con artists, had she just developed that good of a nose?

He sat back down at the table with Lilly.

"Ready?" She still had a few scraps left on her plate, but the important thing was that her glass of juice was now empty.

"I'm stuffed." She patted her stomach. "But I thought you wanted more coffee. And you barely touched your orange juice."

"Changed my mind. And I've already paid. Let me make a quick trip to the john and we'll get this show on the road. I don't want to keep Rose waiting."

He slipped into the restroom and pulled out the phone Rose had sent to Lilly.

Only one bar.

He typed his message, then hit *send*.

The sound of a tone signaled his plan going into motion.

Chapter 30

Sunday
Road to Taravao Plateau
Tahiti Iti

Anna, it's me.
I hope you've found your way to Iti by now because I've left
you a present.
Find your last chance before the road ends—to eat.
You'll recognize the place because there is no other.
Screened in porch and the waitress is holding your package.
Tell her you have diabetes and collect your medicine.
Bring it and the thumb drive to Gauguin's Gold II.
You have one hour.
So does Lilly.
If you're late, she dies.
I can't save her now.
Only you have the power to keep her alive.

The countdown begins now.

Tick tock.

ROSE REREAD THE message for the hundredth time, clenched her fists, and cursed under her breath. It had taken her almost six hours to cross the isthmus between Nui and Iti on foot. But at least she'd made it.

She powered off the phone and buried her face in her hands.

Why hadn't she taken care of Tommy Preston six months ago when she'd had the chance?

She'd been right there in his yard. She'd slipped past Vader and into his kitchen without being detected. Tommy's back had been turned, and she'd had her chance to protect Lilly from his menace once and for all.

But she'd been too weak.

She hadn't been able to bring herself to shoot a human being in cold blood.

Not even as Anna.

When she'd looked through the gun sights at the back of Tommy's skull, doubt had made her lower her weapon. She hadn't been able to convince herself that killing him was the right thing to do.

She'd told herself then she knew nothing about the woman she'd seen lying in that hospital bed.

What if Pamela Jean had been wrong?

What if she'd been lying?

Now Rose's nails dug into her palms, pricking through the skin.

If only she could go back to that day, six months ago.

She'd pull the trigger in a heartbeat.

Of course Pamela Jean knew who'd beaten her.

And any doubt in Rose's mind that Tommy Preston was a cold-blooded killer had been erased on her wedding day.

He'd tried to drown Rose.

He'd seen her lurking on his computer that morning, and later he must have spotted the gun she'd secured in the bodice of her wedding gown for her own protection—she was that terrified of the man she was about to marry. After the ceremony, he'd carried her into deep water, locked his arms around her, and held her under. He was stronger than she was by far, but she'd been able to hold her breath longer. He'd weakened from the lack of oxygen sooner than she had, and they'd struggled. She'd shot him then, because he'd left her no choice.

On her wedding day, it had come down to his life or hers.

But six months before, when it had really counted, when it had been for Lilly, she hadn't pulled the trigger.

She stared at her bleeding palms, but didn't register the pain.

Now Tommy had Lilly in his clutches because Rose had been stupid and weak. No matter his promises, Rose knew he had no intention of letting either of them live.

There was no turning back now.

This desperate scheme of hers to keep him away from her sister by marrying him and gathering enough evidence to put him behind bars had backfired horribly.

Rose had never trusted the police before, and she didn't trust them now.

It went against every instinct she had to send off a copy of the SADIE file to the FBI. But just as she'd had no choice but to pull the trigger of her gun underwater, not knowing—only hoping—that it would fire—she'd had no choice but to turn over the evidence she had to the cops. She didn't trust Caitlin Cassidy to do the right thing—she could only hope that she would.

She saw no other way out for Lilly and her.

Tommy would not be blackmailed, nor would he be satisfied with the return of the file. Once she gave it to him, he'd kill them both. But what was she to do now?

Her worst nightmare had come true.

He'd called her bet and taken Lilly. Rose had nothing left but to play the hand she'd been dealt. A hand far worse than the cards she'd been holding six months ago.

Stupid, stupid Rose.

This time she *must* save Lilly—somehow—no matter what it took.

She opened the door of a screened-in front porch.

Last chance before the road ends.

"Do you want to rest or keep going?" Tommy slowed his stride to allow Lilly to catch up with him on the trail—or semblance thereof. It was poorly marked and if not for the occasional cairn they'd be lost by now. In truth, he wasn't sure they weren't. He surveyed Lilly. Sweat dotted her upper lip, her skin was pink, her eyes confused.

The way he'd read the map, they should've taken the low trail, but Lilly had insisted on the high. And she was the one who was familiar with the area.

He checked his pocket watch.

Thirty minutes left in the countdown and already Lilly was acting strangely.

Had he miscalculated how soon the drugs would begin to impact Lilly's brain? If so, and they didn't meet up with Rose soon, Lilly might not make it to Gauguin's Gold II alive.

Then he'd have to come up with a new way to persuade Rose to hand over the thumb drive—he doubted she'd willingly trade it for her sister's corpse.

"Rest please." Lilly wiped her brow with her T-shirt and he wanted to pull it over her head and suffocate her with it.

But he needed that thumb drive and they had to keep moving.

Even assuming he had *not* miscalculated, and there was still time before Lilly succumbed to the dose of heroin she'd ingested, at this rate, Rose might make it to Gauguin's Gold II before them.

And Rose already had the benefit of home turf since, according to Lilly, the girls had picnicked there several times with their father—whereas Tommy was completely unfamiliar with the terrain.

He wanted to get the lay of the land before Rose arrived.

But Lilly looked like hell—they'd better rest a minute.

He found a boulder flat enough for sitting and used a frond to brush the dirt off of it. "Take your time," he said, motioning Lilly to sit.

He'd keep her comfortable for now.

But once they reached their destination he was done playing the gentleman. No need to put on an act for Rose.

Rose.

ROSE DIDN'T DARE open the package until she was well past the little diner, for fear someone might see what it held. Now she halted, undid the brown paper that wrapped the elongated box, opened the lid—and screamed.

Tears streamed down her face in a blinding rage. *Damn Tommy to hell.*

He'd told her Lilly only had an hour to live.

He'd said Rose was the only one who could save her life, and here, clutched in her hand was the reason why—a naloxone injector to reverse an overdose of heroin.

If Rose didn't get to Lilly in time, Lilly would die. Rose supposed Tommy thought his ruthlessness made him invincible.

But he was wrong.

And she had been wrong, too. Dropping to her knees, she summoned every ounce of strength she had left—not only in her body—but in her spirit. Too many times she'd made the mistake of pretending to be someone other than herself.

Anna: a woman who cared for no one.

Rose had been taught to believe that emotion made her weak and vulnerable.

But it wasn't true.

Why had it taken her so long to realize she didn't need Anna?

Rose was the invincible one—precisely because she *did* care.

Tommy might have all the nerve in the world, but he wasn't willing to sacrifice his life for someone else's. She didn't want to die, but if it came down to her life or Lilly's she'd take a bullet, or worse, without hesitation. It was Rose's beating, human heart—something Tommy Preston didn't possess—that would deliver her victory.

Get up.

She wiped her eyes, and stood, clutching the map to Gauguin's Gold II to her chest. If she followed it closely, at the end of the road was a treasure worth more than a mountain of gold coins.

Lilly.

Her little sister.

She'd promised Papa on his deathbed that she would look out

for Lilly—her twin who'd always been a step behind when it came to just about everything. Rose had preceded Lilly from the womb by five minutes. She'd uttered her first words five weeks before Lilly and had taken her first steps five days ahead of her. She and Lilly might be twins, but in every sense of the word, Rose was the older sibling.

She was supposed to keep Lilly safe.

And she'd failed miserably, because even though she'd known what Tommy had done to Pamela Jean, she'd let him live. When Rose had tried to see Pamela Jean again, to find out more about Sadie, Nurse Prosper had given her terrible news—Pamela Jean had succumbed to her injuries. Internal bleeding had sent her into systemic organ failure.

Pamela Jean was dead.

And there wasn't a word about her in the papers.

Tommy was that powerful—he could kill a woman and make it seem like she'd never even existed.

But Rose had known exactly how dangerous he was.

Stupidly, she'd hoped she could save Lilly without resorting to taking a human life—by finding Sadie, as Pamela Jean had urged her to do.

But Sadie turned out not to be a person.

After Rose had seen the file name on Tommy's laptop, she'd spent nearly a month working hundreds of variations on names and numbers, trying to figure out the password that opened SADIE. And when she finally succeeded, on the morning of her wedding, it was only to find that the file had been encrypted.

She couldn't read it at all.

So she'd copied SADIE, not knowing what secrets it contained.

She'd tucked the drive in an envelope and had it delivered to the desk clerk at a local no-tell motel along with a one-hundred-dollar bill and instructions to hold the envelope for Anna Parker.

She might not know what was on the drive, but she knew it held power over Tommy. Yesterday, she'd made more copies of SADIE at an internet café before sending it to Caitlin Cassidy.

One of those copies was in Rose's pocket now.

She had to give it to Tommy so he would let her administer the antidote to Lilly.

But first she had to correctly follow this damned crazy map.

Many times, she and Lilly had travelled to Tahiti Iti with Papa. He'd made a set of two maps, leading to two separate spots. One version led his marks toward Mana Falls and past a magnificent wall of hives. But Papa's preferred picnic ground was at the site he called Gauguin's Gold II, outside of Taravao that led the opposite way past a swinging bridge. If you had a jeep, you could off-road it almost all the way to the bridge.

She and Lilly had loved to rock that bridge until they made themselves scream.

But it had been too long ago for her to recall the journey completely by heart. Luckily, she remembered pieces along the route, and despite the map's poor condition, she could follow it well enough.

Still, she was on foot, and Tommy must have known the way would be difficult. There was a real chance she might not make it in time.

Tommy hadn't been satisfied with poisoning her sister with heroin.

He wanted Lilly's life or death to rest on Rose's shoulders.

He had to turn the screw.

Chapter 31

Sunday
Heritage Townhomes
Papeete
Tahiti Nui

CAITLIN BELIEVED THERE was time to talk with Lilly and still get back to the hotel and dress for the ceremony. So they were off to have a tough conversation with her now. Lilly hadn't listened to her own sister, making Caitlin doubt she'd listen to them, but she felt obligated to try. Hopefully, if she heard from an objective source that Tommy might be dangerous, she'd at least keep her guard up around him. As they pulled into the Heritage Townhomes, the dash of their rented 4x4 vibrated.

"That's yours," she told Spense.

"Grab it for me, okay? What's mine is yours, or it will be soon."

"Damn straight." She checked the caller ID. "Jacques, it's Caitlin."

Inspector Brousseau? Spense mouthed.

Do we know another Jacques? she mouthed back.

"I'm putting you on speaker, Inspector," she said. "I've got Spense in the car."

"*Bien.* How quickly can you get to Heritage Townhomes?"

"We're here now. Just pulled in to the complex. We're headed over to Lilly Parker's place." Obviously. "Do you have any news we can bring her?"

Every time they saw Lilly, she assumed they were bringing her information about Rose. Maybe this time they wouldn't have to disappoint her. Brousseau and his men were searching the area near the falls again today. Caitlin found herself hoping against the odds. "Did you find Rose?"

"*Non.*"

There was a long pause.

Spense pulled into a parking space near Lilly's home. The wind was threatening to blow over the potted hibiscus on her porch. "Inspector, we're here. What is it you want us to tell her?"

"I need you to check on her welfare. I've spoken with your associate, Dutch Langhorne."

"He told you we have evidence of Preston's illegal business dealings in the States, then," Spense said.

"Whatever he's done in the United Sates is of no concern to me—except that it calls into question his claim against Rose Parker Preston. I have to presume that a man hiding a dangerous secret may himself be dangerous."

"We're in agreement on that point, which is why we're here. To suggest to Lilly she exercise caution—"

"I would check on her myself, but I'm with my men on Tahiti Iti near Mana Falls." The inspector spoke over her.

They knew that already. And Caitlin didn't mind doing a welfare check, but he hadn't told them why he was concerned now, when he hadn't been before. He'd all but dismissed them from the case. In fact he'd all but dismissed the case from the case. "We're happy to do it. Was there any special reason, other than what you learned in your talk with Agent Langhorne?"

"Probably nothing. But I'll feel better when you find both her and Mr. Preston."

Her heart took a short rest. "Say again?"

"We think Lilly is with Mr. Preston. I've received word that the two of them went on an excursion last night, and that Mr. Preston never came home."

"Who put out the SOS?"

"Heather Preston."

Caitlin's heart was beating again, and quite a bit faster than usual. "Does *she* think her son might hurt Lilly?"

"*Mais non.* She's afraid *Lilly* might hurt her son. She thinks if one sister is crazy the other might be, too. And when he didn't come home last night, she panicked."

"I've got to go, Inspector. We'll call you back."

Caitlin jumped from the 4x4. Her knees took a hit, absorbing the impact when her feet landed on the pavement.

"Stay back," Spense said, reaching for his Glock.

She gave him a quick nod. He was the FBI agent. She was the psychiatrist. In the field, she did as she was told—came in handy for staying alive. It occurred to Caitlin just how great a threat Spense posed to Tommy Preston. If the FBI so much as looked like they were surveilling him, it could land him in terrible trouble with his "associates." In fact, Preston had far more motive to have tampered with that rope's anchor than Rose did.

Spense edged quietly onto the porch, keeping his body flattened against the frame of the house—gun out front. Brousseau had asked for a simple welfare check, but if Spense's gut told him to clear the house rather than saunter up and announce himself with a knock, she wasn't going to debate the matter with him. It was Spense's instincts that had kept him alive, and alive was how she liked him.

Though it was daylight, the windows were screened, and she couldn't see into the house. She watched with her hands clenched as Spense breached the door in a split second. "FBI freeze!"

The door slammed behind him.

Her heartbeats counted down the seconds until Spense reappeared on the porch. "We're clear."

He was back inside before she finished exhaling. Her legs trembled as she climbed the porch and joined him inside. She reached out her hand—she needed to touch him.

"Don't worry, baby. I always land on my feet."

"Except for a couple of days ago on the side of a cliff. As your future wife, you can't stop me from worrying."

"Suit yourself." Then without missing a beat, he added, "This place is a mess, but not *tossed*, no sign of a struggle. If Tommy does have Lilly, my guess is she went willingly."

"*Have* her?" This was the first anyone had suggested Tommy might be holding Lilly hostage, but it fit. If Tommy knew Rose had that micro memory card, he might try to exchange Lilly for it. "You think he's using Lilly for bait."

Spense nodded. "From all accounts, she's not as bright as her sister. I'm gonna take a look around."

When Caitlin didn't object he arched an eyebrow. "You're not going to complain about a lack of a warrant?"

"I don't even know if they have warrants in French Polynesia."

True enough, but she did know French regulations were just as strict if not stricter than back home. But she and Spense were unofficial here, and that meant they had the leeway of private citizens.

She hoped.

The flat-out truth was that though she cared about following the rules, she cared more about keeping Lilly and Rose safe from harm.

"I knew you'd come around eventually," Spense said. "Good to know we're seeing eye to eye."

"Don't get used to it. What are we looking for exactly?" she asked as they swept the small apartment, removing cushions and peeking under stacks of clothing. Going through cabinets and dresser drawers.

"A piece of the puzzle, unknown shape and size. Keep your eyes peeled for anything."

She began sorting through her umpteenth pile of papers with that in mind. When you're looking for anything, you have to scrutinize everything. Then the sudden absence of furious activity from Spense drew her attention. "What?"

"Passport. Name of Anna Parker."

The words made her do a double take. "I thought *Rose* was Anna."

He frowned. "This photograph is definitely of Rose. Dimple in the right cheek. Same passport photo Fontaine showed us."

"What's Lilly doing with Rose's fake *Anna* passport?"

"Don't know. Maybe Rose left it with Lilly for safekeeping after she went to the bank."

"But if Rose was planning to leave the country as Anna, she would need to have that fake passport with her."

Spense let out a low whistle. "Look here."

Caitlin peered over his shoulder at a *second* passport. Also in the name of Anna Parker. Only this Anna had a dimple in her left cheek. This Anna was in fact, Lilly.

"So *both* women have 'Anna' passports. Must come in handy when you want to be in two places at once. Just think of the possibilities. Anna can be in one place pulling a con and in another establishing an alibi at the same time. I bet they both have birth certificates and driver's licenses in Anna's name, too."

"But that still doesn't tell us *why* Lilly has Rose's version."

"Or where she and Tommy Preston got off to."

Caitlin's arm dropped to her side, and the papers she'd been holding fell to the ground. She got on her knees to gather them up.

Maps.

"Anything important down there?"

"Just more photocopies of the phony treasure maps."

Spense tucked the passports they'd found into his jacket.

Caitlin felt a sting when her finger grazed the sharp edge of one of the maps as she stacked them on the tabletop.

A big drop of blood fell right on top of the spot marked X. Her palms started to tingle. "Spense, you know how I was so sure Rose would hide out somewhere along the route to Gauguin's Gold?"

"I seem to recall we both were, and that it led us into a hell of a mess. If you're suggesting we retrace our steps, I've gotta say I don't think that's wise. Brousseau's already up there with his men and—"

"Up *there*, near Mana Falls, yes but not *here*. This is a different map. It even has the roman numeral II stamped in the corner."

Spense leaned over her shoulder and studied it. "It looks a lot like the same map to me. Here's Mana Falls. Here's the chutes and ladders trail."

She nodded. "But X is in a different spot. You don't need to go down chutes and ladders or past hives to get there. It's in the opposite direction, on a different section of the island. There's a *road* leading almost all the way there, and a swinging bridge. This is definitely a different spot. I'm pretty sure we'd remember a swinging bridge."

"I'm pretty sure we'd remember a *road*."

Papers flew as they sorted through all the maps, looking for more versions. More spots where Rose Parker might be hiding or where Tommy might've taken Lilly. But in the end, there were only two.

Two sisters.

Two maps.

Two potential hiding spots.

And Brousseau's men had one area covered already.

"I hate to admit when I'm wrong," Spense muttered.

"Then don't."

He holstered his Glock and handed her the map. "I'll drive. You navigate."

Chapter 32

Sunday
Road to Taravao Plateau
Tahiti Iti

NOTING THE TIME on his cell—fifteen minutes left on the clock, Tommy checked yet again to be sure there'd been no message from Rose. Reception was spotty, and she probably couldn't get through, but it was worth a look.

"Can I have my phone back, now?" Lilly asked. Her speech was beginning to slur.

"I'm keeping it safe aren't I?"

"Yes, but I want to text Rose."

"No service."

"Then why do you keep checking it?"

"To see if there's service." He tweaked her nose. "Babe, are you sure this is the right trail?" Because if she was leading him astray in an effort to give Rose time to beat them to the spot, she was going to regret it later—in just about fourteen minutes or so.

She stopped and did a three-sixty. "I think so."

"Think?"

"I'm almost positive. But I didn't see the swinging bridge. When did we cross it?"

He counted to ten. Forced himself to breathe. Clearly, she wasn't thinking straight, and he couldn't exactly blame her for that. But if they were on the wrong trail, which they clearly were, she had led him astray right out of the gate—long before the drug could have crossed the blood-brain barrier. So maybe he could hold her accountable after all. "We should turn around. The X should be only a couple of miles from the end of the pavement, right?"

"How far do you think we've come?"

"More than that." He envisioned himself dragging Lilly's dead body across the swinging bridge—he didn't relish the thought.

He could only hope they would get there before the clock ran out.

ROSE SPIED THE rickety old swinging bridge just ahead.

She'd made it!

But then, her stomach began to churn.

Clever of Tommy to have chosen this place.

Not only was it remote, once she started across the bridge she'd be unable to conceal her approach. The bridge swaying and singing in the wind would give her away, and there'd be no place to take cover.

She blew out a breath, then patted the Glock tucked into the back of her shorts—the one she'd stolen from Pierre and then hidden under a banyan tree until she could safely return for it.

Tommy would be a damn fool to shoot her before he had SADIE in his hands.

If she had indeed reached this spot first, she could get herself into a good hidey-hole and get the drop on him instead—let *him* be the sitting duck crossing the bridge.

She checked her phone—dead. Which meant she couldn't see how many minutes were left on the clock. *Act on the best-case scenario, prepare for the worst.*

She hoped she was the first to arrive, but that Lilly would be only minutes behind.

The only thing that made sense to her was to race across the bridge as fast as possible.

She stepped onto it, and her foot set the thing in motion—big time. She grabbed the cable that served as a handrail. The wind was high, and the bridge far less steady than she'd remembered. Papa had never brought Lilly and her here in conditions like these. All those games of swing and scream had been played in fair weather. She took another step and nearly lost her balance.

Widening her stance, she tried again.

Better, but only a little.

At this rate it was going to take forever to cross, and she only had minutes—*Lilly* only had minutes.

She closed her eyes against the stinging wind and concentrated.

There must be a better way. Maybe if she crawled on her belly the bridge would sway less. Snaking her way on her stomach would be steady, and less likely to leave the bridge in telltale motion.

She hit the deck, then used her hands to drag herself from rung to rung. Through the spaces between them, she could see the verdant valley below with its rolling hills, tall trees, and vibrant tropical flowers. The wind presented her with a sweet-smelling bouquet.

Another time, she might've enjoyed the view.

But not today.

"I'm coming, Lilly. I won't let him hurt you." She spoke aloud, hoping her words would somehow wend their way into her twin's brain.

Then she stretched out her arm and pulled her body forward yet again. Her shirt climbed up her chest and a splinter scraped the tender skin of her exposed stomach. She dragged herself another few feet.

This method was working. She was getting across with very little extra motion to hinder her progress or give her away. One rung at a time, she moved, until she was but ten yards to the end.

A break in the wind made her pulse race.

Voices.

She heard them behind her in the distance.

Ones she'd recognize anywhere: Lilly and Tommy.

Hurry!

THEY ARRIVED AT the bridge, the point of no return for Lilly.

It was swaying, but after all it was a swinging bridge, and Tommy couldn't be certain if Rose had recently crossed ahead of them, or if the movement was only due to the wind.

Tommy had been patient, attentive, and downright saint-like with Lilly to this point. In return, she'd led him the wrong way, potentially costing him the chance to optimally set his trap before Rose arrived.

Lilly was lucky she was still breathing.

Now she'd better hope her sister hadn't gotten here first.

Because Lilly could die the easy way, or the hard way.

He envisioned allowing Rose to revive her with the rescue injector. Then, once Lilly came to, he'd close his hands around her neck, squeezing until she lost consciousness, reviving her, doing it again . . . and again.

And all in front of dear, dear Rose.

As soon as they got across that bridge, he'd punch Lilly in the throat.

But for now, he wanted her upright and crossing under her own power. He gave her a little shove, and they both stepped onto the bridge—Lilly walking a bit ahead—creeping, really.

At a maddeningly slow pace.

When at last they reached the other side, Lilly suddenly slumped and fell forward onto her knees.

Dammit.

He'd estimated he'd have at least five minutes more before she passed out.

This was all Lilly's fault for getting them lost along the way.

Then, up ahead, a flash of movement caught his eye. *Rose.*

She'd beaten him to the meeting place after all.

Adrenaline, with a sidecar of anger, raced through him.

He grabbed Lilly around the waist and hoisted her to her feet. "Hang on, sweetie, I've got you."

She looked up at him with dazed eyes, still filled with trust.

Poor Lilly.

ROSE PEEKED OUT from her hiding place.

Lilly!

Tommy carried her to the fat trunk of a tree and sat down out in the open, not bothering to hide, with Lilly's limp body propped up in front of him.

Please, please let her be breathing.

Rose raised her pistol.

Do not falter.

Then just as quickly, she lowered her arm.

Not because she wasn't willing to shoot Tommy Preston in order to save her sister's life, but because she didn't trust her aim enough to fire on him while he was using Lilly as a human shield.

Think.

Tommy was looking straight at the boulder where Rose had taken cover. Just as if he knew exactly which outcropping of rocks she'd be hiding behind and exactly what moment she'd choose to come out to face him.

She steeled her jaw and stepped out into the open, Pierre's Glock pointed at Tommy. "Move away from Lilly. I'm going to give her the antidote."

"Sorry, but I've got a gun in her back. You're not the one giving the orders. You're the one taking them."

She wrapped her finger around the trigger.

This was her fault.

If both she and Tommy had to give their lives for Lilly's so be it. "And I've got SADIE, so yes, I am the one in charge. I'm coming over. Shoot me if you want, but if you do, everything you've spent your life building will be destroyed. Just let me give her the medicine and then we can talk."

As she crept toward her sister, her eyes filled with tears. If Lilly lived, would Rose ever be able to make her believe that all her actions, wrong though they may have been, had been motivated by her desire to protect her?

Had a plan ever failed more miserably?

Rose's stomach soured at the memory of Tommy's hands on her. She'd let a man she despised touch her, enter her, claim her.

Then she'd married that man, even though he made her blood run cold. All of it had been for Lilly, and all of it had backfired.

"Stop right there." Tommy's voice had a quiet calm about it that terrified her more than if he'd yelled out in anger.

She drew up short, keeping her pistol trained on an imaginary dot in the middle of his forehead.

"I'll let you give Lilly the naloxone. After all, that's why I provided it. But first you need to show me the thumb drive and to prove you're acting in good faith, put down your pistol. Are there any other copies of the file?"

"No. But if I put down my pistol, what's to stop you from shooting me and taking the drive out of my hand?"

He grinned. "Nothing except my word. And your word is all I have that there are no copies. You must know by now that when I bargain with the devil, I keep my end." He placed one hand near Lilly's lips. "I don't feel her breathing. Do you want to stand around and negotiate? Or rescue your sister?"

Lilly was out of time, and only Rose could save her.

She pulled a clear baggie from her pocket and waved it in the air. "Here's SADIE. I'm putting it here, on the ground . . . next to my Glock."

"GOOD GIRL." KEEPING his pistol in hand, but lowered, Tommy gently laid Lilly on the ground beside him. Then he climbed to his feet and waved Rose over.

In an instant, she was kneeling beside her sister, the auto-injector in hand.

Wordlessly, she pulled it from its case and yanked the red stopper from the bottom to activate the pen.

An eerie robotic voice sounded in the air, speaking instructions.

Rose raised her hand, and then gasped.

Bile rose in Tommy's throat.

What the holy hell was going on?

Lilly had a tight grip on Rose's wrist, blocking her from jabbing her with the needle.

Rose jumped back, and Lilly rolled, catapulted to her feet, then charged.

Before Tommy could move, she crashed her knee into his groin, doubling him over with a sickening pain.

Bitch!

Lilly's teeth gouged his cheek, and her heel slammed onto his foot. She grabbed his balls and twisted.

His stomach went woozy.

She kicked him again.

And again.

Then he was on the ground, rolling downhill heading straight for a heap of jagged boulders.

The last thing he saw before his world went black was Lilly— she was laughing.

Chapter 33

"TURN AROUND. LET Brousseau go instead." Dutch's voice blasted out of Caity's speakerphone as their 4x4 bounced over the rocky terrain.

The Jeep slipped and Spense steered into the skid to correct it.

Just minutes ago, they'd reached the unpaved section of road. It was slipperier than black ice, and when you were driving like hell, more dangerous.

As the Jeep flew over another rut, Spense's teeth slammed together, rattling his skull.

"Lives are at stake, Dutch," Caity yelled back, above the roar of the road and the wind. "We can lose reception any minute so listen up. Brousseau's on the other side of Iti near Mana Falls. We can't get a connection with his phone, but you can try to radio him. I just sent you a photo of a map. When you reach him, talk him through it. Tell him to meet us at the X by the swinging bridge."

"I'll get him there. Will you turn around?" Dutch yelled.

"He might not be in time. His men have to hike out. We're on wheels," Spense said.

An ear-splitting screech sounded.

"Wheels that squeal." It was Gretchen.

"Is Dutch on the radio to Brousseau yet?" Spense asked.

"Yes," Gretchen said. "Your vehicle sounds like crap."

"It does. Now that's settled," Spense said, and spit blood from his mouth, careful not to hit Caity with it. "Tell us about the interview with Jessica Prosper. Talk fast."

A slew of static came over the line and Caity pounded her fist onto the dash. "Dammit. We lost . . ."

But then the phone crackled and they heard Gretchen's voice once more. "It's big. And you're right about this reception so I won't leave you in suspense. Nurse Jessica Prosper filed a complaint against Anna Parker after Prosper got fired from Riverbend Memorial. Seems 'Anna' hired Prosper as well as an actress to pull a scam. Prosper lost her job and 'Anna' disappeared without paying her. So a very ticked off Prosper filed a report. At the time, the cops thought it was BS."

"Why the hell would a nurse help anyone pull a scam?"

"I say it was for the money, but Prosper claimed she thought she was doing a good deed. 'Anna' told Prosper that her sister, Lilly—I hope you're paying attention here."

Caity yanked at her hair.

Like they needed a reminder.

"Anna said her sister, Lilly, was in an abusive relationship. That she needed to make her see how bad this man was. Scare her off of him."

Spense muttered a curse and went back to focusing on keeping them upright.

"Anna got a makeup artist to fix it up like this actress was bruised and beaten. Then they set her up in a closed wing of Riverbend Memorial for the day. Texted Lilly to come down there on urgent business."

"You just lost me," Spense said. "The way we heard it, *Rose* went to visit Pamela Jean and then warned Lilly off. But Lilly didn't believe her."

"That's right. It was Rose who met the fake Pamela Jean."

"You said Lilly."

"I *said* pay attention. *Nurse Prosper* said it was Lilly. But when we e-mailed her the photos of the twins, she insisted that Rose, claiming to be Lilly, came down to visit with Pamela Jean—I mean the actress who played Pamela Jean."

"So if Rose was in fact pretending to be Lilly when she met Pamela Jean, then Lilly was the one who hired the actress," Caity said.

"Correct."

The phone tried to jump from Caity's hand.

"How the . . . what the . . . did she say why?"

"Prosper doesn't know why. And frankly, neither do I."

Lilly.

"Thanks. Hanging up to save my battery."

"Wait . . . your wedding . . . what should we tell the moms?"

The phone spewed more static.

"Can you hear me?" Caity asked. "Gretchen?" Shaking her

head, she powered off the phone. "Service bars disappeared. What do you think Lilly is up to?"

"I'm still trying to get it straight in my head. If the whole Pamela Jean scenario was a con, and *Lilly* is the one who set it up, that means we can't rely on anything she's told us. And if I have to leap to a conclusion, I'm betting that whatever game she's playing has a lot to do with those life insurance policies."

Chapter 34

Sunday
Taravao Plateau
Tahiti Iti

"ROSE!" LILLY THREW herself into her sister's arms. "I've been so damned worried. How the hell could you disappear and put me through all of this?"

"I'm sorry, sorry, sorry. I made a terrible mess of things. But I was so afraid Tommy would hurt you. I thought I could fix everything, but . . ." Rose's face felt hot and soaked with tears, her mind jumbled. ". . . how did you? I thought you were dying."

Lilly stepped away and brushed her hair from her dirt-streaked face. "If Tommy had his way I would be. When I was coming out of the restroom at the diner, I saw him putting something in my orange juice, so I switched my glass with his—it's just too damn bad he didn't drink it."

"But, I saw you. You were unconscious. You weren't even breathing."

"I was faking it. I'm a con woman. Remember? I started to figure things out after you shot Tommy in the water. I knew you wouldn't have done that without a good reason. That's when I understood that everything you'd told me about him was the truth. I should've believed you when you told me he killed that poor girl, that Pamela Jean." Lilly sidestepped down the hill to where Tommy lay unconscious on the ground. "And Rose, now that I know what Tommy's capable of, I understand why you want him dead."

This should've been music to Rose's ears, but it wasn't.

Something was off.

This didn't sound like her dear sweet Lilly at all.

"It's not that I wanted him dead. It's that I wanted you safe, and now you will be." She held up the thumb drive. "Pamela Jean told me to find Sadie, and I did. I've sent a copy to the FBI, and together, we can make them believe the truth about Tommy Preston."

"You shouldn't have done that." Lilly sighed. "That file has the numbers of all Tommy's offshore bank accounts. We could've been richer than even Papa ever dreamed." She fixed her gaze on Rose. "Anyway, you have to kill him now."

Rose's arms were shaking. Sobs clogged her chest. A few yards away, at the bottom of the incline, Tommy lay prone. "I brought rope in my pack. I'll hold the gun on him while you tie him up," she said.

"Where did you get rope and a pack?"

"Does it matter? I bought them with the money I stole. I've been watching over you in town, as best I could with the cops swarming everywhere. And I've been trying to find a way to get us out of this mess. Good thing I bought the rope, because it looks like we're going to need it."

Lilly's eyes darted back to Tommy, who lay on the ground, his pistol just out of his reach. "We can't just let him go."

"We're not going to let him go. We'll tie him up and hold him at gunpoint."

"Until what? The cops have a blaze of insight and realize we're out here in the middle of swinging bridge nowhere?"

"I'm a fugitive. They're *looking* for me. Sooner or later they'll find us." But in her gut she knew Lilly was right. It probably wouldn't be sooner. And it was too risky trying to walk Tommy back across the swinging bridge. "We shouldn't wait for them to stumble onto us. I'll stay here with Tommy, and you can go for help." She retrieved her pistol off the ground, lifted her pack and edged down the hill to join Lilly. "Tie him up. I'll cover you. I can shoot him in the foot if he starts coming around."

"I don't want to go for help. What if I get lost? What if something happens to you while you're alone with him. We have to stick together, Rose."

"Lilly, you can do this." She rattled the rope. "Help me tie him up before he comes to."

Lilly took the rope from Rose's hand, and then, slowly, she turned. "Kill him."

"I can't."

"You have to do it for me. He tried to *poison* me. And he beat that poor Pamela Jean woman to death."

Tommy groaned. Rose whirled, training her pistol on him. He lifted his head and then dropped it again. It hit the dirt with a soft thunk.

"I can't do it, Lilly. Not like this."

"You haven't even tried."

"I tried six months ago—and failed. After I warned you about him and you wouldn't listen to me." Her head was throbbing like it never had before. "Why didn't you listen to me back then, Lilly? Why did you believe him over me—your own sister?"

"I wish I had listened to you about Pamela Jean. I said that already. But I *loved* him. I couldn't see him for the monster he is. But now I do. Go ahead. Shoot him for *us*. It's the only way."

"Just hurry and tie him up."

Tommy stirred again. This time he got his head and his shoulders off the ground. Rose had to use both hands to straight-arm the Glock. Pierre's pistol was a heavier gun than what she was accustomed to.

"I don't know any fucking Pamela Jean," Tommy whispered.

"You beat her to death." Lilly moved closer to Tommy.

He raised his arm.

"Don't fucking move!" Rose ordered.

Tommy looked her in the eye. "Rose, listen to me. I admit I gave your sister heroin—at least I thought I did. But I swear I was going to let you give her the antidote. And I don't know Pamela Jean."

Why admit to the heroin and keep on lying about Pamela Jean?

"Lilly's a con."

He crawled onto his knees and then got into a sitting position. Rose was too numb to try to stop him. "Lilly's conning you right now. Please don't shoot me. Just tie me up and wait for the police. You've got everything you need on that drive to break me. And if you say you shot me in self-defense on our wedding day, I'll back up your story. But please don't kill me. I'm all Heather's got left in this world."

Tears filled his eyes.

In the time she'd known him, she'd never seen him cry.

Lilly kicked him in the face, and he fell forward onto the dirt.

Rose's head seemed too heavy for her neck. She stared at Lilly, feeling oddly distant, as if she'd never seen her before. Then she gave herself a mental shake. If they didn't hurry and tie Tommy up, he might regain his strength, and then Rose really wouldn't have a choice except to shoot him. "Tie him up, and *then* we'll talk."

"I—I can't bear to touch him."

Rose pressed the gun into Lilly's hand and took the rope back. "Then I'll do it while you cover me."

Lilly shrugged. "Suit yourself."

A frisson of surprise traveled down Rose's spine. She'd expected Lilly to resist the idea of holding the Glock on Tommy. Lilly had never wanted anything to do with firearms before.

And now she'd taken the pistol almost eagerly.

As strangely as Lilly was behaving, Rose had to admit she'd outsmarted Tommy, and shown a great deal of courage. "I'm proud of you, Lilly." Rose unwound the rope and knelt beside Tommy.

"Don't let her shoot me, Rose."

"Shut up and don't move." She turned her head to give Lilly an encouraging smile and her breath caught in her throat.

With a raised arm, Lilly stepped close.

Rose released her breath. Lilly was only trying to protect her. "Don't worry about me. He's weak, I'm sure it'll be okay." She ran the rope around Tommy's wrists, once, twice, thrice, then tightened it. "I'm going to tie your feet next," she explained, not wanting to startle him into making some crazy move.

"Don't shoot me," he whimpered. "Please, just look at me. There's no Pamela Jean. Lilly is conning you."

"The police will decide what to do with you." But it was odd. He knew nothing could make up for the fact that he'd tried to poison Lilly and drown Rose, so why was he so insistent about Pamela Jean? What difference did it make?

"I saw her with my own eyes," she said, then tightened the ropes and went to work on his feet.

"Don't let Lilly shoot me," he pleaded. "If not for my sake then for hers. She'll spend the rest of her life in prison if she does."

"Lilly is not going to shoot you." But the way Lilly was looking at Tommy, not with hate, but with indifference, made Rose's gut twist.

She'd tied his hands and feet.

He was helpless, begging for his life.

Lilly aimed the pistol.

"No!"

A deafening boom preceded the stench of gun smoke.

In slow motion, Rose turned her head and saw the gaping hole in Tommy's back, blood pooling on the ground around him.

"Is he dead?" Lilly asked, and then shifted her aim to Rose.

CAITLIN LUNGED ACROSS the last rung of the swinging bridge and fell headlong into the dirt.

"Freeze! FBI!"

She stayed down as Spense skirted her, Glock out front.

"Lilly Parker, drop your weapon! Hands behind your head!"

Caitlin heard soft weeping. She eased her shoulders off the ground and saw Rose on her knees facing her sister, tears streaming down her face. Lilly's pistol was trained on Rose.

"Get up, Rose," Lilly ordered.

"Drop your weapon! Now, Lilly!"

Rose climbed to her feet. Across the distance she made eye contact with Caitlin.

Dammit.

Caitlin got to her knees and then eased into an upright position. Rose had been protecting Lilly all along. And past behavior was the best predictor of future behavior.

Do not take the fall for Lilly. Not this time.

"Drop your weapon!" Spense had his gaze lasered onto Lilly.

Caitlin took a step closer to Spense. He didn't object so she figured that was the same as a *go for it*. If he gave the signal to back off, she would. "Lilly put down your gun. Use your head. You're no match for Agent Spenser, and the French police are on their way."

"Please put it down," Rose said, her voice choppy and low. "We can use the money Papa left us for a lawyer. But if you don't put the gun down something terrible might happen."

"More terrible than prison?"

"You won't go to prison." Rose looked at Caitlin and then Spense. "I shot Tommy. Lilly's afraid of me. That's why she won't put the gun down."

The silence seemed to stretch eternally, and then Caitlin took one step closer to the twins. "Is that true, Lilly? Was it Rose who shot Tommy?" She tried to make her tone credulous, though she knew it was a lie.

Lilly looked to her sister and her face screwed up. She nodded. "Yes. I—I tried to stop Rose but she wouldn't listen. She kept talking about money. About life insurance and how we needed it for the yoga studio. I—I tried to tell her I *never* wanted that studio. But Rose is obsessed. She's obsessed with me. She couldn't stand the idea of Tommy taking me away from her."

"Drop your gun," Spense said. "And we can talk about it."

Lilly gave a shaky smile. "I'm sorry, but I just don't trust her. If I put this down, she'll lunge for it."

"If you don't put it down, I'll shoot you."

Lilly scoffed. "You wouldn't. My sister just explained that she's the guilty party."

Caitlin moved one more step closer. "Lilly, listen very carefully to me. Agent Spenser does not bullshit. He's not a gamer. I know how hard that is for you to understand, but if he says he'll shoot, he will."

"With me aiming this at Rose? I don't think so."

Suddenly, Rose's chin jerked up. "Put it down, Lilly."

"Why should I? You're dangerous."

Rose didn't drop her gaze. "No," she whispered. "I see it now. I guess I had to be staring down the barrel of *your* pistol before I finally did. You've been conning me our whole lives. You're standing there holding a gun on me, and somehow, I'm taking the blame for everything you've done. And do you know why?"

"Because you're stupid," Lilly sneered.

Spense jerked his head, and Caitlin stepped back. She knew he wanted her out of the way in case he needed to fire.

"Because I love you. But you don't know what love is. You never wanted us to go straight at all, did you?"

"Well, gee. You finally heard me. How many times did I have to say it for it to sink in? The only thing I like about yoga is the smokin' body it gives me."

"Wow," Caitlin said. "Seems like you two have a lot to talk about, maybe we should have this discussion somewhere else. You must be tired and there's a lot to sort out. Put the gun down, Lilly."

Lilly shook her head. "Stop shrinking me, lady. You think Rose is such a great sister. Well, I'm here to t-tell you she's not. All m-my life, she's been underestimating me. She thinks because I s-stutter I'm stupid."

"I never, *never* said that."

"I heard you and Papa talking about *poor Lilly*. You think you had it rough living with him? All you had to do was be Rose, pretending to be Anna. I had to be Lilly pretending to be *poor Lilly* pretending to be Anna." A hysterical noise came out of her mouth. "It was fucking exhausting."

Caitlin's gut tightened. Lilly was losing it right in front of them.

"I'm *not* poor Lilly. I'm smarter than you and Papa and Tommy all put together."

"I'm sorry, Lilly. I truly am. I never meant to hurt you. I underestimated you, and that was wrong of me." Rose's face had paled, but her voice remained steady.

"Damn straight. I'm a better con than you'll ever be . . . I heard Tommy telling his lawyer on the phone that if anything ever happened to him, all his secret account numbers were on a file labeled SADIE. So I hired an actress to play Pamela Jean and convince you Tommy had beaten her. I told her to whisper *find Sadie* in your ear. I pitted you and Tommy against each other and I didn't give a damn which one of you came out on top. As long as one of you wound up dead, I'd win three million dollars. If you killed each other, I'd hit a jackpot worth six million. And when you screwed everything up by marrying him instead of getting rid of him, I adapted. After you shot him in the water, I kept on fueling the fire. I gave him the phone you sent me. I set you *both* up. But guess what? I don't even care about the money anymore. I don't even care if I go to prison. All I care about right now is getting you out of my life forever." Lilly's shoulder lifted slightly.

Boom!

Lilly's arm jerked, and then her gun tumbled to the ground.

"Stand down," Brousseau told his men.

They lowered their weapons.

Spense rushed over and scooped up the fallen pistol.

Caitlin hurried to Lilly to check her wound. The inspector's bullet had grazed her right shoulder. Caitlin motioned and several deputies arrived with radios and bandages. Rose, too, came to her sister's aide, attempting to hold her good hand. "It's going to be all right, Lilly. We're going to get ourselves the best lawyers money can buy."

"With what?" Lilly jerked her hand free. "I moved all Papa's money to the Cayman Islands."

"Let's get a tourniquet above that wound," Caitlin said.

Under Caitlin's watchful eye, Rose accepted a cloth from a uniformed officer and wound it around her sister's arm.

Brousseau placed his hands on his hips and looked to Caitlin and then Spense. "I've got this," he said. "You two have somewhere else you're supposed to be."

"We do," Caitlin replied. "But I want to say something before we go." She leveled her gaze at Rose. "Tell the truth. Tell Inspector Brousseau what really happened here today and on your wedding day. You think you're helping your sister by covering for her, but all you're doing is helping her game the system, and in the process you'll be killing your own chance for a decent, normal life . . . and I promise you, such a thing really does exist."

Chapter 35

DOLPHIN BEACH WAS more than an hour's drive from the swinging bridge. Spense and Caity made a mad dash across it, and then back to the Jeep, arriving at the beach only a few minutes before sunset. Spense parked right up on the sand, just yards away from a cabana.

"Stay where you are," he ordered Caity.

This was their wedding day.

At least it was supposed to have been and damned if he wasn't going to get her door for her. He came around and helped her down from the 4x4.

Caity fixed her eyes on him.

He tore his gaze away to check out the sky. "If we hustle, there's still time for a sunset wedding."

During the course of the day they'd been attacked by branches and brambles. An odd mix of dirt, sand, and sweat streaked both their faces.

Caity's hair, as untamed as he'd ever seen it, had twigs sticking out of it.

So beautiful.

"The bride wore brambles?" She flashed him a smile, and he trembled at the thought of ever having to live without her.

This wasn't how he'd planned it.

She deserved a perfect wedding, not because she was a perfect person, but because she was perfectly Caity. He took her hands in his. "I promised you nothing was going to ruin our day. I never meant to let you down."

"You didn't let me down." She brought his palm to her lips. "We had to get involved, Spense. If we hadn't, then right about now Brousseau would be bringing us news that Lilly not only killed Tommy, but Rose, too. I realize we said we'd say *no*, but sometimes *yes* is the right thing to do. And honestly, *yes* is kind of our deal, so maybe we should just learn to go with it."

"I wanted to give you your dream wedding."

"I'll settle for my dream husband. It's no tragedy to have to reschedule the ceremony."

"Maybe the preacher's open tomorrow."

She laughed out loud. "Tahitian priest."

A strong thump landed between Spense's shoulders. He'd been so focused on Caity, that with the sand muffling the sound of their footfalls, he hadn't noticed his family's approach. He turned to find his brother grinning at him. Next to Dutch stood Gretchen, her gorgeous blond hair billowing in the breeze, her olive skin darkened by the tropical sun.

And there were the moms, too, a little ways off, standing at the entrance of the cabana, arms crossed with a determination he didn't dare defy.

Everyone was dressed for a wedding, and from the looks on their faces, they were still expecting one.

"You take the big guy. I've got Caitlin," Gretchen told Dutch who, strangely enough, had a box of baby wipes tucked under his arm. Gretchen pulled Caitlin in the direction of the cabana where the moms awaited. Arlene swept open the draped doorway, and Spense heard a sharp intake of air from Caity.

He had a hard time controlling his breath, too, when he saw what was inside.

"Oh my goodness. You brought my wedding dress to the beach." Caity's eyes brimmed with tears.

"And Spense's tux and a hairbrush. Shoes. I've got your makeup kit and a mirror. Spense can get dressed first, and then you're up," Gretchen said.

"But how did you manage all of this?" Caity asked.

Spense, too, was dumbfounded they'd pulled something like this together—even a cabana so they could dress on site.

"When Dutch told us what was going on . . ." Agatha beamed proudly at Spense. ". . . Arlene and I figured you wouldn't make it back in time. So we called the concierge at the hotel, and he was eager to help—since you two are local heroes and all. He arranged to have the cabana delivered, and the gendarmes are going to look the other way, because I hate to tell you, but we don't have a permit for this tent."

"You two deserve a magical wedding, and we just wanted to be sure you got it." Arlene motioned for Spense to hurry up. "That's what moms are for, isn't it?"

He pressed his fingers to his eyes, speechless, for once.

To say he was the luckiest man alive didn't cut it.

He was the luckiest man who'd ever lived.

Fifteen minutes later, he stood before the preacher, in front of the moms, Dutch and Gretchen, and a handful of gendarmes. When he looked up, there was Caity, gliding over the sand in a white satin gown—the most beautiful bride he'd ever seen.

Her makeup was flawless.

But from where he stood, he could see a twig she'd missed, sticking out of her hair.

Perfectly Caity.

MY SPENSE.

"Did this really happen?" Caitlin asked her new husband.

Spense's arm came around her waist, and he drew her in close and planted a soft kiss on her forehead. "Yes, ma'am."

She held his gaze for as long as she could, but she was afraid if she kept on looking at him, her heart would explode. When she looked down, she literally saw it pounding in her breast, above the sweetheart neckline of her wedding gown.

She placed her hand on her fluttery stomach and willed herself to breathe.

"The photographer's here," Gretchen called out.

Caitlin shaded her eyes as the wedding photographer the moms had found approached. She elbowed Spense and laughed softly under her breath. "Is that the same guy?"

He nodded.

"Think so."

The very same photographer who'd been taking photographs of Tommy and Rose on the beach.

Click. Click. Click.

He was already snapping candid shots and never broke stride. If he recognized Spense and her he didn't let on. The man was a professional.

She liked that.

"Okay, then. Everyone get in a line. Bride and groom you're in the center. Moms on either side. You two . . ." The photographer indicated Dutch and Gretchen. "Split up on the ends."

It seemed like a thousand photos, and then he said, "Time for the money shot. On three, everyone jump."

"You mean in the air?" Agatha asked, her mouth slightly agape.

"I do," he replied.

"Ready?"

"Well. . . ."

Spense drew his mother into a hug. "She's ready."

"On three then. One . . . two . . . three!"

Catlin's feet hit the ground, and she doubled over laughing. Not only had Agatha jumped, she'd actually clicked her heels. There were other poses in various groupings, and then it was time for the bride and groom photos.

By now the sun was low in the sky, and it was growing dusky.

"You're welcome to stay and watch," Caitlin told no one in particular, "but please don't feel you must. We've made arrangements with the hotel dining room. Order all the drinks and appetizers you like and Spense and I will join you in less than an hour."

After waves and hugs, the family loaded up into Dutch's car.

Spense and Caitlin mugged for the camera. There was the hand-holding stroll down the beach. The obligatory shot of the bouquet and the rings. The bend-over-backward kiss . . . and then . . . Spense shed his shoes and nodded, pointing to her wedding sandals. She kicked them off, smiling, unsure what he had in mind until he lifted her off the ground and carried her in his arms toward the shoreline.

"Spense!" she cried. "You can't be serious."

"Oh, but I am." He bent his head, and the sight of him smiling down on her made her heart stop in her chest. "As long as you're okay with it. I haven't forgotten the look on your face when Tommy carried Rose into the water, *before* all hell broke loose."

It was true. She'd thought a trash the dress photo shoot was wild and bold and wonderful. "I do think it would make an incredible memory. A great way to start a life together. Just the two of us, throwing away convention."

Then to break the spell he'd cast on her, she gazed out at the ocean . . . and gasped.

Straight ahead, a pair of dolphins leaped from the waves.

"I think that's a good omen." Spense nuzzled her neck.

"Me, too." There was no reason at all to let Tommy Preston and Lilly Parker stop them from having their wedding day any way they wanted it.

"You in?" He pressed his lips to hers for the millionth time.

"All the way." She sighed against his mouth.

He crushed her protectively to his chest and waded into the ocean, then dropped her with a loud splash into the shallow waves. She scooped water and shoveled it over his head. Laughing, he chased her around and around as the camera clicked and her wedding dress turned into a memory.

Chapter 36

Six Months Later
FBI Field Office
Dallas, Texas

DALLAS WAS THE Bureau's nearest field office to Riverbend, Texas, and that gave Dutch, the special agent in charge, jurisdiction over the Tommy Preston financial crimes case. Caitlin was grateful he'd invited Spense and her to the wrap-up meeting—not only to satisfy her curiosity, but also because she was eager to check in with Rose. While they waited in the conference room for Dutch and Rose to make an entrance, she drummed her fingers on the long glass table.

Spense took her hand and stilled it. "Impatient much?"

"Just a little antsy." Caitlin had a case of nerves for Rose's sake. From the beginning, she'd had a strong sense of empathy for the woman, and she wanted to be there to lend support when Rose learned the final disposition of the case.

In addition, Rose had suffered quite a loss.

Rose loved Lilly.

A great deal of her identity had been tied up in being Lilly's sister and protector—to an unhealthy extent. And the way Lilly had turned on her had to have been devastating. Now, in exchange for a full confession to the murder of Tommy Preston, and reckless endangerment by tampering with hives and a rope anchor, Lilly had been sentenced to life, but with a chance of parole.

To be served in a prison outside of Papeete.

Lilly had declined to put Rose's name on her approved visitors list, doubling down on her position that she never wanted to see her again. That couldn't have been easy for Rose to hear, but in the end it would accomplish one good thing: It would give Rose a chance at the honest life she longed for—and a chance to be her true self.

Maybe now she could learn to relate to people without filtering everything through the warped lens of the Parker clan code.

She only had to open her eyes to find that a whole new world awaited her.

Rose had a number of legal issues of her own, both with the Tahitian government and the FBI. In exchange for her full cooperation and as a bonus for exposing Tommy Preston's money laundering schemes, a deal had been made, but Caitlin didn't yet know all the details.

She did know Rose had spent the past six months under house arrest in Dallas, and had been cooperating with Dutch on Tommy's financial crimes case. Caitlin was privately hoping Rose would get off with time served.

Caitlin held her breath as she heard footsteps approaching.

The door creaked open, and Dutch entered the room with Rose at his side. He pulled out a chair for her.

Rose acknowledged Spense and Caitlin with a nod, and then took her seat. "Thank you for being here."

"We wouldn't miss it," Spense said, then aimed his gaze at Dutch. "I'm not one for small talk so please don't keep us in suspense."

Caitlin had to smile.

Spense might truly be impatient, but she suspected this was more about him looking out for her. She'd barely slept last night, and he knew she was on the edge of her seat.

"Rose Parker, you're okay to proceed without your attorney present?" Dutch asked.

Again, Rose nodded.

The deal had already been hammered out with counsel, but apparently Dutch had additional information he wanted to present in person. "The FBI has wrapped its investigation into Tommy Preston and his criminal dealings in Texas. I'm afraid that for you, his widow, the news isn't good."

Rose's face blanched. "Am I criminally liable for his actions? My attorney said I had plausible deniability."

Caitlin braced herself. She knew Tommy's crimes were extensive, and the FBI had even found evidence implicating him in the deaths of several women due to heroin overdoses over the past decade.

"You won't be charged as an accessory to any of Tommy Preston's crimes."

Rose let out a long breath. Her shoulders visibly relaxed.

"The bad news I'm referring to is this: Your husband's amassed fortune is tainted with ill-gotten funds from illegal drugs, extortion, human trafficking, the works. Though he didn't participate directly in those endeavors, his partners did. The government is seizing all his assets. The bank accounts, the house . . ."

Her eyes widened. "What about Vader? He's been with me since Tommy's death, and I worry what would happen if he's sent to a shelter. I don't know if you know, but black dogs aren't adopted as often as—"

Dutch put up his hand and smiled. "Vader's all yours if you want him."

For the first time since she'd entered the room, a smile crept over Rose's face. "Thank you."

"No problem," Dutch said.

Caitlin leaned forward. "So you were saying Rose won't be charged with any financial crimes . . ."

"Or other crimes uncovered in the future that Tommy committed, as long as she had no direct involvement in them. We're also granting her immunity for any wrongdoing related to her father, George Parker's, dealings. Uncle Sam is very appreciative that Rose delivered the SADIE file into our hands. We've forgiven far more in exchange for far less."

"And the Tahitian government?" asked Spense.

"Not interested in pressing charges against Rose." Dutch turned his attention to her. "However, your immunity at home is conditional upon your keeping your nose clean for the next five years. That's part of the terms of the agreement. Did your lawyers explain this to you clearly?"

"They did," Rose said. "And believe me, there's nothing I want more."

Caitlin reached out and touched Rose on the wrist then drew back her hand. "That's what we all want for you."

"I don't look at these terms as a burden, I look at it as assistance. Someone helping me to break old habits."

Dutch tapped his fingers together. "We want to see you break those habits, too, Rose. We want you to succeed in your new life." He smiled broadly. "Which is one reason I've been cooperating with the insurance companies in their investigations. And this is the rest of the news I brought you all here today to share."

Caitlin had been wondering how this whole life insurance mess would play out. It seemed complex enough that the insurers would have grounds to protest any claims Rose might make. But since Rose's father's assets and Tommy's had been seized by the government, Rose would be left with no financial resources to make a fresh start.

"First off, *Lilly* will not be entitled to any proceeds from Tommy's policy—since he died by her hand. Also, the company has canceled the policies that Rose and Lilly hold on each other."

"I was prepared for that," Rose said. "In fact I don't expect anything from anyone. I can't see how I deserve a windfall from someone else's tragedy. The money should go to Heather Preston. Tommy would want her to have it."

"Which is exactly why he provided a policy for Heather. Tommy's adopted mother has already received a three-million-dollar payout."

Rose nodded. "I'm glad. I really liked her, and I feel sad that we can never have a relationship again, after what happened with Tommy and Lilly . . . with Tommy and me, too."

"But—" Caitlin started.

"I wouldn't be too sure about that," Spense interrupted. "Heather Preston's been in contact with us since we returned from

Tahiti. She mentioned something . . . I don't want to misquote."
He looked to Caity.

"Mrs. Preston said she felt terrible. She said she misjudged you.
I think you should give her a call." One thing Heather and Rose
had in common: they were both alone in the world. And from
what Caitlin could tell, they both had big hearts. "But what about
the policy Rose held on Tommy? That's what I'm waiting to hea~'

"Be patient, Caitlin. I was just about to tell you," Dutch
"The insurance investigators believe there are grounds to co.
Rose's claim to her husband's benefits. Even though it was *Lilly*
who caused his death, Rose did shoot him underwater on their
wedding day."

"I understand." Rose looked down at her hands like a child
who'd just received a well-earned slap.

"But, I pointed out to them that argument didn't hold water—
pun intended. Not only did Tommy *not die* due to that gunshot
you inflicted. We believe that your ripped wedding gown and your
statements as to what occurred along with your record of truthful testimony in the other matters before us, support a finding of
self-defense. I also made it clear that by Lilly's own statements,
you made every effort to dissuade her from shooting Tommy. I
explained I would testify as to your intent to find a law-abiding
solution to Tommy's threats to you when you messengered over
the SADIE file to Dr. Cassidy. Given that set of circumstances,
the insurance company believes that if the matter went to court,
a judge would likely rule in your favor. They don't want the bad
publicity surrounding a refusal to pay a legitimate claim."

As Dutch spoke, Caitlin watched Rose's face change from re-
signed to hopeful to something she couldn't quite read.

"What I'm telling you, Rose, is that as Tommy's widow, you'll receive the full three-million-dollar payout from his death benefit."

She covered her mouth with a trembling hand and shook her head. "I don't deserve it. I want to do the right thing, but I'm not sure what that is."

Silence filled the room.

Was it possible Rose would truly refuse the settlement, and with it her best chance for a clean slate, a fresh start?

Rose pushed her chair back from the table. And then her face brightened as though someone had suddenly opened a curtain and let the light into her life. "I'm going to take the money. I know exactly what to do with it. I still love my papa, and my sister, too, though I know we haven't lived our lives as we should have. Papa's code . . . the one that says anyone who gets conned out of his money deserves it, because it's his own greed that brings him down—that's bull. My papa was small-time compared to Tommy. Papa conned folks out of around a million dollars collectively. And with this insurance payout, I can hire an investigator to track down as many of our marks as possible. I'm going to do more than say *sorry*, I'm going to pay them back every last penny."

Caitlin had had enough of being objective and professional. "I'm so happy for you, Rose. I think this is a wonderful idea. You told us you always wanted a normal life. So I say go get it." She jumped up and went around to Rose and put her hands on her shoulders. "And there'll be enough money left to open up that yoga studio on your own if you want. Please don't forget about your own dreams . . . because you deserve to make them come true."

Acknowledgments

THANK YOU, READERS! I am so grateful that you take time out of your busy lives to read my books. I really hope you enjoy them. I love hearing from you, so don't hesitate to e-mail me. You can find my contact information and sign up for my newsletter at www. CareyBaldwin.com. I welcome your feedback and appreciate your reviews.

As always, I want to thank my family, Shannon, Erik, Sarah, and Bill. You guys are my world.

Thank you to my wonderful friends Leigh LaValle, Lena Diaz, Tessa Dare, Courtney Milan, and Brenna Aubrey for always being there for me.

K and T ladies: Sarah Andre, Diana Belchase, Manda Collins, Lena Diaz, Rachel Grant, Krista Hall, Gwen Hernandez, and Sharon Wray—you are all amazing and talented, and I can't thank you enough for all your support.

Carmen Pacheco, my beta reader, I am truly grateful for your help and your friendship.

I'd like to thank my amazing editor, Nicole Fischer. Nicole, on this story in particular, you have done an incredible job in guiding me. So thank you again . . . and again.

And finally, a huge thank-you to my fantastic agent, Liza Dawson, and to Caitie Flum and everyone at Liza Dawson Associates for all your help and support.

About the Author

CAREY BALDWIN is a mild-mannered doctor by day and an award-winning author of edgy suspense by night. She holds two doctoral degrees, one in medicine and one in psychology. A *USA TODAY* bestselling author, she loves reading and writing stories that keep you off balance and on the edge of your seat. Carey lives in the southwestern United States with her amazing family. In her spare time she enjoys hiking and chasing wildflowers. Carey loves to hear from readers so please visit her at:

www.CareyBaldwin.com
https://www.facebook.com/CareyBaldwinAuthor
https://twitter.com/CareyBaldwin

Discover great authors, exclusive offers, and more at hc.com.